Beloved

The Duel, Book 4

Mary Lancaster

Text by Mary Lancaster
Cover by Dar Albert

Dragonblade Publishing, Inc. is an imprint of Kathryn Le Veque Novels, Inc.
P.O. Box 23
Moreno Valley, CA 92556
ceo@dragonbladepublishing.com

Produced in the United States of America

First Edition August 2023
Trade Paperback Edition

The characters and events portrayed in this book are fictitious. Any similarity to real persons, living or dead, is purely coincidental and not intended by the author.

ARE YOU SIGNED UP FOR DRAGONBLADE'S BLOG?

You'll get the latest news and information on exclusive giveaways, exclusive excerpts, coming releases, sales, free books, cover reveals and more.

Check out our complete list of authors, too!

No spam, no junk. That's a promise!

Sign Up Here

www.dragonbladepublishing.com

Dearest Reader;

Thank you for your support of a small press. At Dragonblade Publishing, we strive to bring you the highest quality Historical Romance from some of the best authors in the business. Without your support, there is no 'us', so we sincerely hope you adore these stories and find some new favorite authors along the way.

Happy Reading!

CEO, Dragonblade Publishing

Additional Dragonblade books by Author Mary Lancaster

The Duel Series
Entangled (Book 1)
Captured (Book 2)
Deserted (Book 3)
Beloved (Book 4)

Last Flame of Alba Series
Rebellion's Fire (Book 1)
A Constant Blaze (Book 2)
Burning Embers (Book 3)

Gentlemen of Pleasure Series
The Devil and the Viscount (Book 1)
Temptation and the Artist (Book 2)
Sin and the Soldier (Book 3)
Debauchery and the Earl (Book 4)
Blue Skies (Novella)

Pleasure Garden Series
Unmasking the Hero (Book 1)
Unmasking Deception (Book 2)
Unmasking Sin (Book 3)
Unmasking the Duke (Book 4)
Unmasking the Thief (Book 5)

Crime & Passion Series
Mysterious Lover (Book 1)
Letters to a Lover (Book 2)
Dangerous Lover (Book 3)
Merry Lover (Novella)

The Husband Dilemma Series
How to Fool a Duke

Season of Scandal Series
Pursued by the Rake
Abandoned to the Prodigal
Married to the Rogue
Unmasked by her Lover
Her Star from the East (Novella)

Imperial Season Series
Vienna Waltz
Vienna Woods
Vienna Dawn

Blackhaven Brides Series
The Wicked Baron
The Wicked Lady
The Wicked Rebel
The Wicked Husband
The Wicked Marquis
The Wicked Governess
The Wicked Spy
The Wicked Gypsy
The Wicked Wife
Wicked Christmas (A Novella)
The Wicked Waif
The Wicked Heir
The Wicked Captain
The Wicked Sister

Unmarriageable Series
The Deserted Heart
The Sinister Heart
The Vulgar Heart
The Broken Heart
The Weary Heart
The Secret Heart

Christmas Heart

The Lyon's Den Series
Fed to the Lyon

De Wolfe Pack: The Series
The Wicked Wolfe
Vienna Wolfe

Also from Mary Lancaster
Madeleine
The Others of Ochil

CHAPTER ONE

OLIVIA STARED AT the raindrops falling against the window and trickling slowly down. She had not noticed it growing so dark.

Behind her, Aggie bustled into the room, tutting because the candles were not lit. A cozy glow soon filled the small cottage parlor, and with a word of thanks, Olivia moved to take the cup of hot chocolate that Aggie had brought.

They sat on opposite sides of the fireplace in a familiar pre-bedtime ritual. Olivia felt a rush of affection toward the kind, outspoken woman who, for years, had been the closest thing she knew to a mother. Servant, nurse, and friend—Aggie was all of those things and more, which made what Olivia had to say particularly difficult.

"I think I have to go to Cuttyngs," Olivia said quietly, when she had taken her first sip of chocolate.

A flare of fear surged in Aggie's eyes. "I thought you had decided not to."

"So did I. But our visitors…Miss Wallace and Lord Frostbrook—"

"I remember their names," Aggie said impatiently.

"They believe the late Duke of Cuttyngham did not die of the pistol ball that hit him in the duel."

"I heard, though it hardly concerns you."

"I was there," Olivia said with a shiver. "I saw him fall. I think… I think it is time I met his son."

"The monster?" Aggie said aggressively.

"The new duke," Olivia corrected her.

"If you were going to do so, why did you not obey Mr. Severne and go when he commanded you? When he was here to protect you?"

Aggie's agitation pierced Olivia. She could not upset her more by voicing the terrible suspicions that had floated through her head while Lord Frostbrook, who had been the late duke's second in the tragic duel, told her of his doubts. That the duke had fallen and probably died in the instant *before* the pistol ball hit him. Frostbrook had mentioned a possible illness. And Olivia was afraid.

Aggie leaned forward, both hands clutching her cup. "You mean to keep the iniquitous promise? *You* did not make it, Livie!"

"Mr. Severne accepted a great deal of money on my behalf."

"Money you have never seen! And why do you imagine the duke had to pay a stranger to marry his son? Because the boy is a monster!"

"No one called him a monster," Olivia said tiredly. "An unfortunate cripple, too disabled to appeal to a lady of his own class. It must be very lonely for him."

"And very unpleasant for you," Aggie retorted. "We talked before about the physical demands of marriage, and you would have to bear such intimacy with this mon…cripple," she corrected herself.

Olivia blushed. "Mr. Severne told me that the young man was not…capable. That it would be a marriage in name only. I would merely provide some appearance of normality for the young heir, and in time be the duchess."

"Respectability," Aggie mocked her. "Security. I wish those things for you, but you do not need a duke to acquire them. Any man would be honored and delighted to marry you. All you need do is choose one. A *whole* one, not one physically and mentally corrupted!"

"Those are mere rumors," Olivia said, more calmly than she felt. "Mr. Severne said the boy was reclusive and odd, no more."

"And you would truly marry such a creature? Just to keep Mr. Severne's iniquitous promise?"

"No," Olivia said patiently. "I am going to call upon him, find out what I can." *And warn him...* "I have no intention of marrying him."

Aggie sat back. "No point in going, then," she said in relief.

Olivia laughed. "Aggie, I love your tangled logic. I'll go to the George tomorrow and take the public coach to Cuttyngham. From there, I imagine I might easily walk to Cuttyngs."

Aggie's fright was back. "You can't! What if this duke won't receive you? What if he murders you?"

"In a house full of servants?"

"The dowager duchess is not there. Nor the monster's sister. You cannot go there alone."

"Don't be silly, Aggie. I have been used to going everywhere alone."

Aggie closed her eyes, then opened them again and glared at Olivia. "Well, you won't be going into this lair alone. *I* shall be with you. And I will be taking the *sharp* umbrella."

AGGIE'S COMPANIONSHIP WAS both a comfort and an annoyance. She took up space in the public coach and tended to glare at any man who dared to speak to Olivia, even with perfect courtesy. And then, her visage grim, she grasped her umbrella with both hands throughout the remaining journey after a local farmer kindly gave them a lift on his cart from the town of Cuttyngham to the Cuttyngs estate. It was rather further than Olivia had imagined.

They had left home at dawn and made excellent time, so

when they clambered down from the cart at the grand Cuttyngs gates, the late-afternoon sun was still warm. The gates were open, so Olivia walked through at once, with Aggie flapping after her.

An old man emerged from the tiny lodge inside, looking surprised, though he tugged his forelock respectfully enough. "Afternoon, ladies," he greeted them just a little too loudly. "What can we do for you? Where can I direct you?"

"To the duke, if you please," Olivia said calmly. "Is His Grace in residence?"

The old man, who had watched her lips so intently that she realized he was deaf, took off his cap and scratched his head thoughtfully. "Always in residence, ma'am, but rarely receiving. You can ask at the house, but I don't make you no promises."

Olivia smiled, thanked him, and walked on up the sweeping drive.

Aggie seized her arm to slow her down. "He won't see us. Might as well go home."

"He might see us," Olivia replied. "And if he doesn't, we might learn something from the servants."

Aggie stared at her. "Like what?"

Like if he is safe. "Anything."

Aggie scowled at her. "You're not thinking of getting them to take you on, are you?"

Olivia laughed. "Don't be silly. I'd make a useless servant. I've always relied on you too much, and I would answer all the wrong people back."

Aggie seemed comforted by this to some degree, although she still glared about her as though expecting the ducal monster to leap out of trees to assault them.

The house came partially into view as they rounded the curve of the drive. It was huge, its frontage one of classical splendor, rows of windows gleaming in the sunshine. As they drew closer, Olivia saw that two large wings graced either side of the house, the whole set in very formal gardens and parkland.

Her courage did quail slightly, but she had known she would find the ducal residence magnificent. She kept going. Beside her, Aggie was silent, apart from her labored breathing, as Olivia climbed the steps to the front door and knocked.

A tall, liveried footman opened the door and regarded them somewhat superciliously. "Yes?"

"I am Miss Rainey. Is His Grace at home?"

The servant's lip curled. It seemed likely he was about to tell them to be off, or at least to use the kitchen door, when quick footsteps sounded behind him.

"Thank you, Albert. I will deal with this," said a commanding voice. The footman stepped back at once, and his place was taken by an older man in a dark, immaculate suit. Another family member? Olivia wondered.

"I am Betts," the man informed her regally. "His Grace's butler. Perhaps you would be good enough to repeat your name and your business?"

"My name is Olivia Rainey, and I would like to speak to His Grace when he can spare a moment."

The butler's piercing gaze moved from her and flickered over to Aggie.

"My companion, Mrs. Arnott," Olivia said.

The butler inclined his head and, rather to her surprise, opened the door wide and stepped back. "Of course. Please come in. I am afraid His Grace is not available at the moment, but he should return in the next couple of hours. I shall inform him then of your call. Would you care to wait in the salon?"

Olivia hesitated. Would there still be time to book a room at the local inn in another couple of hours? Then she glanced at Aggie's exhausted face and said, "Thank you, we shall wait."

The butler led them across a magnificent marble hall, with a gracious staircase curving from two sides up to a curved gallery. A huge chandelier holding hundreds of unlit candles hung from the upper floor's ceiling. Opulent cabinets, mirrors, tables, and sofas graced the space, almost crammed in to show off antiquity and wealth.

It was something of a relief to be shown into a much barer salon—presumably where unimportant guests were abandoned until His Grace or his people could spare them a moment of their valuable time.

"May I send you tea, ma'am?"

"Thank you. That would be lovely." Olivia removed her much-mended gloves, and pushed Aggie gently into one of the room's four chairs before unfastening the woman's cloak and removing her hat. "You might as well be comfortable. His Grace will be some time."

Aggie sniffed. "He's here already. Mark my words. Didn't Mr. Severne say he never went out? The quality say they're not at home when they don't want to see you."

"Then why give us tea? I believe he means to consult the duke at least."

Aggie was silent until the tea was brought by a different footman, who offered to pour and then departed with a bow. Aggie and Olivia both fell upon the sandwiches immediately. Olivia hadn't realized how hungry she was until she smelled the ham, which was delicious between daintily cut soft bread and butter. Having almost swallowed her sandwich whole, she poured the tea and passed a delicate porcelain cup and saucer to Aggie, before reaching for the plate again.

"At least he has decent servants," Aggie said grudgingly.

"He's a duke."

"I mean, they haven't yet fled in terror."

"From the monster?" Olivia said sardonically. "You have listened to too much gossip."

"Maybe," Aggie allowed, pursing her lips. "But the old duke hid him away. He never went to school, never attended social events at Cuttyngs or anywhere else. Why would his own father do that unless he was ashamed?"

"Or overprotective," Olivia pointed out.

Aggie snorted and helped herself to one of the duke's scones.

Hunger satisfied, Aggie sat back in her chair, her eyelids drooping. Haring across the country was no longer good for her. She was getting old, and the knowledge gave Olivia a pang of sorrow as well as guilt. She rose and went to the long French window looking out onto a somewhat regimented garden.

A maid came in. "May I take the tea things away, ma'am? Anything else you need?"

"Oh, no, thank you. Might I walk in the garden, do you think? Or is His Grace expected imminently?"

"Not for another hour, I doubt," the maid said cheerfully. "Just unbolt the door and go out, ma'am. I'll fetch you when His Grace returns."

So, they were keeping to the fiction of the duke being "not at home." Perhaps everyone, including His Grace, expected Olivia to get fed up and leave. As she would have to soon, to see about beds at the village inn. If there was one…

When the maid had gone, and Aggie was snoring gently in her chair, Olivia unbolted the French door and let herself outside.

As gardens went, this one was rather too uniform for her taste. In many places the beds were set out in rows of colors, like troops of infantry, hussars, and riflemen waiting for inspection. It was not a relaxing kind of garden, although she was probably influenced by her own tension concerning her visit and the duke. At any rate, it was pleasant to stretch her legs after a day crammed into various vehicles.

She allowed herself twenty minutes, using the small watch she wore on a chain around her neck, to walk as far and fast as she could. She soon strode out beyond the garden through a gate in a wall and onto rougher ground. She veered off the path toward a fallow field and then, after consulting her watch, dropped down to lean her back against a hedge and rest.

Two minutes, she thought, *and I shall run back…*

The galloping hooves came out of nowhere. At first, she paid no attention, but they grew louder so quickly that she felt the ground shake beneath her. With sudden alarm, she realized they were coming from behind the hedge, straight for her.

Her instinct was to spring up and get out of the way, although as soon as she rose, she realized she would probably have been safer huddling into the hedge while the horse and rider jumped it. At any rate, there was barely time to stagger back out of the way of the horse's hooves. She had a glimpse of the rider, a dark man with wild black hair and thick, dramatic eyebrows, an impression of power and beauty that seemed to hit her like a blow.

But the big horse had caught sight of her in mid-jump and squealed in fright, flailing its legs as if it no longer knew where to land. With horror, she watched it stumble and fall, while the rider managed at least to throw himself clear of the animal's weight.

She moved quickly to soothe the horse as it regained its feet, terrified it would trample the rider in its outrage. She caught it by the bridle, uttering soft, calming words and stroking its damp neck until it stopped pulling away from her. As it calmed, she turned with fear to the rider, who lay perfectly still, his fallen hat some distance away.

Oh God, is he dead? With a last, distracted pat on the horse's nose, she released it, and crouched down by the rider. He lay on his back, one leg at a peculiar angle and his open eyes staring upward. With unspeakable relief, she saw that his fist was clenched in the grass, and that he was breathing in short, shallow breaths that he seemed to be making every effort to lengthen. His face was white.

"Sir, I am so sorry," she said. "I'll run and fetch help, but is there anything I can do for you first to make you any more comfortable?"

He turned his head to look at her directly, and there was a wealth of pain in his eyes that tore at her heart. A shudder shook him, and she hastily tore off her cloak and threw it over him. Only then did she realize he hadn't been shivering but silently laughing.

"What is this for?" he demanded. "I'm not dead."

"I-I thought you were cold," she said. "With shock, you know? I'm afraid your leg is broken."

"No more than usual," he said. "It's just wrenched a bit. I'll get up in a minute. I see you caught my cowardly horse."

"He isn't cowardly. It was my fault for looming up so suddenly. I should have stayed where I was."

He didn't debate her guilt, though his black frown deepened. "What the devil were you doing there, anyway? In fact, *who* the devil are you?"

"No one. I am waiting to see the duke."

His eyebrows flew upward. "Not very good at it, are you?"

"Good at what?" she asked, bewildered. Perhaps the poor young man had hit his head?

"Waiting." He shifted, hauling himself into a sitting position. Her hands flew out instinctively to help him. He gritted his teeth, and she fell back.

"Well, *you* are not very good at accepting help," she retorted. "You needn't be so angry."

He blinked. "I'm not angry. I'm damnably sore. If you wish to help, bring me that stick sheathed by the saddle."

She thought at first he meant a whip of some kind, but when she jumped up and found the leather sheath, it was far too big, and what she took from it was a stout wooden walking stick. A terrible suspicion began to enter her head.

But this man was no monster, no inarticulate idiot. No one could ever be ashamed enough to hide him. Dear God, he was *beautiful*.

She carried the stick to him, and he grasped it like an old friend. Then his eyes—profoundly dark eyes—lifted to hers and he said, "Oblige me by turning your back. This won't be pretty."

"I'll fetch your hat," she said calmly, and walked away to retrieve it from where it had rolled in the fall. Behind her, she was very conscious of the hiss of his breath, a grunt of what was surely pain. She picked up the hat and turned in time to see him upright but stumbling. She ran to him, throwing her arm around his waist to steady him.

It worked, but his face was even whiter than before. Even his lips seemed bloodless.

"Thank you," he muttered. He drew in a breath and said shortly, "The horse is lame. Oblige me by leading him back to the stables. I'll follow."

She stared up at him, very conscious of his pain, and the power of his determination. And of the tension of his body under her arm. She let it fall back to her side and eyed the stick with some doubt.

"With your current injury," she said, "the stick is not enough. You will have better balance if you lean on my shoulders."

He tore his gaze free of her. "You are a tiny little creature, and I find I do not mind hurting the stick."

"You won't hurt me."

"No, because I have no intention of using you. Please lead the horse."

"And send people back to pick you off the ground with some greater injury?"

He swung his gaze back to her in surprise. "Tiny but vocal," he observed. Expressions flitted across his face faster than she could read them. Then his breath hissed. It might have been laughter, or a surge of pain.

"Very well," he pronounced. "But only because I want to, and it's the only time you'll let me." He transferred the stick to his other hand and laid his arm gently around her shoulders, as though he expected her to bolt or flinch. When she didn't, his lips quirked. She felt the muscles in his arm flex and realized how strong it was.

"Come here, horse," he commanded, without taking his gaze off her. Rather to her surprise, the horse ambled toward them and let Olivia take it by the reins. "Are you ready for the indignity? Then let us begin."

With the first step, she threw her arm around his waist to balance them better, but it clearly caused him agony to put any weight on his bad leg.

"Are you sure the bone is not broken?" she asked anxiously.

"Quite," he said between his teeth. But as they moved forward, there was a certain weary stoicism about him that showed how used he was to pain. He just bore it and waited for it to lessen.

"Where are we going?" she asked.

He nodded toward the big house.

"I thought so. You are the duke, are you not?"

"I am. Don't mistake the inquiry for rudeness, but who are you and what the devil do you want with me?"

"My name is Olivia Rainey," she said ruefully. "And believe it or not, I came to warn you."

CHAPTER TWO

VICTOR SEVERNE, NEWLY ascended Duke of Cuttyngham, was very pleasantly distracted from the intolerable pain in his leg. He had been afraid it was making his whole body shake, but the deceptively fragile frame beneath his arm and the feel of her very feminine body against his side encouraged quite another turn of mind. He had learned long ago that management of pain was largely a matter of the mind.

He liked her arm about him too. He could easily imagine them much more intimately entwined. She might even understand his jokes.

Her name meant nothing to him, and he was as sure as he could be that she did not belong to the neighborhood. Although she spoke like a lady, her cloak and the drab gown beneath did not, to his mind, belong to someone of that class. Not that he was acquainted with many ladies.

"Warn me," he repeated when her words finally filtered through the pain of an awkward step. "Of what? If my father swindled you or neglected you or anyone of your family, I'll make decent reparation. There is no need for threats."

She stared at him with such total incomprehension that he realized he was wide of the mark. He had an insane urge to drop his stick and use his fingertips to smooth the frown tugging at her brow.

"So, no threat," he said. "You must forgive my lack of social graces. Tell me, in plain words, what it is you want of me."

"Nothing," she said, her eyes sparkling with such indignation that he laughed.

"I beg your pardon," he said with a self-mockery he doubted she would recognize. "Allow me to rephrase. What might I do for you?"

"Nothing," she repeated, "except listen."

"I am all ears," he said flippantly, trying to ease some of his weight from her narrow shoulders. Her hand felt warm at his side, her fingers surprisingly strong.

She drew in an audible breath. "I recently received a visit from Lord Frostbrook and Miss Wallace. I believe they are known to you."

"They are," he said, gazing at her now with some glimmer of understanding. "Never tell me you are the mysterious lady from the George Inn? Who saw His Grace's duel?"

She flushed, which intrigued him, until he realized it was probably merely the exertion of supporting his weight and his clumsy gait.

"I observed it, yes, though I have no idea why you might consider me mysterious."

"Oh, just the fact that you were there. Aren't females meant to have fits of the vapors at the very mention of duels?"

"You don't know that I did not have a *huge* fit of the vapors," she pointed out.

"True. To be honest, I'm not perfectly sure what such vapors are, though I suspect I shouldn't like them. But I feel you are not such a poor creature."

"I'm not," she admitted. "Though I confess I am out of patience with such behavior as dueling to prove the right of a quarrel. Who could possibly believe such nonsense?"

"No one, I'm sure. And I'm very glad to see you are not prostrate with grief over His Grace's death."

She blinked. Her lashes were long and curling. He could

almost feel them tickling his cheek. In his dreams.

"I am sorry he is dead, but since I never met the man, my grief is minimal."

"So is mine," Victor said, and found her gaze on him, eyes wide with astonishment. An unbecoming sentiment, no doubt, for a son. Well, he couldn't help that. "But if you didn't know His Grace, what were you doing there?"

"I went to meet my father and found the inn full of soldiers and noblemen. I kept to my own chamber most of the time."

"And your father?" he asked, with sudden unease. He didn't want her to be His Grace's by-blow, though God knew it made no difference to Victor's chances with the lady.

"Not the late duke," she said, holding on as he veered to the right, away from the front of the house. "Don't you mean to go in the front door?"

"On no account." He tried not to speak between gritted teeth but wasn't sure he succeeded. "Loop the reins around that tree. He'll stand until someone comes to retrieve him."

The girl obeyed, keeping one anxious eye on Victor, no doubt in case he fell over without her to hold him up. Then she slipped under his arm once more and put her own around his waist, which now felt dangerously natural.

Victor nodded toward the garden at this end of the house. "There is a side door, or one of the French windows might be open."

"The one I left by is unbolted."

"That would be quicker," he said with some relief. The effort not to lean on her too hard was making him shake, and he was terrified he would faint from the pain. He had once, when he fell down the stairs, but that had been years ago. He had also lost the thread of their conversation, concentrating only on putting one foot in front of the other, through the rose garden that his stepmother and Hera both hated, to the French window into the blue salon, which no one ever used.

She must have only closed it over when she had left, for it

gave easily when he pushed it with his stick. They lurched inside together. Two more steps and he fell into the nearest chair with a muffled groan of relief.

For a moment, the blood sang in his ears and the pain washed over him like a tide. There was nothing he could do until it eased back as he knew it would. But somehow, her capable little hand was in his, and he had to stop himself squeezing her fingers as though they were his own.

As though from very far away, he heard her say, "Aggie, ring the bell." And somehow, that brought back his senses.

Someone else was in the room. Not one of his own servants but a plump, elderly lady in a mobcap, looking concerned, though whether for him or for the girl, he couldn't have said. The latter possibility made him laugh, though, a short, husky sound.

"Sir, allow me to present my companion, Mrs. Arnott. Aggie, His Grace, the Duke of Cuttyngham."

He saw the woman's jaw drop with astonishment—well, he was a poor creature for such a splendid title—but there was no time for more, for Jenny the housemaid bounded in and skidded to a halt when she saw him.

"Send Black to me, if you please," he said, and she ran out again. But he should have known she couldn't do *only* as she was told. Before Black arrived, Betts did, striding into the room in some distress.

"Your Grace, what has befallen—"

"My Grace befell," Victor interrupted sardonically. "Send to the stables to take care of Julius—he's lame and liable to eat all the flowers besides." There was nothing else for it. Taking a deep breath, he dug his stick into the floor and hauled himself to his feet once more. The girl—Olivia?—uttered a little mewl of distress. Which was, sort of, the noise he felt like making himself.

If only they would all go away, he could go up the stairs on his backside, which would be so much simpler…

But no, Black appeared in the doorway as well, and Victor wanted to grind his teeth.

"With one of us on either side," Betts began, "we could manage him. Or Albert could just carry him."

"No," Victor ground out, "Albert could not. If you would just—"

"Grip crossed hands like this to make a seat," Black interrupted, and Victor blinked at the chair they presented. They moved behind him, and the girl pushed him gently to sit.

"I'm sorry," Victor managed. "I will be more the thing by dinnertime. You will join me, I hope. Mrs. Irwin will show you to rooms."

He wanted to look back over his shoulder to see her for longer, but part of him couldn't bear to. He had, as his father had often prophesied, thoroughly disgraced himself. It should not have hurt so much. The pain in his leg at least should have been able to distract him.

Fortunately, he had made his bedchamber on the first floor, next to the library, so there was only one flight of stairs to negotiate, and that was accomplished with surprising ease. They set him on his bed, and he lay back on the pillows with some relief.

"I'll find you something to ease the pain," Black murmured.

"No laudanum," Victor said at once.

"No, sir. Just the medicine Her Grace mixed. It helped once before, if you recall."

He did recall. Also, his stepmother's unexpectedly profound knowledge of herbs and medicines.

While Black went into the dressing room, Betts said, "I hope I did the right thing in allowing Miss Rainey to wait for Your Grace?"

"Yes, of course. Though I never did discover what the devil she wants."

Betts held his gaze. "Miss Olivia Rainey, Your Grace."

"So she told me," Victor snapped. "The name means nothing to me."

Betts blinked. "I believe her to be the natural daughter of

Your Grace's cousin, Mr. Anthony Severne."

Victor opened his mouth to say something dismissive before the obvious reality came clattering down about his ears.

Her. This was *her*. And damn it all, he'd liked her, had even imagined...

What? His lips twisted, and he forced himself to stare at the butler. There was a certain pity in the man's eyes, damn him to hell. He knew. He knew it all.

Of course he did. Victor's servants were all his father's creatures. He didn't much care, but he must never forget it.

Her Grace's medicine took the edge off Victor's pain, at least enough to allow him to bear through gritted teeth the agony of the local quack examining his leg. In his head, he translated chunks of Homer until the ordeal was over and the doctor pronounced nothing broken.

"Still, you must give it absolute rest for at least a week. No walking, even, until the damage has healed. I must tell Your Grace that it is pure folly for you to be riding. The late duke, your father, was right to forbid it."

"The late duke, my father, was killed in a duel," Victor snapped. "Which says little for his judgment. I thank you for your time. You may go."

The doctor opened his mouth to say more.

"Good afternoon, doctor."

The doctor departed, an expression of surprise on his face, as though he couldn't quite work out why he had left before saying all he meant to. Victor refrained from throwing his stick after him.

For a time, he lay deep in thought. Part of him wanted to confront Olivia Rainey now, make her suffer, frighten her into an early departure. Another part wanted simply to dismiss her as he had every other unwanted hanger-on at Cuttyngs, including his Aunt and Uncle Hadleigh, and Cousin Anthony, who had clearly imagined he would have his feet well under the table by now. Being the duke had some advantages.

Was Olivia here to fulfill her part in her father's bargain? Presumably. In which case, this "warning" nonsense must be merely an excuse. He should go to dinner, listen politely, and make sure she knew to be gone first thing. He didn't need to frighten her. To do so, surely, made him no better than his father. Unless she deserved it, of course.

He drifted into sleep, grateful for the oblivion.

OLIVIA, HAVING BEEN informed that His Grace was confined to bed by his doctor, was not surprised to dine alone. Aggie, appalled by the formality of the dining room, had gone to speak to Mrs. Irwin, the housekeeper, and told her she would be more comfortable in the kitchen, with the status of Olivia's maid.

It was not a comfortable meal, observed by the footmen who must all have wondered what on earth she was doing here. She occupied her mind by imagining the oppressive room with different decoration, made welcoming and airy in summer, cozy in winter. Different hangings, less furniture…

She retired to her room as soon as she had eaten dessert. Like the rest of the house, her bedchamber was large and grand, the curtains heavy and dark, the whole somehow cold, even on a pleasant May evening. She sank down on the rigid sofa and wondered how the duke was faring. She pitied his pain, suspecting he lived with it constantly in varying degrees. She wondered about his strange, reclusive life.

There was nothing of the monster or the idiot about him. The mystery was why the old duke had thought it necessary to bribe anyone to marry him. Or had Anthony, her own father, made that up? She could not imagine why, unless it was to encourage Olivia to the altar, to make his daughter a duchess. It would certainly explain why she had never seen any of the money Anthony had supposedly received for the bridal.

Not for the first time, she wondered what she was doing here. Loneliness washed over her, but she would not ring for Aggie. The poor old thing was exhausted with the journey.

In this, however, she was proved wrong, for Aggie appeared without her ringing only a few minutes later.

"Is everything well below stairs?" Olivia asked her anxiously. "Are they kind to you?"

"Oh yes, kind enough," Aggie said comfortably, laying out Olivia's night rail. "And I've learned lots, too. The late duke was a right old tyrant, controlled everything and all but imprisoned his wives to the house. Though that may be an exaggeration. They all seem to like the current duchess, though, and aren't remotely surprised she bolted as soon as the duke was buried. Even left her companion behind—that would be the Miss Wallace, who came to the cottage with Lord Frostbrook. The daughter's gone, too—Lady Hera, off to visit friends no one has heard of in Lincolnshire."

Olivia wanted to know what they said of the new duke, but the words stuck in her throat. There had been enough gossip about him, lies that had come as far afield as her own isolated village. Lies at least partially endorsed by her father, who had thought little of "Victor."

Aggie unfastened her gown for her. "They're all a bit frightened of the new duke."

"Why?" Olivia asked blankly, until she recalled that first glimpse of him, all raw power and an almost satanic beauty—although that was ridiculously fanciful.

"Mostly because they're amazed he's still alive. He wasn't expected to survive childhood, but he did. He's fantastically clever, apparently, but he wasn't physically fit to go to school or Oxford. Couldn't play with other children, so never went outside further than the home wood. Until his sister took it into her head to teach him to ride. Since the old duke died, he's been riding all over the estate, taking note of everything. Half the tenants are expecting eviction. And since the servants mostly come from these families, that's probably one source of their fear."

"Is he a cruel landlord, then?"

"They don't know, but the old duke was bad enough. Some of them seem disappointed that Mr. Severne didn't succeed to the dukedom."

"He couldn't," Olivia observed, pulling on her night gown and padding over to the dressing table where Aggie had left her hairbrush.

"Not while the old duke's son lives. But then, no one expected him to live, and they're all wondering why he's still here. The kitchen maid said witchcraft, though she was slapped for it."

Olivia stopped brushing to turn and frown at Aggie. "Why shouldn't he live? Is he ill as well as lame?"

Aggie shrugged. "They're guessing. The doctor was here a lot until the old duke died. The young duke apparently forbade him from the house until today, and even then he was here for a mere ten minutes."

Uneasily, Olivia dragged the brush through her hair once more.

"Makes sense if you think about it," Aggie mused. "That's why Mr. Severne wanted you to marry him. He thought he would trouble you little and die, leaving you a duchess and set up for life."

Then why was he paid for it?

Aggie shivered. "I don't like this house. You did right not to obey your father for once. We should go. First thing. The servants suspect we'll be dismissed at breakfast in any case."

"I haven't had the chance to speak to him yet."

"Then go to breakfast before we leave."

Chapter Three

The maid Jenny showed Olivia to the breakfast parlor the following morning. Disappointingly, the duke was not there.

"Has His Grace breakfasted already?" Olivia asked.

"Oh, he has his in the library, ma'am. Has most of his meals there. Though he did come out for tea with Miss Wallace."

That was interesting. Olivia had liked Miss Wallace. Apparently, the duke did, too.

She ate some egg and toast and drank two cups of coffee. Then, resolutely, she rose and walked out into the passage.

Catching a passing footman, she said, "Direct me to the library, if you please."

"Round the corner, and the first door on your right, ma'am."

"Is His Grace well enough to be disturbed?" she asked.

"He doesn't normally *like* to be disturbed," the footman replied cautiously. "Though I took him his breakfast an hour ago."

She thought of asking him to announce her, then decided against it. His Grace did not appear to be a man who stood on ceremony. Accordingly, she marched along the passage and rounded the corner to the large double doors on her right. She knocked, and hearing no voice telling her to go away—in fact, she heard no voice at all—she opened the door and went in.

The library was a large, elegant room, filled from floor to

ceiling with bookshelves. Two large desks were piled high with volumes of various size and copious papers, but visible over the top was the figure of the young duke swathed in a gorgeously embroidered dressing gown, sitting in the middle of the sofa surrounded by even more books.

He looked up with the almost permanent scowl deeply etched on his face, and his eyes widened. To her surprise, a tinge of color crept along the bones of his pale cheeks. She pretended not to notice, since she knew she was blushing much more obviously from the embarrassment of discovering him *en déshabillé*.

"You must excuse me, Miss Rainey," he said sardonically. "I was not expecting visitors, and I have got into the habit of using the library as something of a boudoir."

"It's a very pleasant boudoir," she allowed, with the first hint of envy she had felt since coming here. "Forgive me for interrupting, but I wished to speak to you before we leave."

"What about?" he asked indifferently. He neither made any effort to get up—for which she was glad, considering his injury—nor invited her to sit.

"First, to thank you for your kind hospitality," she began, and his lips curled into an amused smile. His mood made her uneasy. Where was the brave, blunt young man who had managed to laugh even through considerable pain? She persevered. "And to wish you a speedy recovery from your injury. I hope you are in less pain today. Also… to give you my reason for intruding on you here in the first place."

"Don't trouble, Miss Rainey," he mocked her. "I'm well aware of your purpose."

She regarded him more closely. "You are?"

"No one ever accused me of being slow-witted, ma'am. Not to my face, anyway."

"Is it well known, then?"

"Apparently. His Grace was not the most discreet of men. In fact, you might say he talked himself to death."

Olivia frowned now in total incomprehension. "His Grace was aware of the danger to his life?"

"Even the biggest fool would be aware of the risks in dueling."

"Yes, but… Your Grace, Lord Frostbrook implied that you are aware of his view that the late duke did not die of the dueling injury."

"And what is your view?" the young duke inquired with an exaggerated interest that appeared to be more insulting than courteous.

"That Lord Frostbrook could be right," she said, determined to say the words. "I too thought the duke fell the instant before he was shot. If that is so, then it seems likely that someone deliberately harmed him. And if they did, you also might be at risk."

The duke drew back his head, an involuntarily gesture of surprise. At last, it seemed, she had said something unexpected. "From what? I am unlikely to be challenged to a duel. It would reflect poorly on my opponent, even to accept a challenge from me."

His self-mockery was apparent, but she read no self-pity in the dark, beautiful face.

"Why?" she asked, distracted. "I imagine you shoot as straight as anyone else."

"More so than most. Though beating one's sister in a contest is hardly the accolade for a gentleman. To return to your curious warning, Miss Rainey, exactly what do you imagine this risk is?"

"If I knew I would tell you," she muttered. "I am just uneasy."

"And thought you would come here and try to make me uneasy, too?"

She glared at him. "Make you *careful,*" she corrected him. "But I suppose if you're a duke that isn't necessary, because you can always blame someone else!"

"Very true. Only that's not a very useful privilege once you're dead. Who would kill either my father or me? Leaving aside

Major Butler, who probably did *not* dispatch His Grace."

She turned away because even now she could not play the traitor, not without proof, at least. "How would I know? I merely urge you to take care, and so take my leave. My thanks for your time. Goodbye."

He said nothing, though as she turned and walked to the door, she thought she caught an ironic glint in his eye. He was undoubtedly an odd creature, but she was disappointed to find no trace of the likeable young man she had encountered yesterday. Either she had been badly mistaken or he was excessively moody. Or both.

She closed the door quietly behind her and climbed the stairs to the chamber she had slept in last night. Aggie was already there, having packed her own and Olivia's overnight bags.

"Well?" Aggie asked.

Olivia sighed. "I have no idea. I tried to warn him, but who knows if he took me seriously."

"Did you mention…?"

"Of course not. I have no proof, and I would not destroy their relationship. The duke is *not* a fool. He will look out for himself. Come, we should be able to find transport from the village to Cuttyngham."

They descended to the front hall, each carrying their own bag, and were bowed out by the same footman who had been reluctant to admit them the day before. Olivia refused to glance up at the windows to see who, if anyone, was watching their departure.

Aggie scowled as she walked, clearly deep in troubled thought. Well, they could compare anxieties on the journey.

However, they had not reached the first curve in the drive before the same footman—Albert?—ran after them calling, "Ma'am! Miss Rainey!"

They both turned in surprise, and the footman slowed to a smart walk. "His Grace begs you will return and accept his hospitality for the next few days."

"Please thank His Grace and send our regrets." Olivia nodded and turned aside once more, but to her amazement, Aggie spoke.

"On the contrary. Tell His Grace that Miss Rainey will be glad to accept."

Olivia stared at her. "I am not."

"Of course you are."

Albert the footman glanced from one to the other with an air of superior amusement.

Aggie stepped closer to Olivia. "Something is wrong here. Very wrong, and we both know it. I'm afraid you were right to come. And there is no one else here but us."

So to Aggie's mind, the duke was no longer a monster. To Olivia's, he was more of one than he had been yesterday, but that was her own pique. For the rest, Aggie was right.

"Very well," Olivia said slowly. "We shall stay another night."

IT WAS, APPARENTLY, expected that Olivia return to the library and take tea with the duke. She did not rush, but went to her room to leave her bag and remove her bonnet and cloak and pin a stray lock of hair back into place. She regarded herself doubtfully in the glass. Smooth chestnut-brown hair without a hint of a curl, grave gray-blue eyes, unfashionable, country-made gown, although the fabric was decent quality.

The overall effect, she felt, was plain. Her reflection never looked as she imagined, as though some other strange, serious female gazed back at her, disapproving of her imagination, her desire to laugh and spread her wings.

With a quick shake of her head, she stepped back, took a deep breath, and left the room for another interview with His Grace.

When she knocked this time, she was answered with a curt "Enter." She walked in to find no sign of the sumptuous dressing gown. Instead, His Grace was fully dressed in loose pantaloons and dark coat, plain white cravat, and an unexpectedly colorful tartan waistcoat. Even his unruly hair had been brushed into some semblance of order.

And he seemed to have remembered his manners.

"Miss Rainey," he said politely. "Please, sit down."

A pile of books had been removed from the sofa. Presumably she was meant to sit there. The duke sat now on one side of it, his legs resting on a long footstool. One lay at an odd angle as though permanently twisted.

Olivia stood where she was. "Why did you command—I beg your pardon, *invite*—us to return?"

A gleam, perhaps of appreciation or amusement, flashed in his dark eyes. "I never meant you to leave in the first place. I just wanted to see if you would go."

Irritated, she walked forward. "I don't understand you. What are you trying to prove? What do you want of me?"

"There is no need to panic. It is not marriage."

She paused, and he regarded her mockingly as he lifted the teapot from the table beside him.

"Nor any less honorable arrangement," he continued. "You should know that my father's death releases you from any bond. I shan't even ask for the return of the money."

So he *did* know. He had always known. The heat of shame flooded her.

She said, "I had nothing to do with any bond. It was between your father and mine."

"It seems neither of us has been fortunate in fathers." He replaced the teapot and pushed the cup of tea he had just poured to the far side of the table.

She sat on the sofa—mostly because her legs seemed reluctant to support her—with the low table between them. Like an automaton, she lifted the cream jug and added a dash to her cup.

"I barely know mine," she admitted. "But I understand why you are angry. Such an arrangement was infamous and incomprehensible."

He inclined his head somewhat sardonically, but she refused to be cowed.

She said calmly, "You thought I had come to claim my prize."

"Didn't you?" he said, depriving her of breath. "Don't misunderstand me. I don't underestimate the difficulties, to say nothing of the strong stomach required. But being Duchess of Cuttyngham is quite a promotion for Cousin Anthony's…love child."

She lifted her chin. "You may say the word bastard. I shan't be offended."

His gaze fell. Perhaps he was ashamed. Perhaps he was just looking for his cup, which he lifted distractedly to his lips. "Is that what you really came to tell me? And then lost courage? Or interest, since I was being unpleasant?"

"You are still being unpleasant," she retorted.

"And yet you are still here. Without answering the question."

"I came to warn you because I felt I had to. I did not believe you could even be aware of my father's disgraceful arrangement with yours."

He laughed with a genuine amusement amongst the bitterness. "You imagine His Grace had so much delicacy?"

She frowned. "When…*why* did he tell you?"

"Just something else to beat me with," he said. "Why did Anthony tell *you*?"

"Because he expected me to go to Cuttyngs when he summoned me."

"Ah, he has summoned."

"He summoned me a few weeks ago," she admitted. "Immediately after the duel, in fact. I ignored him."

"Cold feet?" he asked with entirely false sympathy.

"Much the same revulsion of feeling I imagine you are experiencing right now," she retorted.

With insulting deliberation, he looked her up and down. "Oh, I don't know. You are a beautiful girl, delightful figure, you speak like a lady. We would both be regarded as marrying better than expected."

She stared at him. "You said we were released from any such agreement."

"You said you were warning me of some danger, the same that killed my father. If we allow that the duel did not account for him."

This time, it was she who looked away, to her teacup. She did not answer, for there was nothing she could say.

"Where is Anthony?" he asked.

"I don't know. He stopped writing to me."

"Where do you send your letters?"

"I stopped writing to him," she admitted.

Silence stretched between them. "You are indeed a mystery," he said at last. "But I understand you are prepared to stay at Cuttyngs another few days at least?"

"Oh no," she said at once. "I said we would stay tonight. Neither Aggie nor I have enough with us to stay longer."

He shrugged. "You may borrow. The house is full of female garments."

She blinked at him. "I can just imagine the duchess's reaction to such an arrangement."

His lips curved into something like the spontaneous smile she remembered from yesterday. "I doubt it. She is very easy-going and happy to share. Besides, I would like you to stay. We are cousins, after all."

"Several times removed and on the left-hand side."

"Be grateful. There is bad blood in my branch of the family."

I rather think there is bad blood in mine, too…

He put down his cup with an air of finality. "At any rate, you must treat the house as your own. Walk, ride, go where you wish, order what you need."

It was clearly a dismissal. She didn't know whether to be annoyed or relieved, but there was nothing to do but rise and leave.

His voice stayed her. "Would you mind passing me the book on the nearest desk? The one on the top there."

"This one?" She lifted the book from the top of the pile she suspected had been resting on the sofa during her previous visit.

"That's it."

As she handed it to him, she noted its title. "Egypt!" she exclaimed.

"Indeed."

"Might I have a look at this when you're not reading it? Or perhaps you have others?"

His eyebrows rose. "You are interested in Egyptology?"

"One of my teachers introduced me to the subject. Her brother had been in Cairo. But I'm aware the study has moved on."

"So I am discovering. I have been distracted from my classical studies into a magnificent civilization I knew nothing about." For an instant, in the eagerness he could not hide, she saw the appealing young man of yesterday, and then his dark eyelashes swept down, and his voice reverted to its indifferent tones. "I shall look out for some volumes for you."

Dismissed again, she could only thank him and depart.

As she walked thoughtfully along the passage, she noticed Betts, the butler, hovering around the corner. Perhaps he was eager to help. Or perhaps he had been eavesdropping. Olivia decided to assume the former.

"Betts, is Mr. Anthony Severne expected at Cuttyngs in the near future?"

"Not to my knowledge, ma'am." He seemed to consider for a moment, then added, "His Grace requested some privacy in this time of mourning, for himself, Lady Hera, and Her Grace the duchess."

"And yet I believe neither of those ladies is in residence?"

"Not at the moment, ma'am."

Olivia nodded and walked on. There was nothing more she could ask in all decency and expect an answer. But it bothered her that the duke was so alone, despite his lack of obvious mourning. Why had his sister and his stepmother abandoned him?

Aggie presented a fresh perspective on this when she accompanied Olivia on a walk in the nearby woods.

"*They*," she confided, meaning the staff below stairs, "reckon the duchess bolted even before the old duke died. She came home again for the funeral, for decency's sake, but she left again as soon as she properly could. They reckon she was the next best thing to a prisoner here, with the old duke allowing her no freedom and no responsibilities beyond the dinner menus. Mind you, he was hardly ever here in later years."

"And Lady Hera?"

"She was with her aunt in London latterly, but after the funeral she went off to stay with friends to the north somewhere. With His Grace's approval, apparently. The staff reckon they all hated the place and couldn't wait to get away."

"Except the duke," Oliva murmured.

"No, including the duke. He had planned to go to Oxford this autumn, in the teeth of his father's disapproval. Apparently he had wanted to study there since he was a boy, and could pass the entrance examinations standing on his head. But the old duke forbade it. Then, when he'd decided to do it anyway, he became the duke and got saddled with responsibilities he's been ill-prepared for."

"Was he not brought up as the heir?" Olivia asked, surprised.

"Up to a point. He bore the heir's title, Marquis of Dean, but he was taught nothing of the estate management or his responsibilities in the House of Lords. He wasn't even taught to ride, or any other manly sports, because the old duke considered him too weak. Only Lady Hera taught him to ride secretly, and now he's learning about the estate by riding around with his father's steward."

"The old duke did not treat him well," Olivia murmured.

"Didn't trust him, either." Aggie looked up at her, her eyes anxious. "Have you considered there might be a reason for that? That we have it all wrong?"

Olivia frowned. "All what?"

"We discounted the heir from harming the old duke because we thought he was a crippled imbecile. He isn't."

"No, he isn't," Olivia said fervently. "On the other hand, he never left the estate, so I don't see how he could have poisoned him at the George Inn."

"He could have paid someone else to do so," Aggie argued.

"So could anyone."

"Just bear it in mind," Aggie said. "I'm sorry I suggested staying now I've considered it. But we must be cautious, Livie. It's possible the young duke is no victim but the murderer of his father."

Chapter Four

As the morning wore on, Victor remained afflicted with rare indecision. He could not make up his mind about Olivia Rainey. His instinct was to believe her, but he was painfully aware how little experience of the world he had to judge her by. Apart from the staff and tenants, he could count his acquaintances on his fingers—and that included family. He had never had to deal with feminine wiles, though he had always imagined they came with artful dressing and fluttering eyelashes.

Olivia's dress was ordinary to the point of drabness, and she did not flutter. And yet he would be lying if he tried to pretend she did not affect him. The anxious face gazing down at him through the pain of his fall had winded him all over again, and he had no real idea why. It was more than her beauty, of which she seemed genuinely unaware, much more than her concern and compassion, which in her he found oddly bearable. There was a clarity in her eyes, a delightful spirit and humor in her speech. He had imagined a kind of *seeking* in her that spoke to his own.

But she had not been honest.

Could he trust her explanation? Certainly, he had given her little time to tell all in their walk from the accident to the house. And though she was well aware of his father's bribing her to marry him, she had not volunteered the information. To protect his feelings? Or had she her own reasons for being here?

Letting her leave had been a test. He had been sure she would find a way not to go, but Black had watched from the window as she and her "companion" walked down the drive with their unimpressive bags. And so Victor had sent a footman scurrying after them.

The girl, apparently, had wanted to go. Well, he had been rude and insulting to her. In such circumstances, most people would have made the same choice. It was the companion or maid or whatever she was who had persuaded Olivia to change her mind.

She was either full of guile or had come only for the reasons she had given him. Warning. And yet she hadn't told him the full truth. He knew that much without doubt. She knew something, something to do with His Grace's death, that she had not confided to Frostbrook or Sophia Wallace. Something she did not want to tell Victor either.

So he would keep her close and learn what that secret was.

Even now, staring unseeing at the same page of Champollion's book, he knew there was more to his motives. He liked her physical effect on him. He liked to look at her, spar with her, whether in banter or interrogation. And he wanted to believe in her too much, which only warned him that he should not, not without incontrovertible proof.

Victor had been too angry for too long with his father to seriously mourn his passing. But if there was more to his death than His Grace's own pride and idiocy, then it could affect the whole family, and Victor would not allow that. If he loved anyone in the world, it was his sister Hera. Rather to his surprise, he also found he was fond of his stepmother, Rosamund, and would include her in any protection he could devise.

He blinked so that Champollion's book came back into focus. Olivia had claimed an interest in Egypt. Well, then… He began to smile.

He left Olivia to her own devices until teatime. In the weeks Sophia Wallace had spent at the dower house, he had rather liked the civil companionship of the tea ritual, so he contemplated going to the drawing room and joining Olivia. Reluctantly, he decided to give his leg the rest of the day to calm down before he walked further than his bedchamber next door. Instead, he sent a message asking Miss Rainey to take tea with him in the library.

Then he wondered if she would refuse. He probably appeared to her to be autocratic and unpleasant, and in a way, he would think more of her if she declined. In another way, he would be disappointed.

But the acceptance came back via James the footman, and the lady herself appeared in the library at the same time as the tea tray.

"Thank you for joining me," he said civilly, waving his hand to the same place beside him on the sofa that she had occupied this morning. "Would you care to pour?"

She cast him a quick glance but, without fuss, sat and poured the tea. She even offered him the plate of sandwiches that was furthest from his reach. He took one, though he left it on his plate while he watched her small white teeth bite into a buttered scone.

"Tell me about yourself," he said.

"What would you like to know?"

"Everything. Start at the beginning. Who was your mother? A Rainey, I imagine?"

She shook her head and set her scone on the plate. "No. Mr. and Mrs. Rainey were the people who took me in. I don't know who my mother was, but she could not care for me."

"Did she give you to the Raineys?" he asked. "Or did Anthony?"

"I don't know," she said. "But I know Anthony paid them for my board."

"You are fond of them?"

Another quick glance, as though searching him for signs of mockery. But then, he had surprised himself by asking the question.

"To own the truth, I was not. Nor did they care a great deal for me. They took me in as a matter of Christian charity, not affection, and I suspect they were too set in their ways to deal with a lively child. They sent me away to school when I was eight, and I did not often go home for holidays. Aggie came to visit me, though. Took me to the seaside sometimes."

"Aggie is the lady who came with you here?"

"Mrs. Arnott, yes. She was Mrs. Rainey's servant, who had mostly looked after me in my early years. When I was sixteen and left school, I went to live with Aggie in the cottage in Farnton Heath."

"The cottage is Mrs. Arnott's?"

"My father pays the rent for it and gives me an allowance."

"Does he visit you?" Victor asked steadily.

"No. We correspond via the George Inn. I have met him only twice in my life."

Victor, who would have given much to have run into his own father so seldom, could not tell if she was hurt.

"I have wondered," she added, "if he was protecting me from accusations of bastardy, or perhaps my mother."

Anthony, it seemed, had hidden parts. He certainly kept a damned good secret. "What was your school like? Were you happy there?"

She wrinkled her nose. "Miss Harvey's Select Seminary for Young Ladies. I did not care a fig for deportment and etiquette, though I suppose they were dinned into me in spite of myself. I liked to learn about literature and history and other countries, and some of the teachers were very kind. Like Miss Arbuthnott."

"Did she tell you about Egypt?"

She smiled spontaneously, which caught at his breath. He reached for his tea like a shield.

"Yes," she replied.

"I was wondering," he said, "if I might ask for your assistance?"

Her eyebrows flew up in clear surprise. "Of course."

"My dear cousin," he said, "you should not agree so quickly

until you have heard the proposal."

A hint of color stained her cheeks, but she retorted, "I said you might ask, not that I would agree."

His lips quirked of their own volition, and he inclined his head in acknowledgement. "Do you think you would be able to fetch and carry books for me? Just until my leg is more the thing. And perhaps put my notes on Champollion and others in some kind of order? I wish to organize my thoughts on his discoveries and interpretations, particularly concerning hieroglyphs."

Her eyes sparkled. Oh yes, he could swear she had told the truth about her interests. "I should be happy to."

"I would pay you, of course." He smiled more deliberately. "*You*, not Anthony. An independent income is always advisable."

"You make it sound like a long task."

He shrugged. "Let us try a few days and see if we can bear each other. I am not an easy or likeable man, as I'm sure you have noticed."

She met his gaze and gave that challenging tilt of her chin. "On the contrary, I believe it Your Grace who has taken *me* in dislike."

"You are quite wrong. I like you very well. Which does not mean I trust you."

"I don't trust you either," she said.

He had expected nothing less, and yet something inside him twisted in pain. "Then we appear to be in agreement."

"When should I begin?"

"Now, if you wish."

She jumped to her feet, as though with relief. "Where are your notes?"

AT FIRST, IT was difficult to concentrate with her in the room. For years he had been used to working completely alone, except for the odd occasions when his sister was home. But Hera never bothered him. She was not a chatterer, and she always found something to study herself. Victor missed her companionship.

Olivia Rainey was nothing like Hera. She was too…distracting. He wondered if she could decipher his handwriting and his system of abbreviation, if she understood what he had written and if that mattered. He wondered if she would merely jumble his notes up and leave him worse off than before. Mostly, he gazed at the curve of her slender nape as she bent over her work at the desk in front of him and felt the beginnings of desire simmer gently.

Somewhere into the second hour, he regained his train of thought. There was, actually, a kind of peace in her company, and if it was edged by a little forbidden excitement, well, now that he was used to it, it made his brain sharper and stopped him noticing the throbbing ache in his leg.

He progressed steadily, making copious notes, only marginally aware of the rustling of papers on the desk in front, and the scratching of her pen.

Eventually, she said, "I believe it is the dinner hour. Shall I dine here and carry on with the work?"

It was curiously tempting, for there seemed to be a glow about her that he had not noticed before.

"No, you deserve a break." *From me and the work.* "You can begin again tomorrow at ten, if you like."

"Thank you—it's quite fascinating!" She smiled at him and danced off.

If she was pretending, she was very, very good.

IN FACT, OLIVIA was not pretending. As she ate her solitary dinner and went for a brisk evening walk with Aggie, her head was full of what she had read, and of the sharp connections revealed by the duke's notes. He was a true academic, not a dabbler. He really should have gone to Oxford. He was not so disabled that he could not have found a way to thrive there.

She retired to bed that night much happier than on the night before, looking forward to the following day with interest.

In fact, it began with a visit from Mrs. Irwin the housekeeper, who accompanied Aggie bearing a load of gowns and assorted shawls and chemises.

"Choose whichever you like and they will be altered to fit you," Mrs. Irwin said.

"But…won't the actual owners mind?" Olivia said, staring at the sheer quantity of garments.

"No," came the immediate answer. "They were already set aside to be given away."

"Truly, one change of clothes will be quite adequate, and if your laundress is busy—"

"The laundresses are there to launder," Mrs. Irwin said severely. "That need not concern you. Let me advise a walking dress, a morning dress, and an evening gown for immediate use. And a riding habit, if you ride."

Olivia merely goggled, while Aggie did the choosing and the fitting. Mrs. Irwin supplied the pins and took the lot away with her again. Bemused, but once more in her familiar gown, Olivia went down to the breakfast parlor, where she enjoyed another solitary meal before bearding her host in his library.

She found him seated at the desk she had used yesterday, looking through what she had done.

"Your leg is better?" she asked, pleased.

"Considerably. You have made an excellent list. I congratulate you on your understanding."

"I was merely born with it. I can take no credit."

"Why not? The rest of us do. Will it trouble you if I sit here and leave you to the chair beside me?"

"No, not in the least." This was not strictly true. There was enough distance between them that there could be no accidental touching, and the desk was broad enough that they need not interfere with each other's papers or books. All the same, the strong, handsome profile was always at the corner of her vision, tugging her gaze away from the page.

A few times, he asked her to bring him another book, directing her to where to find it on the shelves or on the other desk. She had the feeling he watched her at such times. Her face and neck heated as she climbed the little ladder to reach the upper shelves, and she had to force herself to concentrate to find the title he sought.

"Were you lonely in this village of yours?" he asked with odd abruptness as she returned to solid ground.

"No. There was always plenty to do, and the people were kind." She stopped. "Perhaps I was. I did not belong there. I don't really belong anywhere, neither lady nor villager. I wanted to be a governess, but my father wouldn't hear of it."

"You'd have had the same problem then, too," the duke observed, "judging by Hera's governesses, who were treated as neither family nor servant."

She smiled a little, moving forward again to lay the book on the desk beside him. "Much as now, in fact."

A frown marred his brow. He wasn't really used to dealing with social situations after all. It was he who was lonely. At least Olivia had always had Aggie.

"I have informed the household that you are my cousin, which makes you family. If anyone speaks or behaves with anything less than total respect, you will inform me. If you please."

"I don't expect anyone will. I have been treated with every courtesy." She sat back down and continued working, but his gaze lingered on her face, and she had no idea what he was thinking. Except that she very much doubted he trusted her.

Well, she did not trust him, did she? Aggie's words rang in her mind like a warning bell. *"It's possible the young duke is no victim but the murderer of his father."*

Except… "Will you still go to Oxford?" she blurted.

He replaced his pen in the stand. "Who told you that?"

"I don't recall."

"Do you think I should?" he asked with apparently genuine curiosity.

"I suspect you far outstrip the average intake of undergraduates in both knowledge and diligence. But if it is your ambition to obtain a degree, why not?"

"It was my ambition to immerse myself in the life of an academic. That is no longer possible." His lip twitched. "Actually, it was never possible, but everyone needs a goal in life. What was yours?"

Without thought, she answered honestly. "That my parents—even just one of my parents—would give me a home."

He held her gaze. "*This* home?"

"God, no," she said with genuine revulsion. "I only discovered my father's connection to Cuttyngs recently."

The duke sat back in his seat, watching her, rather like a cat eyeing up its prey and wondering whether to play with it first or go straight for the kill.

"Anthony was always available around His Grace," he said. "Being useful in small matters and great ones, playing messenger boy and diplomat to mend the many mistakes of my father's overlarge mouth. In many ways, he was His Grace's right-hand man. And yet the old man left him nothing in his will. Not so much as a horse or a set of—ah…artistic books. Why do you suppose that was?"

Olivia felt her face whiten. She forced her fingers to release the papers she was gripping tightly enough to tear. "Because His Grace considered Anthony had been left the best of all—a life interest in the dukedom through his daughter being the duchess."

"Well, you needn't look so terrified," the duke mocked her. "I have already released you from the obligation."

She blinked and glared at him. "I released myself, for I made no such undertaking. And since you were not involved in our fathers' infamous—"

"How do you know I was not?" he interrupted.

An involuntary frown pulled at her brow.

"I am a cripple with deformed limbs," he said deliberately. "I know no marriageable women. Why would I not jump at the chance of a beautiful wife who at least has aristocratic blood in her veins, from whichever side of the blanket?"

"Because a baseborn cousin is not a suitable bride for a duke, and you find the whole idea as demeaning and disgusting as I do," she retorted. "Are you fishing for my sympathy? For you won't get it." Furiously, she looked him up and down. *"A cripple with deformed limbs,"* she repeated. "You are hardly paralyzed, at least when you aren't falling off horses. And you have *one* abnormal limb, upon which you appear to be fixated to the exclusion of everything else."

"You sound surprised."

She had the impression he spoke only to fill the silence after her outburst. But she chose to answer anyway. She had gone too far not to.

"I am," she snapped. "I had not taken you for a man wallowing in self-pity."

He drew his head back in the gesture of astonishment she had seen before.

She rose. "I shall pack immediately and be gone before luncheon."

She had not taken more than a step before his hand closed around her wrist. His touch was a shock, firm yet gentle enough that she could delude herself into imagining she could break free. She tugged hard, but his fingers might have been a steel trap. His strength was frightening.

But then, he had been compensating all his life for the weakness of his leg. A man who had controlled that great horse as he had was no weakling. She stopped struggling.

"You agreed to help me with my work until my leg was better," he pointed out.

"We did not agree to quarrel and insult each other."

"I do not feel insulted," he said calmly. "Do you?"

"Yes! You do not believe what I say, and you are constantly accusing me of some unknown crime." She glared at him, but he held her gaze without difficulty.

"Then why did you come back yesterday? What did Aggie say to convince you?"

"That something is wrong here. And until we find out what—or whom—you and your household could be in danger."

He released her, and she had to stop herself rubbing her wrist. It was not sore, but she felt the imprint of his fingers as though they were still there.

"You believe someone secretly killed His Grace at a time it could be blamed on Major Butler and the duel. And that now they might turn their attentions to me? Why?"

"I get the impression your father was a man who made enemies."

"As understatements go, that one is huge. And you would have to include his family, most of who are indubitably happier without him. Including Her Grace and my sister." He smiled. "And me. We all benefited in one way or another."

"And Anthony?" she said, as though going along with his train of thought.

"Not Anthony. He's the only one who got nothing. No bequest, no bridal. I even threw him out of the house with the servant he was using as a spy."

Olivia's jaw dropped. "*Spy?*"

"Don't be too hard on him. He learned from my father, who had several servants spying on us all for him."

Olivia sank back into her chair without meaning to. It just seemed her legs would no longer support her. Her father had employed a spy in this household, a man already employed by the old duke in the same capacity. Were there others still here that the young duke knew nothing of?

She bit her lip to stop the questions spilling out. What kind of a daughter was she?

"I think, perhaps, you have worked long enough for this morning," the duke said. "I shall be out this afternoon."

Distracted, she gazed at him in horror. "But the doctor told you to rest your injury for a week!"

"He's an old quack. Besides, I shall be in the coach. I have decided, you see, that there is more to learning than the classics. Or even the ancient Egyptians. I have much to learn of land management, and it cannot all be from books."

She gazed at him, realizing she had been dismissed—again—but unable to move for her own thoughts.

"Will you be a good duke?" she asked.

"No. I am a terrible duke. But I shall be a good steward of the land."

She opened her mouth to pursue the subject until she saw the deliberate patience in his eyes and realized he needed her to leave before he would move. A man should be allowed some dignity.

She rose. "Have I your permission to continue with this work while you are out?"

He inclined his head. "And my gratitude."

Impossible to know if he meant it. She could only dip a brief curtsey and walk out of the room.

CHAPTER FIVE

LEFT TO HER own devices, Olivia spent some time exploring the house and grounds, including the stables and the dairy, and the public portions of the huge house. She found a magnificent ballroom, many ornate salons, and a chapel.

"Is it used?" she asked the maid she had discovered dusting the altar.

"Only for weddings," the girl replied. "His late Grace was married here both times. But the funeral service was at the parish church. There's no chaplain here anymore."

"And the ballroom?" Olivia asked.

"Once a year for the autumn ball," the maid replied. "But I suppose it won't happen this year, since we're in mourning. And besides, we might all be under the heathen French by then."

"You don't expect the Duke of Wellington to defeat Bonaparte?" Olivia asked in some surprise.

"He never has yet, has he?" the maid replied.

"No, I don't believe they've met personally in battle at all. Are you worried?"

The girl laughed. "Bless you, no, ma'am. Makes no difference to us, though it might put the hems on a few balls."

Not judging by the news from Brussels, where the Duke of Wellington was preparing to meet his foe. Apparently, the town in general, and the British visitors in particular, was in the grip of spectacular gaiety.

Leaving the girl to her dusting, Olivia made her way back to the library. She spent a little time investigating the shelves, and then returned to her desk to get on with her work.

About an hour later, she heard a sound behind her and jerked around to see the duke's valet, Black, closing a door she hadn't even known was there. The man halted, apparently confused to see her there.

He bowed. "Excuse the interruption, ma'am. I am merely in search of any garments abandoned here by His Grace."

"Carry on," Olivia said, pointing to the sofa. "There is a coat there, and a cravat, I think. Is His Grace returned?"

"Not yet, ma'am."

She replaced her pen in the stand. "Is his injury really recovered enough for this expedition?"

"His Grace believes so."

"Do you?"

Black shrugged and picked up both coat and cravat from the back of the sofa. He added a pair of old slippers Olivia hadn't noticed. "His Grace lives with the disability. He has, presumably, decided he can bear the consequences of his expedition."

"He is very…determined," Olivia observed.

A smile flickered in the man's otherwise austere eyes. "He is, ma'am. And clever as they come."

"And yet the late duke did not see fit to involve his heir in estate matters."

"Apparently not, ma'am," the valet said, in unmistakably repressive tones.

Olivia had no experience of dealing with domestic servants, let alone the upper and haughty variety, but she was not easily intimidated.

"Have you worked long for His Grace?"

"Nine years, ma'am." And he was, no doubt, one of the old duke's "spies." With deliberation, Black added, "I am honored to take good care of His Grace."

Was that a warning? If so, she could probably trust him to give the young duke whatever protection he could. She nodded and returned to her notes.

"Forgive me, ma'am," the valet said. "But is His Grace aware of your presence here? He does not care for his papers to be moved about."

"He has given me the task of putting them in order," Olivia said.

There was a short, stunned silence. Then, "Very good, ma'am." Black retreated as silently as he had come, leaving her with little idea whether he approved of her or not.

Much like his master.

She worked on, happily lost in the fascinating notes and references until a maid knocked and told her tea was served in the drawing room. Olivia thanked her and found she was glad to stretch her legs after sitting so long. After tea, she would go for another walk and ask some more questions…

She walked into the drawing room and came to an abrupt halt. The duke glanced up from a newspaper, his lips twisting into a sardonic smile. "Behold My Grace, being hostly. If my presence spoils the peace of your teatime, one of us might easily go somewhere else."

"How could your presence anywhere in your own home offend me in any way at all?" she retorted. "I expect your leg hurts after being bumped about in the coach all afternoon, and now you're looking for an excuse to quarrel."

He blinked. "Damn it, now you make me sound like my father."

"Did he swear in front of ladies also?"

For an instant, he stared at her, then he let out a bark of laughter. "You are obliging me with a quarrel," he said appreciatively. "Well, I've gone off the notion, and I apologize for my language. I have no social graces."

"Like Egyptology and land management, they can be learned." As soon as the hasty words left her lips, she was sorry, for a stricken look of abject misery flashed across his face and was gone almost before she registered it.

"*Touché,*" he drawled.

She dropped her gaze to the teapot and began to pour. "I'm sorry. As you perceive, I did not learn such lessons very well either. I have grown too comfortable arguing with you."

"Oh, don't back down now," he said as she rose to bring him his tea. "I am not offended." He took the cup and saucer from her, his face a polite mask. "Thank you."

Olivia hesitated, for everyone was entitled to privacy, to hide their hurts, but her overwhelming impression of this house and family was one of repression and oppression, and she could not be silent.

She brought him a plate and offered him the choice of sandwiches and scones. He took one of each. She said, "I think you are too used to being unfairly criticized. I should not have added to the list, certainly not while committing the same infringement. Perhaps I have not had enough people to quarrel with either."

"My felicitations. I quarreled royally with my father and solved nothing."

"Perhaps," she said delicately, "you both said things you did not mean."

A glint of mockery entered his eyes, but it did not appear to be aimed at her. "Oh no, we meant them. By the very act of saying something, my father believed it and never, ever backed down. Which is how he came to die in a duel."

She sat and poured herself tea. "What were his criticisms of you?"

His lips curved, but it was not a smile. "I shan't tell you that. I daresay you can imagine, and I hesitate to offend you again. What did you do this afternoon?"

She accepted the change of subject, because anything else seemed cruel, and after a little, he told her something about his inspection of some piece of land and the plans he was concocting with Jenkins, his steward, to improve it.

"You plan to make many changes on the whole estate?" she asked, rising to refill his cup.

"I do."

"Will you be obliged to make evictions?"

"Oh, no. The improvements will benefit the tenants." He frowned. "Why do you ask that?"

"Something Aggie overheard in the servants' hall. Some of your tenants are apparently convinced you're taking notes in order to turn them out."

He threw his head back. "For the love of... Why do they not speak to *me* of such fears? Or even Jenkins?"

"Probably," she said, "because they would not have dared speak to your father."

She had just returned to her place while he mulled over her words, scowling blackly into his teacup, when Betts entered, bearing a silver tray, which he presented to the duke.

The duke blinked. "What?" He lifted the card. "Who the devil is Lady Mountjoy?"

"Your Grace's neighbor at Carnstow Hall. Their land marches with yours to the west."

"What does she want?"

"I imagine, Your Grace, she is making a condolence call."

"Well, I'm not at home." His scowling gaze lit on Olivia, as if by accident. "Wait."

Betts stood impassively before him.

"Word will have spread of Miss Rainey's presence," the duke said.

"I imagine so," Betts agreed. "With Your Grace's cousin as hostess, the ladies have no reason *not* to call."

"And if I damn their impudence and send them away, there will be further speculation. Should I see them?" He flung the words at Olivia.

"Unless there is a reason not to," she said carefully, "I have generally found it helpful to be on terms with my neighbors." And no one had been starved of company more than this irascible, vulnerable young nobleman.

"Lady Mountjoy is accompanied by her daughter," Betts informed them.

"Oh, bring them up," the duke said ungraciously. "What?" he added as Betts departed and he caught sight of Olivia's expression. "They've come to gawp at the monster."

"Then they will be disappointed."

"Were you?"

The question took her by surprise, but she was spared the necessity of answering by the sounds of footsteps in the passage. The duke reached for the crutch propped by his chair and hauled himself to his feet.

"Lady Mountjoy and Miss Mountjoy, Your Grace." Betts bowed in a handsome matron and a befrilled and pretty young girl.

The visitors did not at once see Olivia, so she had leisure to observe them as well as the duke. Lady Mountjoy sailed in, a gracious, practiced smile on her lips, and was clearly brought up short by the handsome young man standing upright before her—without the aid of the crutch, which once more was propped against his chair.

Lady Mountjoy's smile wavered, then broadened in genuine delight.

The duke inclined his head. "Lady Mountjoy, how do you do?"

"Your Grace." Her ladyship curtseyed deeply, as did the girl beside her. More obviously than her mother, she was stunned, the somewhat avid fear in her pretty face giving way to something approaching awe. "Allow me to present my eldest daughter, Elizabeth."

"Charmed to make your acquaintance. This is my cousin, Miss Rainey."

"Ah, of course." Temporarily, at least, Lady Mountjoy had clearly forgotten the cousin who had enabled her to call with propriety. Now she turned and inclined her head to Olivia's curtsey. "How do you do, Miss Rainey?"

"How do *you* do, my lady? Miss Mountjoy."

A footman arrived bearing a tray with a fresh teapot and more cups. While the visitors sat, Olivia poured the tea and marveled with some amusement at her changed circumstances—from a cozy mug of tea shared with Aggie in their cottage, to playing hostess in a ducal mansion, handing fine porcelain cups and saucers to local gentry.

Lady Mountjoy sipped her tea and lowered the cup. "You will allow me to express our profound condolences on the loss of His Grace, your father? I know my husband will have said all he ought at the funeral, but sometimes a little feminine sympathy can be kinder. I know Eliza, who is particularly tenderhearted, feels deeply for you."

Eliza flushed but offered the duke a hopeful smile.

"Thank you," he murmured. "And it was kind of Sir Hugo to join us for the burial. I trust he is well? And the rest of your family?"

So he *did* know precisely who the Mountjoys were. Either that, or he had dredged up some memory and made the right connections, for Sir Hugo clearly was her ladyship's husband. The duke needed to say very little else for the duration of the visit, for most of the conversation was carried by Lady Mountjoy. Occasionally, she prompted her daughter into breathless speech, but mostly she fired bland questions at His Grace about the weather and the health of the duchess and dear Lady Hera, most of which she answered herself.

Olivia she mostly ignored, apart from offering her a smile and word of thanks for refilling her teacup or offering cakes.

On the other hand, she did not overstay her welcome, but rose to leave after just under half an hour. The duke, proving he knew his manners even if he did not always exercise them, reached for his crutch and stood politely. Eliza watched the process wide-eyed. He did not look at her.

"I am so glad to see you bearing up beneath the burden of

grief," Lady Mountjoy said. "I wonder… I know you are in mourning, but perhaps you would not find a quiet dinner exceptionable? Just our family, and perhaps the Nasebys? And yourself and Miss Rainey, of course."

"You are very kind," the duke said noncommittally, propping up the crutch again and inclining his head. "And my thanks for calling. Please pass on my regards to Sir Hugo."

He waited until they had gone, guided by the waiting footman in the passage, then all but flopped back into his chair. "Well, that was vapid."

"Courteous," Olivia corrected him, although her eyes danced and his responded with an unexpected twinkle.

"I beg your pardon."

"Will you go to dinner?" she asked.

"God, no. Why the devil did she invite me? In fact, what the devil is all this…*courtesy* about?"

Olivia blinked. "Don't you know? She wants you to notice her daughter."

"Why?" he asked blankly.

"So that you'll marry her and make her the Duchess of Cuttyngham."

"*Me?*" He looked so genuinely flabbergasted, not to say disbelieving, that she wanted to hug him.

"You are more than a catch, sir," Olivia said gently. "You are *the* catch of the decade. An unmarried duke, young, handsome, and rich."

He actually laughed. Though color seeped along the blade of his cheekbones. She didn't know if it was pleasure, disbelief, or embarrassment. But it had to be said.

Olivia held his gaze. "I don't know what bee got into your father's bonnet, or what induced mine to go along with it, but there was never the remotest need for bribery in the matter of your marriage. Young ladies will trample each other to get to you."

CHAPTER SIX

VICTOR SAT STARING at the door long after she had gone. His mind had raced through ridicule, disbelief, and gratitude for her kindness, until he realized it didn't really matter whether or not he believed bribery was necessary. *She* did not believe it. Moreover, she had suggested he go to this wretched dinner at the Mountjoys'.

These were not the words, beliefs, or actions of a scheming woman come to flatter him into marriage according to her father's wishes. She quarreled with him, stood up to him, wanted him to meet marriageable young ladies. Unless she was playing a very deep game indeed, she was exactly as she appeared—a poor young woman whose conscience was troubled by the old duke's death.

But he didn't want to think about that right now. He wanted to concentrate on her words. She thought he was handsome, that women would like him.

Well, that being Duke of Cuttyngham outweighed his lameness.

Lost in thought, he waited until the maids had cleared away the tea things and all was quiet. Then he roused himself to reach for his crutch, heaved himself to his feet, and made his ungainly way to his bedchamber next to the library.

He didn't go through the library. He wondered if she was

there, working on his papers. The thought did not displease him. Normally, he was irritated by anyone else's presence in the library. Except Hera's. But now, flopping with relief into the nearest chair in his bedroom, he gazed at the adjoining door and felt a tingling warmth suffuse him.

Just because she said you were handsome? he mocked himself. He turned his head to the glass in front of him and made himself look. Normally he avoided his reflection, unwilling to see the bony contours of his face, the thick black brows, the dark shadow of his jaw, and the unhealthy pallor of his skin.

Riding out had helped with the paleness, but he was still a dark, malformed specimen to frighten any refined lady.

He did not appear to frighten Miss Olivia Rainey. Nor, he supposed, had he appeared to frighten the women his father had so contemptuously bought for him in his teens, though they had been well paid for the purpose and were no guide.

The Mountjoy women hadn't run screaming either—possibly because they had expected him to be swinging from the furniture and the chandeliers like a large monkey or lying gibbering on the floor.

He shoved himself back impatiently, scowling irritably at his foolish concentration on the physical. Fortunately, Black came in to cause a distraction.

"I have ordered a bath for Your Grace before dinner. It will soothe your leg."

Victor nodded curtly, then roused himself to add, "Damned bumpy ride to the Farfield ditch."

Black began laying out soaps, razors, and towels. "I met Miss Rainey in the library while you were gone. She said she was organizing Your Grace's papers."

Victor looked at him. "She is."

"Very good, Your Grace."

Fifteen minutes later, as Black helped him into the steaming bathtub, Victor caught sight of his familiar thin, twisted leg. No one seemed very sure whether it had not formed properly in the womb, or if it had been damaged in his difficult birth.

She would not think that *is handsome.*

"Would Your Grace prefer to dine here, or in the library?" Black inquired some time later.

Victor opened his mouth to reply absently, then said decisively, "No, I shall go the dining room."

In fact, his leg felt so much soothed by the bath that he eschewed the crutch and used only his walking stick to aid his journey to the dining room. Even so, he was glad to arrive first, and stand beside his chair to welcome his guest. He had been a poor host so far.

Though perhaps, since he had thrown out all his other guests since he'd inherited the dukedom, she should consider herself favored.

She came quickly into the room, wearing a high-waisted lilac evening gown he didn't recall seeing before, though it was a pleasant change from the dull thing she had been wearing since her first arrival. She halted in immediate surprise to see him, but a quick, spontaneous smile gave him a clue as to how lonely her previous meals here must have been.

"Your Grace. I am glad to see you so much better."

"Thank you," he said, taken aback. "Shall we sit?"

He allowed the footman to hold her chair for her, and then dropped onto his own, propping his stick against the table.

"Pretty gown," he observed, as the footman served the soup.

She colored. "Thank you. I'm afraid it is one of your sister's. Mrs. Irwin had it altered for me."

"Will you wear it to Lady Mountjoy's?"

Her eyes widened. "You intend to go?"

"You think I should not?"

"On the contrary, I think you should, but you seemed so set against it this afternoon."

"I decided it was time I knew my neighbors as well as my tenants."

Her smile was definitely one of approval, which baffled him.

Why did she care?

With the constant presence of servants, it was necessarily a formal meal. He had endured many such when his father had been at home, glaring and fault-finding from the moment Victor limped into the room until His Grace stormed out of it after his son refused to drink port with him.

That was one of Victor's petty rebellions. When he was old enough to drink with his father, he had refused to do so. Toward the end, his father had even stopped summoning him for meals, apart from the first evening of his increasingly infrequent returns. Latterly, Victor recalled, there had been a hint of suspicion in the old bastard's glare whenever his son spoke, as if he was never quite sure Victor wasn't mocking him. In fact, Victor had never taken the trouble and would not, in any case, have risked subjecting his sister and stepmother to one of his father's rages.

But with this girl, this distant, illegitimate cousin he barely knew, he discovered, to his surprise, that formal meals could be *pleasant*. She asked about the land, and he explained about the improvements he had begun. They discussed his Egyptian studies and possibilities in interpretation. They even talked of poetry. He would have been content enough passing the time in such a way, but she also made him *laugh*. She had an unexpected sense of the ridiculous and a certain quickness of wit that intrigued him. Usually no one, except Hera occasionally, had ever understood his jokes. It was almost disconcerting to be caught out. And he liked to be amused.

He was almost disappointed when the cherry tart and the cheese were all but gone. Olivia rose to her feet and smiled as she bade him goodnight. Victor half rose in the informal courtesy he had used toward his stepmother.

"Goodnight, Your Grace."

It wasn't late. He knew an urge to keep her with him, afraid of breaking the connection. But it made him vulnerable, and he would not ask. "Goodnight, Cousin."

Her smile was slightly uncertain as she turned and walked

away. He hoped nothing had leaked out of his expression.

The footman removed the dessert plates and placed the decanters and glasses on the table by his elbow.

Loneliness loomed, long and cold.

He poured himself a glass of brandy and dismissed the servants. He should have told them to take the decanters to the library, where he would at least have had the company of his books. For the first time, he wished Hera had not gone away, though he had wanted her to spread her wings and be happy. He wished Rosamund, his stepmother, were still here, a lady he had begun to like but never troubled to get to know. Never known how. Even Sophia Wallace, whom Rosamund had left in his care, had gone to some party with Lord Frostbrook's family. He hadn't even recognized the budding friendship there.

Was that what this was with Olivia? Budding friendship? Budding trust?

Not quite. Something *hurt* around her. Warm, delightful, but painful.

He took another mouthful of brandy and impatiently shoved the glass away. He refused to sit here feeling sorry for himself and whining about loneliness. Using the table and the stick, he hauled himself upright and limped out of the room, making for the library.

Only as he pushed open the door did it enter his head that Olivia might have come here. He hated the eagerness with which he stumped in, glancing around for any sign of her.

Of course, she was not here. Why would she be?

He sat down at his desk, trying to banish the loneliness with books, as he always had.

But he felt too tired to concentrate. In fact, come to think of it, he didn't feel too well either. Wearily, he hauled himself to his feet once more and limped through the library to his bedchamber door. There, he rang the bell for Black.

That was when the first pain grasped his stomach like a claw.

OLIVIA PACED HER bedchamber, her stomach in knots. Or was it her heart? At any rate, she was knocked off balance by the duke's...*pleasantness*.

No, that wasn't it. He wasn't always pleasant or good-natured. In fact, he could be downright cutting. But he made her laugh, and she had never spoken to such a knowledgeable, well-read man in her life before. Nor did he ignore or disparage her opinions because she was a mere woman. He had listened to her.

And while *she* listened, she had watched the expressions play across his beautiful face. When that had become too intense, she had let her gaze drop to his hands instead, watching his long, strong fingers curl around the stem of his glass or the handle of his knife.

She liked to look too much. She had almost asked him if he would come to the drawing room for tea but stopped herself in time. For some reason, he was being polite to her, and she must never expect more.

Did that mean he trusted her? She hoped so. For he needed to be encouraged into human company, to discover for himself which attractions were genuinely personal and which were to his dukedom. He seemed to have no concept of his own beauty, only his lameness, as though there were nothing else to the man. It was so far from the truth that she wanted to weep.

Instead, she forced herself to stop pacing. She could either ring for Aggie and have a short gossip and another early night. Or she could go to the library and work for an hour. He might even be there.

The possibility pleased her, though she thrust it to the back of her mind as she snatched up her shawl and made for the staircase. Her heart brightened when she opened the library door, for a few candles were lit against the growing gloom. But the duke was not present.

She sat down and picked up the papers, trying to remember where she had got to. Curiously, she liked the idea that he was probably close by, in the next room…

The house was too quiet. She often thought that. The servants did not laugh or talk in the upper house, only in the kitchen, according to Aggie. The old duke, apparently, had been both strict and miserable by nature.

She found the place on her list and returned to the duke's copious notes. Some indefinable, muffled noise reached her. It seemed to come from behind the door at the far end of the library, where the duke slept.

She turned toward it, just as someone flew out of the duke's room—his valet—and skidded to a halt beside her. He looked demented.

"The duke is ill! We need Mrs. Irwin—damn it, we need Her Grace, but Mrs. Irwin will have to do! And the doctor!"

Olivia sprang up, trying to stay calm before the man's panic. He knew better than she how to find the housekeeper and who to send for the doctor. "Fetch them. I'll stay with His Grace."

He looked alarmed, as though he would argue, but Olivia, terrified what she would find, was already striding toward the open bedroom door. An instant later, she heard his running footsteps going in the opposite direction. Decorum went by the wayside. He was shouting to Albert, one of the footmen, to fetch the doctor, then yelling for the maids to fetch Mrs. Irwin.

His Grace had been violently ill. Olivia could smell it at once, even before she saw him curled on the bed, shaking. The valet had managed to remove his clothes, from what she could see, and the sheets appeared to be clean.

When she touched his cold, clammy skin, his eyes opened onto hers. Racked with pain, they stared as though trying to communicate something to her.

"Not you," he muttered between chattering teeth. "Not you."

She had no idea if he was sending her away or meant something else entirely. She only squeezed his hand and walked to the washstand to pour some clean water. She brought the wrung-out cloth to his bedside, to bathe his hands and face. There seemed little else she could do. His eyes were closed, and he did not appear to notice.

More quickly than she had expected, Mrs. Irwin appeared with an armful of jars and bottles. She looked confident and efficient until she saw her patient, when all the blood drained from her face.

"Dear God," she whispered.

"It must be food poisoning," Black said.

"But I ate everything he did," Olivia said, before one possible truth began to prickle and burn its way into her brain. *Oh, no. Please, no...* She stared at Mrs. Irwin. "We must purge him."

"There's nothing left in his stomach," Black protested.

The duke's hand flew up from the covers and grasped the housekeeper's arm. "Purge," he said distinctly. "And leave me."

Mrs. Irwin and Black exchanged wild, frightened glances. "I can't, Your Grace," she said in anguish. "It might—"

But Olivia knew the duke was right. He harbored the same suspicion she did. But he trusted Mrs. Irwin and her potions, so Olivia had to.

"No," she interrupted. "Give him the purgative. Quickly."

Mrs. Irwin blinked at the force of Olivia's command. Then, with shaking hands, she found the correct potion and poured some into a glass while Black lifted the duke into a sitting position. When the duke had swallowed it, there was nothing for Olivia to do but step back out of the way while the guilt and the terror held her in thrall.

"Leave him to me now," Black said with sudden firmness. "I will call you."

Dare she trust the valet? He had not been near him all evening until, surely, he was ill.

Taking a deep breath, she took Mrs. Irwin's arm and led her from the room, closing the door to the library behind her.

"The food was good," Mrs. Irwin said numbly. "We never

keep bad food, never serve it even to the lowest servant."

"I ate the food too, Mrs. Irwin, and I expect you had the left-overs below stairs. No one else is ill, are they?"

"No…" She seemed relieved. "Then he has just picked up some nasty stomach illness while he was out this afternoon. But oh, miss, he looks so *ill…*"

She sank onto the sofa, the bottles in her lap, as though she couldn't manage another step.

"Is he subject to such illnesses?" Olivia asked. *Please say yes…*

Mrs. Irwin said doubtfully, "On occasions. He was a bit sickly as a child, but it was more fevers and cold, and of course his leg gave him great pain, especially whenever his father decided he had to be like everyone else…"

"Did he?" Olivia asked, staring at her.

For once, Mrs. Irwin had lost her calm. She was pale, worried, anxious, and the words poured out of her. "At first, when he was tiny, His Grace tried to make him walk without limping, forced him to run, to ride until he fell off, whipped him when he could not do what the duke commanded. Then His Grace forbade him from doing anything at all, shut him away from everyone except at mealtimes when there were no guests, and then he said such awful things, even in front of the servants."

"What sort of things?" Olivia almost whispered.

"Cruel things. Belittling things. The wonder is that there's any sweetness left in him at all." Mrs. Irwin drew a shuddering breath. "It got a little better once the new duchess came… His own mother hadn't protected him. Neither did we. We could, we should have done something… But his stepmother at least managed to prevent the public humiliations. Not that she was free of them herself…" She buried her head in her hands. "I am talking too much. You must forget what I've said. We must only pray for his recovery."

"Once he is settled, I'll sit with him," Olivia promised.

"We can take it in turns."

WHEN BLACK APPEARED in the library looking exhausted, Olivia felt her fingers curl into painful fists, for fear of what he was about to say.

"He's asleep," Black said. "And I think the pain has gone."

"He'll need lots of water and nourishing tea," Mrs. Irwin said worriedly.

"Tomorrow," Olivia said, as gently as she could. "Go to bed, Mrs. Irwin. I'll watch over him and give him water if he wakes."

She walked through to the bedroom and sat in the chair Black must already have placed beside the great bed. The duke looked very small and pale, his black hair a tangled shock between the whiteness of his face and the pillows. Like a beautiful little boy in exhausted sleep.

At least he was breathing, and the continuous frown had temporarily gone from his face.

Something twisted in her heart, both pain and sweetness and an unexpected longing. *I will protect you. And this has gone far enough. It is time for the truth.*

CHAPTER SEVEN

HE WOKE WITH the dawn, just as she was nodding off. She sprang back into full wakefulness as his eyes opened wide and held hers. For an instant, neither of them said anything.

"You," he muttered, at last. Impossible to tell if it was surprise or disapproval.

"Are you comfortable?" she asked.

He blinked. "Yes," he replied in apparent surprise.

She smiled with relief and reached for the glass of water on the bedside table. "Can you sit, or shall I help you?"

He hauled himself up on his elbow and took the glass from her. Then he paused, and his gaze flew back to her face, as if he couldn't prevent it. "Not now," he said, shoving the glass back down.

Her heart ached, but she had brought it on herself. Holding his gaze, she lifted the glass and deliberately drank from it, then handed it back to him.

Slowly, he took it and sipped, and sipped again before setting the glass down and falling back on his pillows. "Then I *was* poisoned."

"I'm afraid of it. But I was not ill, nor any of the servants. I have to tell you something."

"I know."

She blinked. "You know?"

"I know you are hiding something. Have been since the day you arrived. Is it to do with Anthony?"

Her breath caught, and she had to look away. "I woke early on the morning of the duel. Too many people were milling around the inn. I told you, I felt something was wrong. I went to..." She closed her eyes. "I went to my father's room. The door was ajar, and I saw a tall, well dressed man who must have been the duke."

"Face like a pinched lemon?"

A sob shuddered through her. "Oh, don't make me laugh. He took a flask from someone in the room. I couldn't see him, but I could only suppose it was my father. The duke hesitated, then took a gulp or two and passed it back. He said something like, *You are right. It does help. Let us to the wood.* I slipped back to my own room, but something made me follow them, some foretaste of disaster, or some suspicion I couldn't bear..."

"You think Anthony poisoned my father?" He sounded remarkably calm.

"I didn't. Not then. I thought I had just mistaken the order of events during the duel. It all happened so quickly, and I am not used to violence. Like everyone else, I assumed he fell because he was shot, and died for the same reason. And then Lord Frostbrook and Miss Wallace came to me, and I realized other people had seen what I had."

She swallowed and opened her eyes again. "But I had seen more. Everyone swore the duke had eaten and drunk nothing, not so much as cup of coffee before the duel. My father told the attending doctor that. And Frostbrook. But it wasn't true. Someone gave him a drink from a silver flask."

"Was it your father's?" the duke asked steadily.

Tears clogged the back of her throat, but she would not release them. "I don't know for sure. I never knew him well enough to tell. It was my father's room. He didn't have a valet, so far as I knew."

"But he had my father's groom." The duke's voice cracked,

and Olivia immediately passed him the water again. After drinking, he lay back on the pillows, apparently exhausted. His eyes fluttered closed. "I think I told you. My father had his favorite spies in the household. Gregson the groom was one. They spied on me and Her Grace and possibly Hera, though His Grace never seemed to consider her as of much account. As soon as His Grace died, Gregson transferred his loyalty to Anthony. I gave him Gregson as a gift…"

"But Gregson is not here," she argued. "Neither is my father."

"Something brought *you* here to warn me. You suspect Anthony."

She wasn't sure she could hold the tears much longer. "I longed for him," she whispered. "I wanted a father so badly, and then I finally met him, and he was kind and distinguished and understanding and everything wonderful. I convinced myself there was a good reason for everything, for why he only came to find me when I was grown up, for his iniquitous bargain for my marriage to you. I nearly did it."

A single tear squeezed out of the corner of her eye. She ignored it, hoping he wouldn't notice.

"Something stopped you."

She nodded. "I hated my suspicions. I could even ignore them, until Lord Frostbrook…" She gasped as something touched her cheek—his finger on her trickling tear. His eyes were wide open, gazing at her. "I didn't come when my father told me to. I wouldn't play my father's role, but I should at least have warned you."

"You did."

"Too late!" she whispered in agony. "I could not bring myself to tell you that I feared it was my own father. I wanted so much to be wrong." Without thought, she caught his hand to her cheek. "*Please* get well."

"I shall be fine." He almost sounded surprised.

"How?" She stared at him. "How can we trust anyone?"

"By making sure it never happens again. We'll shout *poison!*

abroad. The authorities would look askance at two such happenings in one house. For the rest…we need to think. After you give me the rest of the water and send Black to me. And I sleep…"

"I don't think it's Black," she murmured, somewhat doubtfully. "He was nowhere near your food or wine, was he?"

"I'll think when my head stops hurting…"

Olivia poured more water into the glass, then hurried to find Black and Mrs. Irwin.

⁂

WHEN HE WOKE again at midday, the headache was manageable. The muscles of his stomach still ached with their exertions, but he felt hungry and much more like himself.

He had been lucky.

Some instinct, only half thought through, had caused him to make himself sick as soon as he felt the pains. Some of the poison, whatever it was, had undoubtedly gone through his body, but he had got rid of enough of it quickly enough that he was still alive.

There had been dark times in his past when he wouldn't really have minded dying. Now was not that time. For one thing, if it was by bloody Anthony's hand, he had no intention of letting the man get his grips on the dukedom.

And for another…*Olivia.*

She had watched over him, bathing his face, looking after him. His head had known she could be the culprit, but he didn't truly believe it. Her position of a lonely, neglected girl wishing only to believe in the goodness of her father was only too believable. Yet doubt had driven her here.

Mrs. Irwin herself brought him some broth, saying grimly, "No one's touched it but me and Cook. I made sure. But surely Miss Rainey is wrong? Who would harm Your Grace?"

Anyone under orders from my father. Anthony or his minions. Anyone who thinks I degrade the dukedom… "Who is the magistrate around here?"

"Sir Hugo Mountjoy. Oh." She delved into her apron. "A card arrived this morning from Lady Mountjoy."

The promised invitation to dinner tomorrow evening. "I believe I might go after all." *If I have the strength to walk.*

Just as he finished the broth, Dr. Arkwright arrived, bustling into the room as though he owned it.

"Well, now, what is Your Grace's problem today? Further ill effects of the accident, I shouldn't wonder. Let's just have a look at the poor leg—"

"My problem," Victor said coldly, "was last night."

The doctor was brought up short by this tone, his hand not quite touching the sheet. "Your Grace's pardon, of course. I was attending a difficult lying-in and needed to sleep."

"Then feel free to go back to bed, for the problem is solved."

"May I know what it was?"

"Poisoning of some kind."

The man's jaw dropped. "Then Your Grace wants to dismiss your cooks!"

"My Grace can take care of my own household. You behold me purged and recovered and may go."

"No, no, you must tell me more. I suspect bleeding may be necessary—"

"Bleeding is not necessary. I am quite weak enough. Good day, doctor."

It still gave him a certain amount of satisfaction to see the doctor obey him. As a child, he had suffered agonies by this man's hands as, under His Grace's orders, the doctor had manipulated his leg in a futile effort to straighten it. The doctor had explained to His Grace that it would do no good, but at His Grace's command, he had done it anyway.

When the doctor had gone, Victor summoned Black to help him dress and shave. Black behaved with his usual distant good manners until, as he picked up the razor, he said abruptly,

"Someone tried to hurt you last night."

Their eyes met in the glass. Victor did not so much as glance at the razor blade. "Was it you?"

Slowly, Black shook his head.

"But you are not surprised," Victor observed, "let alone offended that I asked."

"No," Black agreed. He set down the razor and picked up the soapy brush.

"You bore tales to my father," Victor said.

"It's what I was hired to do. Valeting appeared to be purely secondary to His Grace's requirements."

Of course. There had been no point in dressing the cripple.

"But I believe I have been a decent valet to Your Grace," Black added, pasting soap all over his lower face and neck.

"You have, and you were far from the only spy."

Black hesitated. "I had nothing to tell him. He never learned from me that you had been accepted to Oxford, and the stable lads and me hid it—even from Gregson to begin with—when you went riding."

"Then Gregson was not his only spy in the stables?"

Black shook his head and lifted the razor once more. "He was the only one who didn't find it distasteful. He spied on the rest of us, too, and got more than one dismissed."

"And who else in the house, Black, were his spies?"

Black hesitated, then, "Albert, the footman," he said, "But he covered for you, too."

He raised the blade, and Victor grasped his wrist. "Gregson changed to my cousin Anthony Severne's employ as soon as His Grace expired, if not before. Who else did so?"

"No one to my knowledge," Black said steadily. "Would Your Grace rather shave yourself?"

Infinitely. But Victor released the valet's wrist and tilted his head.

Black began his work. "Has Your Grace considered that you

have had two accidents now in the space of four days? Since Miss Rainey arrived at Cuttyngs. I believe she is Mr. Severne's daughter?"

DESPITE A NAP, Olivia felt too tired to concentrate properly on the duke's notes. Nor did she expect the duke to grace the library that day. She spent most of her waking hours outdoors, making friends with the horses and tramping around the woods and grounds of the estate, as though the fresh air would clear her head. She tried to think of all the people who might have added poison to the duke's dinner, but not to hers.

Rain drove her indoors at last, in time for tea. But if she had expected the duke to join her again, she was disappointed.

"How is His Grace?" she asked Albert, the footman who carried the tray that day.

"Back to normal, ma'am," he replied cheerfully. "Or so Mr. Black says."

Was she being unreasonable to imagine that "normal" should mean having tea with her, as he had yesterday? He had dined with her too, and that had been oddly…wonderful. She was sure he had liked her then, that some rare bond was forming between them.

But that had been before the poisoning. He had not trusted her enough to take a glass of water from her when he woke in the morning. She thought the truth had cleared the air, but now she began to doubt it.

After a short, lonely tea, she looked into the library and found it empty. But several of his books and his most recent notes had gone, as though he had chosen to work elsewhere. Was he avoiding her?

The conclusion seemed inescapable. She only hoped it wasn't because he thought she would poison him.

After tea, she wrote a short letter to the vicar's wife in Farnton Heath to explain her and Aggie's absence. It turned out to be a much shorter epistle than she had intended, since there was so much she could not say. Unsatisfied, she set it aside to arrange postage tomorrow. If the duke did not throw them out. She hoped he would not, since she could not bear the thought of his being here unprotected.

Without much hope, she went through the motions of changing into the altered lilac evening gown for dinner. She forced herself not to look for the duke in the library on her way to the dining room, though the need to know he was well was like a growing ache. During dinner, she decided, she would ask the footman to relay a message to His Grace.

But His Grace surprised her again. When she entered the dining room, he was standing by his chair, clearly waiting for her.

Relief and pleasure cascaded through her, quickening her pace. "Your Grace! Are you well enough to dine?"

"We are about to find out. I got bored with gruel and broth, but even so, I have ordered a rather light meal. I hope you do not mind?"

"Of course not." She searched his pale face with some concern, for she had the feeling they were both saying words more to pass the time than because they meant anything. Of course, there were servants in the room, holding her chair, setting dishes on the table, and, on the sideboard, pouring wine.

"You may go," the duke said, when the first course was served. "We'll serve ourselves and ring when you are required."

"Very good, Your Grace," Betts said, jerking his head at the footmen, who promptly marched out. Betts followed and closed the door.

It was true that the duke and Olivia were family, but even so, it was not quite proper to be dining alone behind closed doors. Olivia found it hard to care, though perhaps she should. If Anthony cast her off, she would need to work, and then her reputation would indeed matter.

"We have much to discuss," the duke said, picking up his knife and fork.

Olivia nodded. The crab was delicious, and she swallowed the first mouthful before saying, "Whatever the poison was, it could not have been added in the kitchen or on the journey from there to the dining room. To affect you alone, it must have happened during serving. Something added directly to your plate or your glass."

"Exactly. I told Black to get rid of the brandy, but it had already been thrown away."

"You think it was in the brandy? Did it taste strange?"

"No, but then, some poisons don't taste of anything. Arsenic, for example—rat poison."

"*Rat poison?*" she said with revulsion.

He looked amused. "You think it adds insult to the injury? I don't *know* that it was arsenic, but it's probably the easiest to have found. There's bound to be some in the house and grounds."

She swallowed. The crab no longer tasted quite so good. "Perhaps we should concentrate on whom rather than what. Both Albert and Frank poured you wine and served your food. If the poison was in the brandy, it could have been added at any time. And, of course, I was beside you for the entire meal."

The duke set down his knife and fork. "You were. In fact, it was pointed out to me that I have now suffered two accidents since you came to Cuttyngs."

It should not have hurt as it did. She supposed it was natural that suspicions should linger, but if they did, would he trouble to look for the person who had really hurt him? Who might kill him the next time?

She found she was staring unseeingly at her plate. Her presence was not helpful. Could she trust anyone else to look out for him?

"I will go," she said. "But you need someone here you can truly trust." She looked up and met his gaze with conscious bravery.

He said, "You think if you leave, all this will end? I suppose it might, but only in the short term."

She frowned, uncomprehending.

"Think about it," he urged. "Your arrival could well be the reason, and you are, besides, a useful scapegoat. I'm quite sure Betts is not the only person here who knew of my father's arrangements with yours. I acquit you of deliberately scaring my horse—but then, *I* saw your face when I all but rode you down. To everyone else, taken with the poisoning, it could look very suspicious."

She made an effort to close her mouth.

"You have been at pains to avoid acknowledging it," he said gently, "but I think we both know the only possible motive for my father's death, and mine, is so that Anthony can succeed to the dukedom."

Ugly words, ugly truth. But even that made no sense. "Then why try to marry me to you?" she asked.

He shrugged, reaching for her plate and shoving it aside. "Soup?"

She blinked. "Allow me." She stood to place the soup plates and ladle soup into each.

"I suppose," he mused, picking up his spoon, "it would be odd to have a dowager duchess who is the daughter of the new duke, but then, it ensures you are provided for. I suspect that was Anthony's original plan, imagining that until I obligingly died, you and he could run the dukedom between you as he pleased. But you proved to be a disobedient daughter, and I was awkward to the point of throwing him out. He could not rely on either of us, so he needs to be rid of me and inherit himself as soon as possible."

"But there would be scandal, two dukes dying in quick succession. And if the doctors discovered arsenic in your stomach—"

"Why would they look? I am a sickly boy. You are an illegitimate fortune hunter and subject to hysterics."

"But I have turned up here at Cuttyngs. For all my father

knows, I have come to do my duty and marry you."

The duke shrugged. "I suspect that no longer suits him. We are not the pawns he imagined. But the real problem is not our marrying, it is the prospect of children of that marriage. A son would disinherit him."

"But he thinks—" She broke off, appalled by what she had nearly said.

The duke, apparently, had no such scruples. "He thinks I am not capable of fathering a child? He may have told you that to win your cooperation and teach you to deny me, but in fact, he can think no such thing."

"I don't see how he can know one way or the other," Olivia muttered, her face burning with embarrassment.

The duke's lips twisted. He set down his spoon. "How open to be?" he murmured. "My father could not bear the sight of me. My imperfections. He sought to humiliate me, shame me in any way he could. Including, as you know, in explaining how no gently born lady would bring herself to marry me. To show me all I would ever be entitled to, he brought in several… What shall I call them? Soiled doves? Women of ill repute? At any rate, they were well paid for their endurance, and I'm sure my father questioned them before they left. I know for a fact that Anthony was in the house on at least one such occasion."

Olivia found herself staring at him. "You did not send them away?"

"The women? I meant to," he admitted. "But actually, they turned out be interesting people and a great deal of fun." A hint of color seeped at last into his cheeks. "It was hardly what my father intended, either, so he stopped it. The point is, Anthony knows I am as likely as the next man to become a father, given a willing bride. The willing bride was the tricky bit. But the household knows you and I are friends. You help me with my work. You have been included in dinner invitations. You do not avert your eyes from my ugliness."

"Stop it," she said fiercely. "You can never have been ugly, and you never will be. I take your point. Whoever is working for my father—if indeed Anthony *is* our culprit—must be worried that I will marry you on my own terms and produce an heir that will cut him out."

"Succinctly put," he replied. "Which brings us back to the question, who is working for Anthony?"

She finished her soup and laid down the spoon. "Someone who has already shown themselves open to bribery by spying on you or Her Grace for your father? Only it could not have been Black, unless he doctored the brandy hours in advance."

"I have acquitted Black. And Albert the footman along with him. They stopped serving my father in that way."

"Which leaves Frank, the other footman who served us last night."

"And Betts," the duke said reluctantly, "who is in charge of the wine and brandy."

Her jaw dropped once more. "But he is an old family retainer! Surely he could not—"

"Loyalty to my father is no great recommendation to me," the duke said. "Perhaps he knows that. Perhaps they all do. I daresay they would all rather serve Anthony."

She gazed at him in consternation. He did not even speak with resentment, just calm reason. She remembered Black's panic last night, and Mrs. Irwin's distress. She could have sworn they were both genuine.

"I think you have more friends than you imagine," she said. "These people know *you*, not rumors or your father's lies."

Again, a tinge of color crept into his face. He swirled the wine in his glass, gazing into it. "I have done nothing," he said with difficulty, "to win their liking or their trust."

At that, she could smile. "Or mine. You don't need to."

His gaze lifted to hers and held. Something stirred inside her, something warm and exciting and overwhelming. In panic, she rose to collect their soup plates and see what else had been left for them on the sideboard. She brought some roasted vegetables and cold chicken to the table and, without asking or even thinking, served some onto his plate before helping herself.

"Thank you," he said. "I think we should get Anthony down here and finish this once and for all."

"You think he will admit it?" she asked.

"I can make sure he knows that I have made things so difficult for him, should I die, that he will do anything in his power to keep me alive."

"Have you?" she asked.

"Not yet, but I will." He picked up his fork, prodding half-heartedly at the vegetables, then set it down again. "I know this is difficult for you. You wanted a heroic father and you got just another Severne."

"*You* are a Severne," she pointed out.

"I am endeavoring to break the mold. What I mean is, do you wish to be here when he comes? If not, you can either be hidden in a separate wing, or go home until I have dealt with him."

She grasped his hand in fright. "You can't face him alone! We are sure he has an ally in the house. You will be even less safe!"

"Perhaps I should write to Frostbrook, too. And that Rivers fellow, though I suspect he is already abroad with the army. Then we will have our own alliance."

She smiled in relief, and his fingers curled around hers, making her suddenly breathless. "I like that idea," she managed.

"So do I. I shall write to Anthony and Frostbrook in the morning. If I know Anthony, he will be here by nightfall, so I shall be glad to dine elsewhere." He gazed at their joined fingers as though surprised, and released her hand, to pick up his knife and fork once more. "The chicken is good, don't you think?"

A shudder of laughter shook her. "Aren't you afraid at all? You have an unknown enemy who can strike without anyone knowing, and you're talking about chicken?"

"It's a selfish pleasure. I am glad to appreciate food again. On the other hand...no, I don't seem to be afraid. I feel more...exhilarated. Which is strange and probably perverse. But it's as if…when I deal with Anthony, I take charge of my own life."

She raised her glass to him. "You are the duke."

"I am," he agreed. "God help us all."

Chapter Eight

Aggie's observations in the kitchen bore out Olivia's feelings that the staff were appalled by the idea of the duke being taken from them, and not just because servants were always the first suspects in any crime.

"They're outraged that anyone dare lay a hand on their duke," Aggie said, helping to pin up her hair the following morning. "Let alone poison him, which they regard as a pretty low trick."

"Then they believe it?" Olivia asked her. "Are they suspicious of anyone?" *Me, for example…?*

"Oh, they believe it. Some reckon the old duke poisoned the brandy months ago. Apparently, he used to try to make Victor drink it, only he never would, then. Others think that Gregson the groom sneaked back to do the deed. Any other suspicions, they're not likely to let me hear, since I'm a stranger. But Mrs. Irwin told them all roundly that you had saved His Grace's life by insisting on the purgative he demanded."

Thoughtfully, Olivia made her way to the breakfast parlor. She had just helped herself to some toast and coffee when she heard the familiar tap of the duke's stick along the passage. She expected him to go on toward the library, but he came precipitately into the room, a letter clutched in his hand. He threw the letter on the table with apparent disgust and all but fell into the chair beside her.

"We'll have to change our plans," he said.

"Why, what has happened?"

"Anthony is in Brussels. He went to stop my stepmother marrying Giles Butler—yes, *the* Giles Butler who shot my father in the duel—but failed to arrive in time. Does that make Butler my stepfather?"

"I-I have no idea," Olivia admitted. "Do you mind?"

"About the marriage? No, though the old tabbies will have a field day. She committed two outrages in one—married the man who widowed her and did so within a month of his death!"

"Except, of course, we don't think Major Butler *did* kill His Grace," Olivia pointed out.

"There is that. Anyway, apparently Rosamund and Butler have the support of Wellington himself, so no one has dared cut them. Yet. But it does mean we'll have to wait to deal with Anthony, which is annoying." The duke scowled. "I had my heart set on a quick action."

"Unless..." Olivia laid down her toast. "Unless you go to Brussels, too."

He stared at her. "*Me?* I can't go to Brussels. I can't go to—"

"To the edge of the park? To the property boundary? You can ride. You can travel in a carriage. You can go anywhere I can—more comfortably, too, since you have the means to pay for it."

His lip curled. "Ha!" he said derisively, and got to his feet, stomping off without another word.

OLIVIA UNDERSTOOD PERFECTLY that she had thrown too much at him too quickly. She regretted her bluntness, though not the sowing of the seed. If Lord Frostbrook, perhaps, were to accompany him, he would be more comfortable, for they did not yet know for sure which servants were trustworthy and which had poisoned him.

Squaring her shoulders, preparing to meet his hostility, she entered the library.

"Olivia, you have worked wonders with my rambling notes," he greeted her. "I can see where my thoughts are leading now. You must have almost finished?"

Oh yes, he could always surprise her. "I just have your newest ones to add," she said.

"Excellent." He nodded in a friendly fashion and returned to his book.

Still wary, she sat down at the desk beside him, casting a quick glance at his absorbed profile. *I will miss him when we part…*

The knowledge felt like lead in her stomach until he glanced up and caught her gaze. After a moment, a faint smile flickered across his face, and she could only respond. But it was she who dropped her eyes first.

An hour later, she glanced at him again. He was gazing at the page, but his eyes were not moving. He had not turned a page nor made a note in some time. She wished she knew what thoughts occupied him so intensely.

She returned to her notes, just as he moved, grasping the stick propped against the table, and hauled himself to his feet.

"You'll excuse me, I hope. I'll be out with Jenkins on the estate most of the day. But I haven't forgotten dinner at Lady Mountjoy's."

"Of course," she said faintly, and watched him hurry to the open library door.

His gait was hardly graceful, but when his leg didn't pain him, at least it was fast and effective. She could only admire the spirit that fought to rise above what everyone else had thought him capable of. Above the deliberate cruelty, verbal and physical, that his father had inflicted upon him. In many ways he was like a child, slowly learning the possibilities he had never before considered.

It was all part of what made him who he was—not the duke,

but Victor Severne. And she liked who he was. So much that her heart seemed to soar just watching him walk away from her.

⋙⋘

MRS. IRWIN WAS brought in to approve Olivia's gown for the evening.

"Becoming," the housekeeper pronounced.

"Is it plain enough?" Olivia asked anxiously. "At best I am a mere poor relation, and I doubt Lady Mountjoy was even aware of my birth when she invited me."

"I think that unlikely," Mrs. Irwin observed. "No, you will do very well. The gown is simple and pretty, and it suits you to perfection. Go with our thanks."

That dragged Olivia's attention away from her reflection. "Thanks? For what?"

"For encouraging His Grace to go. He wouldn't, you know, if you had not been here."

It gave her plenty to think about as she descended the stairs, Aggie behind her carrying her cloak. The duke awaited her in the front hall. She rather thought he had timed it so that no one would see him negotiating the stairs, and wondered how many staircases were ahead of him at the Mountjoys' house.

"I'm sorry, have I kept you waiting?" she asked.

He turned, and a smile spread across his face, dispensing havoc through her heart and her stomach. He really had no right to such beauty, she thought crossly, and the austerity of his evening dress only accentuated it. From his starched white cravat to his polished black shoes, he was perfectly turned out. Even his unruly hair had been brushed into some kind of order. He was…stunning.

"No," he replied, "but if you had, I would hardly care. You look delightful."

Not so much his words but the warmth of his dark eyes

brought the heat rushing into her face. He offered her his right arm—his left being engaged with his stick—and she laid her gloved fingers on his sleeve as they walked the short distance not to the front door but to the side, where a portico protected the waiting carriage from rain. The duke's step was uneven, but had a rhythm of its own that she easily adjusted to.

Black waited by the carriage, but it was the duke who handed her inside. Black provided his arm for the duke's extra support as he climbed in, and then closed the door.

"Will you manage at the other end?" she asked.

"Black comes with us to preserve my dignity," he said wryly.

"You have dignity," she said. Then, "Do you know everyone who will be present?"

"I know Mountjoy, of course. And Naseby. They came to His Grace's funeral. The Mountjoys have another daughter besides the one who called, and I believe the Nasebys have three children. No idea of their ages, and if I've ever met Mrs. Naseby, I've forgotten her. His Grace did not encourage callers at Cuttyngs, except for the autumn balls, which I never attended."

"Did you ever want to attend?"

"God, no. It must have been horrendous for Her Grace, having to be pleasant to all these strangers she was never allowed to meet at any other time."

"Why not?" Olivia wondered.

The duke shrugged. "Just because he could prevent it. She was only there to produce him babies. And when it became unlikely that she would, he more or less ignored her. Not that he relaxed his prohibitions on her doing anything, you understand. No wonder she bolted and fell in love with the first decent man she met. She is younger than me, you know."

"You believe she rushed into marriage? That her happiness will not be lasting?"

"I'm the last person to judge such matters!" He turned his head and gazed out of the window. "The truth is, though I don't want to admit it, my father made us all the people we are today."

"No," she said, and when he turned back to her in surprise, she added, "I don't know Her Grace or Lady Hera, but it seems to me you have all risen above what he tried to make you. Even the Cuttyngs staff, once his pawns, are now devoted to you."

His lips parted as though he would reply, but in the end he just shook his head. They both knew that someone was *not* devoted to him.

Carnstow Hall, the Mountjoys' home, turned out to be a pleasant manor house, on a much smaller scale than Cuttyngs. For the duke's sake, Olivia hoped this meant the public rooms were all on the ground floor.

The duke's exit from the carriage was managed with casual discretion, and he handed Olivia down with perfect courtesy.

"Do you suppose they're watching from the windows?" he murmured as they progressed the short distance to the front door.

"Do you care?" she asked.

He thought about it. "No." He sounded surprised.

There were a few steps to the front door, but he managed them with ease and handed his hat to the footman, allowing another to remove his cloak.

"Welcome, Your Grace." The butler bowed. "Ma'am. Allow me to show you to the drawing room."

The servants were too well trained to gawp, but Olivia could almost have imagined they were disappointed to find His Grace so *normal*. Since there were double doors to the drawing room, they entered together, to the butler's proud announcement.

"His Grace, the Duke of Cuttyngham, and Miss Rainey."

The buzz of conversation in the room ceased at once, and every head turned toward them. If the duke hated it, he gave no sign, and in any case, their host and hostess jumped up to greet them almost immediately.

"What a privilege to welcome Your Grace!" Lady Mountjoy gushed.

"What kindness to invite me," Victor said, bowing punctiliously over her hand. "How do you do, Mountjoy? You won't know my cousin, Miss Rainey. Olivia, our host, Sir Hugo."

"Pleasure, my dear, pleasure," Sir Hugo assured her, bowing over her hand after he had heartily shaken the duke's. "Come and meet the others. We are a small, cozy party, bearing in mind Your Grace's recent loss. You know Naseby, of course. This is Mrs. Naseby, their son, Francis, and daughter, Anna. And their friends whom we are delighted to welcome for the evening, Mr. Yates and his son, young Tom. And last but not least, my own daughters, Eliza and Nell."

When all greetings and introductions were made, His Grace was invited to sit on the sofa beside Eliza Mountjoy, and Olivia in a cluster of chairs with the other young people. Sherry, ratafia, or lemonade were offered, and the usual inquiries made about the journey and the expected weather. The conversation was very general, and then dinner was announced. Inevitably, His Grace was given the honor of escorting his hostess, who, just as inevitably, expected to take his left arm, as was normal practice.

The duke merely stepped to her other side. "This one is more secure," he said humorously, and the lady blushed. One of her daughters let out a strangled giggle of embarrassment that everyone ignored, and Olivia found herself partnered with young Mr. Yates, who could not have been much more than seventeen years old.

"They've put the strangers together," he said, offering his arm. "My father and I are merely staying a few days with the Nasebys. Our home is in Cambridgeshire."

"Mine is further to the north of the county, and like you, I am merely staying a few days."

Tom lowered his voice a little. "I believe I met your cousin, once."

"The duke?"

"Lord, no, the lady who must be his stepmother, though you'd hardly credit it."

"Sadly, I have never met Her Grace," Olivia said.

Tom grinned. "She is a great gun—you'd never know she was a duchess at all, except when she takes it into her head to be regal. But I probably shouldn't say such things."

"Perhaps not…but you should find a moment to speak to His Grace."

VICTOR WAS NOT having a dreadful time. His companions appeared to be amiable, and curious rather than well informed. The girls made him uncomfortable by gazing at him with a mixture of wonderment and hunger that made him feel like a tasty but misshapen cake, so he was quite relieved when Lady Mountjoy took the females away. Olivia, who had seemed damnably cozy with young Yates throughout dinner, cast him no more than a quick smile as she passed him in the wake of the others. He hoped they treated her with respect, or so help him—

"Your Grace?" Young Yates himself slid into the chair next to his. "Tom Yates."

"I recall."

"I wanted to ask after Her Grace, the duchess," Tom said apologetically.

"I understand she is no longer the duchess, but Mrs. Giles Butler."

"I heard!" Tom grinned, as though relieved. "I wasn't perfectly sure *you* had, so I was keeping it to myself. I had occasion to be of service to Her Grace before she left England, and she is now staying in Brussels with my betrothed."

"She is?" Several questions tried to force themselves from Victor's lips but when he saw the other men all looking toward them in some surprise at such a tête à tête, he held his tongue. "Tell you what. Ride over to Cuttyngs tomorrow and we can talk in peace."

Tom looked both surprised and gratified, and Victor took his turn with the brandy decanter.

⋙⋘

"WELL?" OLIVIA ASKED him when the horses began their journey homeward in the darkness. "Did you hate the evening?"

"No," Victor admitted, and mentioned his thought about the misshapen cake.

She laughed, as he had known she would. "I told you. You are the top prize in the Marriage Mart."

"They really don't care about the leg, do they?"

"No."

"If I were a coxcomb, I might start to imagine myself a damned handsome fellow. I beg your pardon, a *dashed* handsome fellow."

"Well, and so you are," she replied, so lightly that he could not tell if she meant it. She had said it once before. He knew it was kindness, meant to bolster his confidence, but he already knew he was not the monster his father had made him believe in. "I understand the Marriage Mart takes many things into consideration concerning both ladies and gentlemen. Birth, property, and fortune being chief among them."

"And those I have by the cartload." He leaned back against the squabs, letting his hat fall forward over his brow. The light from the coach lanterns and the moon flickered through the windows, casting shadows across her face. They made no difference to her beauty. "What do you bring to the Marriage Mart, Olivia? Has Anthony given you a dowry?"

"He didn't even give me my bribe."

"Well, you didn't marry me."

"True. I am well served. In truth, I have never thought of marriage. I believe I might like to be a governess."

"We never had any remotely like you. My sister thought she would like to be a companion and help look after a child. Seemed an odd notion to me, but it's her life."

"I thought she had gone to stay with friends."

"They probably are by now. Friends, I mean. I think my family is odd. Hera said we are."

"I suspect she is right. It does not make you bad."

"Or good. Were they kind to you?"

"The Mountjoys? Yes, of course. They were curious, inevitably. Oh, and Tom Yates apparently knows Her Grace your stepmother, though I have no idea how that came about."

"I asked him to ride over tomorrow and tell us. I have a feeling we probably don't want it spread around the countryside. Although it's only a matter of time until her marriage is known and gossip rife. Will that affect my chances on this Marriage Mart?"

"I doubt it," Olivia said. She frowned. "Though I suppose it might affect Lady Hera's."

"Hera doesn't want to be married. His Grace's example as a husband appalled her."

"I don't imagine all husbands are like His Grace."

"But women always take that chance, don't they? Given as chattels into the power of…whomever."

"You would at least take care to pick a good man for your sister."

"If she let me. She needn't marry if she doesn't want to. If she does, I doubt I could stop her. Why are we talking about marriage?"

"Because Your Grace has just realized the possibilities."

He curled his lip. "That I could have a beautiful duchess to give me heirs?"

"If and when you want one. The choice is yours."

"And hers."

"I hope so. The prospect does not seem to attract you."

He gazed past her face and out of the window. "Beauty and heirs. It seems so…empty."

"You want love as well."

He could not resist looking at her once more, though he could not read her face. "Is that likely?" he said, lightly sardonic.

"It is not impossible."

"For you also?"

Her gaze dropped to her hands twisted together in her lap. "Not for me."

"Because you are poor? Or because your heart is already lost to some ruffian who broke it?"

She shook her head, smiling a little. On impulse, he reached out and closed his hand over hers. It lay still and soft while her gaze flew back to his face.

"I am glad I met you, Olivia Rainey. We are friends, are we not?"

She nodded. Her fingers twisted, but only to curl around his. "Always. I hope."

He knew he should release her, but he didn't, and she made no effort to pull free. Her breathing might have quickened a little. Or perhaps that was his own, or just a simple longing to hold her hand whenever he wished to.

"Will you ride with me tomorrow?" he asked suddenly.

"If you have a placid horse," she answered, after a slight pause. "I was taught at school, but that was years ago, and I was never able to practice. Do you have business on the estate?"

"No, I just want to ride. First thing? At six?"

"Very well."

A strange contentment stole over him, just sitting in the darkness with her hand in his, a promise of friendship, and an appointment to ride. Had he ever been this happy?

THE HOUSE WAS quiet, shrouded in darkness and silence. Everyone was abed, except him. He crept from the servants' stairs along the passage to the main staircase down to the front hall. He counted down three steps, then sat and set down his candle.

He was not the only man who despised this apology for a duke, but it seemed he was the only one prepared to do anything about it. The others had all gone soft, as if the cripple was a worthy duke who should ever have been allowed to succeed. The truth had been explained to him often enough by the late duke and by his cousin, Mr. Anthony Severne, who would have succeeded had there been any natural justice in the world.

Well, he was happy to aid natural justice, exactly as he had been paid to. And the danger presented by the Rainey girl was considerable. He had seen the way the cripple looked at her, let her assist in his studies, dine with him. The poisoning would have been simple, but the bloody girl had apparently interfered in that, too. He had had a few bad moments when Mrs. Irwin had started wittering about the duke being poisoned.

Well, he thought, screwing the tiny hooks into the wood at either side of the step, this time, no one would be surprised that a cripple had fallen downstairs on his way to ride out with the girl. That was rather a nice touch.

Between his two hooks, he wound several strands of black thread that would never be seen in the poor light of early morning, but would be strong enough to trip a strong, fit man.

Smiling, he pocketed the remains of his threat, picked up his candle, and made his silent way back to his own attic bedroom.

Tomorrow, there would be a new duke, one who could be respected by all. And he, most loyal of servants, would be the recipient of much gratitude—as well as gold.

Chapter Nine

Olivia woke to warmth. The sun had not yet risen, so she knew the warmth came from within—because she and the duke were friends, because they were going to ride together this morning, and because he had held her hand for a good part of the journey home last night.

A man so deprived of human contact could not possibly have merely forgotten that he held a lady's hand. Even a comfortable cousin's hand. She decided, in the end, it was merely an expression of friendship, made with the knowledge that she would not misread it and take it for a romantic advance.

God help her, she wanted to take it as such. She wanted it to *be* such. And that way lay unbearable heartache.

But she would accept the warmth and the pleasure of friendship with him. And remind herself that just because she had discovered her father was not the hero she had wished him to be, she did not need to put another family member on that pedestal.

But she had liked the feel of the duke's strong fingers curled around hers, his closeness in the carriage, the faint scent of his soap, his skin…

She rose quickly, before she could dwell further on that and misdirect her own feelings. She concentrated on washing and dressing herself in the riding habit that had perhaps once been Lady Hera's or the duchess's. She had not asked for a habit when the clothes were chosen from Mrs. Irwin's pile, but one had appeared in her wardrobe all the same, a comfortable garment in dark reds and greens. She managed to fasten it herself with some difficulty and pinned up her hair beneath its matching hat, which, though old, was the smartest head covering she had ever owned.

It was almost fully light as she made her way along the passage to the staircase and ran down. As she reached the main, curving staircase from the first floor to the front hall, she paused, for the unmistakable figure of the duke in an old coat and riding breeches sat on the third stair down, examining something in his hands. His stick was propped against the wall.

He glanced up at her, somewhat distracted.

"What is it?" she asked, relieved that he did not look obviously hurt. "Why are you sitting there?"

"Come and see."

She brushed past him and sat a couple of stairs beneath. He spread a line of threads she could barely see between his hands, and then pointed to the step above his.

"It was stretched across the step with a hook holding it into either side." He opened his hands to show her the tiny hooks and then pointed to the equally tiny holes in the wood at either side of the step. "Designed to trip."

"Dear God," she whispered, rising to the next step to feel the wood where the little hooks had been thrust in. "I take it you did *not* trip? Did anyone?"

"No, the servants don't use this staircase as a rule. I would never have seen it."

"Then how did you?"

For the first time, he looked embarrassed. "If no one is about, I find it quicker to go down—or up—on my rear. Like a baby. So I sat on the thread and saw the hook move."

She seized both his hands. "Victor, this has gone far enough. You must go to the magistrate."

"Perhaps," he agreed absently. His gaze was on her hands, and she quickly slid them off his.

"Who?" Olivia demanded. "Who could have… Surely, no one would have left this all day? The maids would have found it sweeping. Anyone could have been hurt, or killed…"

"They knew in the stables that we were riding out early. It was aimed at me."

"By someone who didn't know how you descend the stairs in moments of quiet."

"Well, no one knows that, except possibly Black. And now you."

"But no one from the stables would have cause to be in the house," she argued.

"The servants were up when we came home. Word will have been passed on of our intentions this morning." He drew in a breath that was not quite steady. "I have to think what is best to do. For everyone. This is not some game, an adventure to best Cousin Anthony…" He caught her gaze. "This is downright dangerous. I believe it was *aimed* at me. But *you* could easily have come downstairs first. Some servant might have used this staircase for speed when no one was up and about. Someone could have *died*, and it needn't have been me."

It would have been you… The thought was terrifying. She had to blink away the vision of his still, broken body lying in a heap at the foot of the stairs.

"Then we'll go to the magistrate," she said. "Is it not Sir Hug—"

"With what?" he interrupted. "He will question the servants and probably arrest the wrong one because he doesn't know them. Even the correct one will not lead to Anthony. We have no proof against Anthony at all. Not of this crime or any other, even poisoning my father before his duel. You did not see or hear the person who gave him the flask."

"But if we find who did this, they will surely implicate Anthony to save themselves?"

"I have no great faith that Mountjoy will find the culprit. And the law is ruthless with the lower orders. An innocent man—or woman—could easily hang."

She stared at him. "But we cannot do *nothing*, just because we are afraid we might be wrong!"

"No, we cannot do nothing," he agreed. His eyes seemed to come back into focus on her face. His hand came up, and he touched her cheek with the backs of his fingers. "It could have been you."

"It very nearly *was* you." She caught his hand tightly, pressing it hard to her cheek. The impropriety hit her suddenly, as did their closeness on the steps in the early light. She wanted to put her arms around him and press her face to his chest, to keep him safe, to comfort herself. But she could not. "What do we do?" she asked helplessly.

"Ride," he said, reaching for his stick.

"No." She caught at his hand and the stick. "Let's go down the easy way and be sure there are no more threads to trip us."

To be sure he would, she began to bump downstairs on her bottom. It brought back the memory of a childhood game that the Raineys had told her off for. Behind her, she heard a breath of laughter, and then he was bumping down beside her. They reached the bottom without incident, and he hauled himself to his feet at the same time she did.

"We check the girths ourselves," he said, staring down at her. "We do not gallop on paths where any further traps might have been left, only in the open."

"Victor, you cannot live like this," she whispered. Then, blushing, "I beg your pardon—Your Grace,"

"Victor will do. *Your Grace* was my father."

They walked out into a fine morning and followed the path to the stables where Victor's large black horse, Julius, and a smaller bay mare had been saddled by yawning grooms. They each stood beside mounting blocks. Olivia made friends with her mount, stroking the mare's nose and scratching her neck. As agreed, she ran her fingers over the girths, which were firm and whole. She saw the duke do similarly. Then, leaning heavily on the stick, he climbed to the mounting block, took the weight on his stick long enough to set his good foot in the stirrup, and hauled himself into the saddle. It might not have been graceful, but it was effective. He stowed the stick in the special sheath tied to the saddle that she had seen before.

When Olivia had mounted, the mare danced a bit.

"She's a good, obedient beast, ma'am," the lad at her head said. "Just got a bit of life in the mornings."

Olivia shortened the reins and petted the mare's neck. She calmed again.

"Ready?" the duke asked.

Olivia nodded and kicked her heels to urge the mare to follow him.

She had come this far largely because she couldn't think what else to do, but she certainly didn't expect to enjoy the outing. Amazingly, she did. In a very few minutes, the awfulness of what could have happened faded into the reality that they were both here on a beautiful early June morning, in delightful countryside.

Perhaps the horses' enjoyment was catching, for as they galloped across the meadow, worry and fear seemed to fall away, leaving only pleasure in the immediate present. The wind in her hair, the mare stretching beneath her, and Victor at her side. If he was not precisely carefree, there was still a sort of fierce gladness in him that told her that, in these moments, he felt as she did.

They drew up at the edge of the meadow, gazing down to the village at the foot of the path.

"It's very pretty," she observed. "I've never even been into the village. Can we go down?"

He hesitated only a moment, then nodded, wheeling his horse around to the path. He never went, she realized. He might visit tenant farmers because he had to, but he never showed himself in the village. No wonder the monster nonsense had grown and spread. Olivia could cheerfully have struck the old duke for his cruelty—it was not even thoughtless. It had been only too deliberate, no doubt caused by resentment that fate or

God had given him a less than physically perfect specimen for his only son and heir. Instead of rejoicing in the sharp, clever mind, in the determination that overcame his physical problems, the basic goodness and compassion…

They walked their horses down the path and through the main street of the village, which was waking up. A bakery emitted the delicious smell of new bread. A plump woman stood in the doorway talking to a carter and paused to gawp at them. Olivia inclined her head, and the duke, as if suddenly realizing what he should do, touched the brim of his hat. The woman bobbed a curtsey. The carter tugged his forelock.

The little incident was repeated several times as the horses ambled slowly up the street. Behind them, there may have broken out a storm of gossip, but Olivia sensed nothing but wary good will. Their duke had shown himself at last.

Victor was quiet as they made their way back to Cuttyngs, through the home wood. "Hiding is playing into my father's hands," he said. "My responsibility is not just to the land but to the people."

"You have no reason to hide. Like the Mountjoys, the villagers might have expected a monster because they hadn't seen the man. Now they know differently."

He was silent another few minutes. Then he said, "In my grandfather's day—according to Jenkins, the steward, who remembers it from his childhood—they held open days at Cuttyngs. A fair day with sports and feasting, and if it rained, everyone piled into the great hall. Perhaps I should consider reviving that tradition. And others, such as the harvest dance for the tenants and laborers. I think our autumn balls grew out of that, but the estate people got left behind."

She could see him mulling over the possibilities, the knowledge that he would need to move among them not on horseback but with his stick and his lame leg. He would have to make conversation with people he barely knew and who had very little in common with him. A bit like last night at the Mountjoys, in fact.

"Life," he said, throwing one arm wide, "is…*broad*, different."

She smiled. "And wonderful."

"Most of the time," he added.

She smiled, and just for a moment, so did he. Gladness flooded her heart, so intensely that it was almost pain.

Once the house came back into view, though, so did the reality of someone trying to kill the duke, and not really caring who else might be hurt or killed in the process.

In the house, a maid was sweeping the front hall and stood aside to let them pass unimpeded. Olivia wondered if the duke would send her somewhere else while he climbed the stairs, but he didn't.

Using his stick rather than his rear, he stumped his way upstairs. He had learned to do it at some speed, though she suspected it exhausted him, especially after the ride.

"We'll talk at breakfast," he said curtly, and limped off in the direction of the library and his own chamber. "Send Black to me," he flung at a passing footman, who happened to be Albert, one-time spy for the old duke. Albert took off at a run.

Aggie was already in Olivia's chamber upstairs.

"Been riding with His Grace?" she said, apparently pleased. Since the poisoning incident, her attitude to the duke had changed again. She regarded him once more as a possible victim and had made only halfhearted attempts to get Olivia to leave.

"Yes, it is a lovely morning. I wondered if I would still be able to ride, but apparently I can. A well-mannered horse helps, of course."

Aggie helped her strip off her habit and don a morning dress, before brushing out and re-pinning her hair.

"Are you comfortable here, Aggie?" Olivia asked abruptly.

"Comfortable enough. It's not my own home, but I've got used to most of the servants, and I can look after you." Aggie dropped her hands to her side and met Olivia's gaze in the glass. "Truth to tell, I never really regarded the cottage as home either.

It was more Mr. Severne's than ours."

"Did you trust him, Aggie?"

Aggie was silent for so long Olivia thought she would not answer. Then she turned away. "I tried to. For your sake."

Which was really all she needed to say on the subject. Olivia cast her a quick, unhappy smile and left the room. Although she knew in her heart that any traps would be set only where the duke was likely to fall into them, she found herself checking each step on her way down to the breakfast parlor.

The duke was already there, a plate of food and a cup of coffee in front of him. There were no servants in the room. By way of courtesy, the duke lifted his rear from the seat and dropped back down again.

"Close the door," he suggested. "I've poured you a cup of coffee."

"Thank you." She took a rasher of bacon with her egg, and a slice of toast, then brought her plate to the table and sat down beside him. For a while, they ate in silence, then Olivia set down her fork and reached for her coffee. "Have you thought what to do?"

He nodded slowly. "Yes. I think I have. Though I need your agreement."

Intrigued, she opened her mouth to ask for more details, but at that moment, a knock heralded Betts.

"Your Grace, a young gentleman has called. He has no card but says his name is Yates."

"Ah. You'd better show him in. And send up some extra crockery."

"Very good, Your Grace."

There was barely time to exchange glances with the duke before they heard the sound of the youth's bounding footsteps on the stairs and Tom Yates erupted into the room.

"Am I too early?" he asked disarmingly.

The duke waved his cup at him. "Not in the slightest. We have, in fact, been up for hours. Help yourself and come and join us."

Tom appeared to have the appetite of a horse, for his plate was piled high as he sat down on the duke's other side and accepted a cup of coffee with a grin. The retreating maid closed the door behind her.

"So," the duke said, "you met Her Grace. I hope you mean to tell us the circumstances."

"I'd love to. Only not sure I should. I don't want to get the lady into any more trouble."

"*Any more trouble,*" the duke repeated. "What a telling phrase. I have not always been the friend I should to Her Grace, but I stand by her absolutely. Nothing I learn from you will hurt her through me or Miss Rainey."

The boy searched his face, then Olivia's, before, apparently satisfied, he sighed and said, "I am betrothed."

"Felicitations," the duke said politely.

"Thank you. It is not a matter of universal rejoicing, however. Izzy is only sixteen, and between us, we don't really have a feather to fly with. On top of which, she can be hugely annoying, as girls often are. Present company excepted," he added hastily with a jerky bow in Olivia's direction.

"You do not wish to be engaged?" she asked.

Tom's eyebrows flew up. "Of course I do! I might have chosen to wait a few years, but at least this way, our families acknowledge that we *will* be married. They don't really approve. In fact, Izzy's family wanted her to marry some rich old goat in Bath, so we were forced to elope, and *that* is where I met Her Grace."

"You met her while you were eloping?" Olivia said, intrigued in spite of herself.

"Got soaked to the skin, and the innkeeper was disinclined to put us up because we weren't married and said he had no rooms, but Her Grace stood up for us and took Izzy into her room, and I slept in Major Butler's."

"I wondered when he would show up," the duke murmured.

"When did this happen?"

"Oh, three or four weeks ago." Tom shifted in his seat. "In fact, just after the duel. Her Grace and the major seemed to have met by accident. He didn't know she was the duchess, and she didn't even know her husband was dead, let alone that Major Butler had shot him." He took a breath. "In any case, the duchess persuaded Izzy's father to let us be betrothed so that we didn't feel the need to elope every time a man showed an interest in Izzy. In return, Izzy and I were able to help rescue Major Butler from the magistrate, but that is another story. And not really why I wanted to talk to you."

"I rather want to hear the story," the duke said, "but we'll leave it for now. You said you knew Her Grace was in Brussels and that she had married Major Butler."

"Turns out it is a small world," Tom said. "Izzy and I always have our ways of communicating. I believe she is using besotted soldiers and official channels to send me her—er—dispatches. Anyway, Her Grace is staying with Izzy's Aunt and Uncle Edwards in Brussels. Your sister is there, too."

"*Hera?*" The duke's mouth fell open. "She's meant to be in Lincolnshire!"

"Someone called Dr. Rivers took her to the duchess in Brussels. There's another fellow called Astley that traveled with them, but I don't quite understand why, or who the devil he is."

"Astley is the name of the family she went to in Lincolnshire," the duke said distractedly. "But Rivers is in Brussels, you say? And I had a letter from Frostbrook this morning saying *he* was headed there, too. Did your Izzy mention an Anthony Severne?"

"She said he was there. Your cousin? He didn't want the duchess to marry Major Butler."

"No, I'll bet he didn't. Any child born over the next year could be legally ruled my father's." The duke's gaze focused on Olivia. "So, Anthony is in Brussels, and the alliance we had hoped for is there, too."

Her stomach twisted. "Does that mean you will go?"

"I think it does…though we have a few matters to agree to first."

"You will take Black?" she said anxiously. "You need more people you can trust for the journey…"

Tom put down his fork and sat very straight. "I volunteer to accompany Your Grace to Brussels."

Olivia blinked at him, and he blushed.

"I want to see Izzy. She'll be getting into mischief with all those army officers falling at her feet."

"You are a stranger," Victor pointed out.

"I know," Tom said humbly. "And I can't pay my way. But I assure you I am a loyal friend and—"

"You misunderstand," the duke interrupted. "Being a stranger is good. It helps."

"It does?" Tom said in pleased surprise.

"In an odd kind of a way," Olivia said.

"Don't say anything to anyone just yet," the duke instructed him. "But I will be in touch. How long do you plan to stay with the Nasebys?"

"Until next week, I believe."

"Well, I'll be in touch before then." Victor held out his hand, and after a moment, Tom shook it, grinning, and stood up to depart. He remembered at the last moment to bow to Olivia.

"Your Grace, *what* are you about?" Olivia demanded as the door closed behind him.

The duke drew a deep breath and held her gaze almost defiantly. "Marriage."

Chapter Ten

Olivia stared at him, uncomprehending. "Whose marriage?"

"Mine."

Her arm crept across her stomach in instinctive comfort, though in truth, she had no idea which part of her actually hurt. "I am to wish you happy? What has that to do with Tom Yates? Or Brussels? Or Anthony?"

"We are central, are we not, to the alliance finding out the truth about Anthony?"

"Yes, but—"

"To make everyone at Cuttyngs safe from idiocy like this morning's trap on the stairs, I need to leave."

"That is probably true, though we don't want the culprit to go with you."

"Hence Tom Yates, the amiable stranger who thinks fast enough to save Her Grace from…whatever."

She nodded, following the argument.

"And you. We have got in the habit of looking after each other. Well, you looking after me." He broke off, with a choke of laughter "I'm not selling this well, am I?"

"Selling what?" she asked, bewildered.

"Marriage. You and I cannot go to Brussels unchaperoned—I cannot think Tom Yates counts on that score—unless we are married."

Her jaw dropped. "You cannot marry someone just to go to Brussels! You are the duke! And I have Aggie."

"Servants don't count."

"Aggie is not a servant."

"To the world, she is."

"*Now* you care about the world?"

He smiled, boyish and a little shy. "For you."

Her throat closed up. Without thinking, she reached out and closed her hands over his where they lay on the table. "Oh, my dear, you are…"

Her voice cracked and she broke off. She tried to remove her hands, if only to dash them against her eyes, but his fingers twisted around her and held them.

She swallowed. "There is no need to marry me. I will come."

"You do not think you are important enough to matter."

"I don't," she said. "Not in your world."

"In the world of my rank," he corrected her. "My father was very keen on his rank. I am very much opposed to being anything like my father."

"That is no reason to marry anyone either."

Another smile flickered. "True." His thumb moved on her skin, softly like a caress. "You do not find me abhorrent. You needn't ever see my leg."

"Victor, it is not about your wretched leg!" She squeezed his fingers, as though to get his attention. "You are… You have not been *out* in the world. Your life, in most senses, is just beginning. No quixotic chivalry should tie you to me."

"Not so quixotic," he argued. "If you ruin your reputation traveling with me, who would take you on as a governess to their children?"

"Governessing is not my only option."

"I won't list the advantages pertaining to the option I have just offered. I know such things don't weigh with you. But they shouldn't weigh against me either."

"You don't understand," she said with increasing agitation. "I would *die* rather than bind you to me in such a way."

"You don't want to take advantage of me?" he said, his eyes suddenly laughing.

She shook her head, unable to speak.

"But if I want it?" he said. "If I want you?"

"You don't."

"You cannot know that." He lifted her hands, brushing them against his lips one after the other. The kisses were soft and made her skin tingle.

"Don't," she whispered. "Please don't."

"Because you dislike me?"

Because I love you, you idiot! "Yes," she said defiantly. "Because I dislike you."

"Liar," he said, brushing his thumb and then his mouth across the inside of her wrist. "I feel your pulse, galloping like a bird's. And I know it is not fear."

She closed her eyes. "It is. It is fear."

"But not of me. You called me your dear."

"I should not," she said in a strangled voice. "But I have come to think of you as a dear friend."

"That is a good beginning, is it not?"

She opened her eyes to find his intensely on hers, wary and unreadable. She swallowed. "Not for you. The world is just opening up for you. Let us go to Brussels and clip my father's wings, make him face justice if necessary. You will meet so many people there—beautiful women, powerful women. You will regret being tied to me, and I…I may be no one, but I would require fidelity in a husband."

"And I in a wife."

"You have no one to compare me with," she said. "Until you do, you have no business offering for anyone." Her mind seized on another vital point. "Besides, if what we believe is true, then your marriage will lead to redoubled assaults upon you—and your bride!—lest you produce an heir."

She felt both triumphant and devastated over that, but it did not have quite the effect she had imagined.

"I have thought of that," he said, his gaze dropping to her lips and causing all sorts of panic and longing, "and we will need to go about it secretly. We will marry on the day we leave. I will obtain a license."

At that, she tugged her hands so fiercely that he released them. "I will not be bullied and forced into this! Understand, Your Grace, I will not marry *anyone*!" She rose and stormed to the door with what dignity she could muster.

Even so, before she could open it, he said mildly, "Think about it, Olivia."

OF COURSE, SHE could think of nothing else. Desperation drove her to the library, in search of alternative occupation for her brain. Had the duke been there, she would have seized a book and left, but for once, the place was empty, and she decided to keep up to date with his notes and follow his references for her own knowledge.

It was a good distraction, and she relaxed considerably. Time would find her a way to live comfortably with this, for she could not run and leave him to face his enemies alone, any more than she could marry him to appease propriety. Even so, she was aware the moment the door to his bedchamber opened and his familiar, halting step sounded on the parquet floor.

She could not bring herself to look around, so she pretended to be lost in the book in front of her while he came nearer. A whiff of his distinctive, clean spice and citrus scent swept over her, and she wanted to close her eyes. He halted behind her, leaning over to see what she was reading. He did not touch her, and yet every nerve end tingled as though he had. He had good, strong yet sensitive hands, and his arms…

"You are diligent," he observed, straightening. "You make an excellent secretary." He moved and sat in his usual chair beside her.

She stared at the same sentence for five minutes without any of the words making sense. Her brain seemed to be aware only of the duke pulling books toward himself, reading with silent concentration, making abrupt, speedy notes, and then returning to his book or retrieving another.

Gradually, an odd shift came about. She remembered how comfortable she had been with him, and that he was no different from the man he had always been. She read her sentence and then the next and began to lose herself in work once more. After all, she had always liked his companionship.

When he asked her politely for another book, she fetched it for him, and took the latest page of notes to transfer to her own system. Neither of them mentioned marriage or even Anthony.

Perhaps, she thought, *he has realized the foolishness of his proposal and is grateful for my refusal.* Perversely, this depressed her, even while she acknowledged it was for the best.

They worked through luncheon, and then the duke stretched his shoulders. "I have an appointment with Jenkins. I expect to be finished by tea. You are, of course, at perfect liberty to do as you wish."

And he rose, seizing his stick and stumping off to the main library door.

No, nothing had changed, she thought with amusement. And yet something painful tugged at her heart. Part of her had not wanted to be right. In spite of everything, she liked the idea that he might want her. But she knew him too well. She had merely become his responsibility to get to Brussels with her reputation intact.

VICTOR WAS NOT, in fact, bowed beneath the weight of responsibility. He was setting a whirlwind in motion that would transport his party from Cuttyngs to Brussels and install them in a decent, rented house. He was applying for a common license to be married in the local church without banns, and he was making sure Cuttyngs and the other estates would run without him for a few weeks. He had written to Rosamund and Hera.

All of it was in secret, courtesy of Tom Yates, whom he had summoned to meet him on the edge of the woods dividing Cuttyngs from Naseby land. The lad's eyes had sparkled with delight as he took the bag of letters from the duke.

"For Her Grace, via Izzy. For your man of business in London. For the bishop," Tom recited. "And I'll be back the day after tomorrow." He hesitated, then said awkwardly, "I'm grateful for your trust. You hardly know me."

"I always found my stepmother to be an excellent judge of character. Though I admit I'm taking a chance. I depend upon your discretion. Won't your father kick up a dust over your deserting your host for the London fleshpots?"

"Expect he'll be relieved," Tom said with a wry smile. "Something to take my mind off Izzy."

"Am I making an enemy of your father?"

Tom laughed. "God, no. In his heart he knows I'll always find a way to get to Izzy."

"Thanks, Tom. We'll talk again when you return."

The lad waved happily and galloped off once more for Naseby's manor. The boy was seventeen and fixed in his affections for a girl he had no illusions about and yet adored. At that age, Victor's intimacies had been with whores purchased by his father. Women who had taught him many things besides the joys of the flesh.

But he could not afford to think of such joys at the same time as Olivia Rainey. The trouble was, she tended to be everywhere in his head, a background or foreground to all his thoughts and hopes and plans.

Of course he would never force her, and he had by no means counted his chickens. But he was intent on courtship. Marriage might elude him for now—after all, there was little time before he planned to leave England—but he would have some time in Brussels, too.

Unless she met someone there who swept her off her feet, someone with less…baggage. Someone whole.

Pain clamped around his heart. If it happened, he would have to let her go. Perhaps he was not even being fair to *try* to tie her to him. And yet it was she who had taught him that he had as much right as anyone to look for happiness, for love. He wanted her love with an ache that left him breathless now that he had acknowledged it.

He wheeled his horse around and cantered back in the direction of the house. This plan had been coming upon him even before he had found the trap on the stairs. Ever since she had suggested he go to Brussels. She had become so necessary to him so quickly that he had been almost surprised to realize he did not regard her as a crutch, or even a friend whose company he looked forward to, as he had to Sophia Wallace's, for example. With Olivia, there had always been more. That tug of physical attraction and liking he had fought so hard against, his determination to distrust because he could not bear his own intense feeling for a girl who deserved more than a broken man.

And he *was* broken. His lameness was the least of the mess that was Victor Severne. He was only too aware he had been damaged inside by his father's cruelty, by his own perception of himself that he had only now begun to alter. He had no idea what he was capable of, but God, he looked forward to finding out. To being a good man and making some difference to the world he had only ever read about. He would do it, if he had to, without Olivia. But something in her spoke to him, and he wanted her so badly he had almost stopped sleeping.

That didn't matter. His own physical lust he could deal with. But if *she* liked *him*, as he had begun to suspect with some astonishment, then he would allow nothing and no one to come between them. He was not there, yet. But he had sown the first seeds, and they made him smile.

The softness of her skin beneath his lips, the excited galloping of her pulse… Even the memory thrilled him, gave him hope. If Hera had been here, or Her Grace, everything would be different. He could take his time, court her slowly and deliciously. But he did not have that time. Not if they were ever to be safe.

And damn it, if Anthony had killed the old bastard, *he* was responsible for catapulting Victor into the burden of ducal responsibility years before he should have faced it.

After leaving Julius in the care of the grooms, he decided, as usual, to enter the house via the side door. It gave him more options for ascending the stairs unseen. Though perhaps it was time he stopped bothering about such things. His route took him through the rose garden, once a bone of contention between his father and Rosamund. His Grace had won, inevitably.

A movement caught his eye, and he spotted Olivia among the flowers, a light shawl around her altered gown. He suspected she was avoiding him. A week ago, he might have let her. Now, he recognized there were many reasons for such avoidance, and they didn't all have to do with dislike.

He changed direction and swerved up the path toward her. "Have I missed tea?" he asked.

"I'm sure the servants would bring you some. Shall I ring?"

"No. I should change. Tell me first, would you alter this rose garden? If it were yours?"

"It is very regimented," she observed.

"Then you would rip it out and begin again?"

"Oh, no, what a waste of beautiful plants! No, I believe I would change the paths to make them curve, and perhaps move a few around for more pleasing color contrasts. Also, I don't believe I would prune them to within an inch of their lives just to make them all the same height. This variety will climb, given the chance, so we should give it a trellis or at least a wall to cling to.

It's as if the garden is here to tame nature, rather than let nature entertain us." She flushed slightly. "You think me fanciful."

"No, I think you've put into words what the rest of us always hated about the place. Only my mother loved it. And I suspect that was only as a task accomplished."

"Do you remember your mother?"

"Vaguely. She was distant, like my father. Hera blamed it on their being of an older generation."

"Perhaps that is true."

"It probably has something to do with it. Mostly, I suspect, neither of them were very pleasant people."

She gazed at him. "Your dispassion on the subject takes my breath away."

He said, "I save my passion for causes I can change."

She understood him, for color seeped into her face and she tore her gaze free. "Did you have a pleasant ride?" she asked with a hint of desperation.

"Most pleasant, if short. Would you have liked to come with me?"

"I doubt I am yet up to two rides in one day."

"Perhaps tomorrow afternoon?"

"Perhaps, if you and the weather are still agreeable."

He offered her his arm, and after the merest instant's hesitation, she took it. He was relieved, for it was no part of his plan to drive her from the closeness he had already won.

CHAPTER ELEVEN

THE DUKE WAS, of course, lulling her into a false sense of security.

He had not touched her, apart from accidentally while passing a plate, or in basic courtesy such as offering his arm to return to the house when they had met in the rose garden. Nor had he brought up any awkward subjects in conversation. On the contrary, he had been more relaxed and amusing than ever before, and she had found herself responding to his warmth despite her determination to maintain a certain coolness.

The only warning bell she noticed was during dinner that night when he asked if there was anything she needed for the journey to Brussels.

"I don't believe so," she replied. "Between what I brought with me and what I have already borrowed, I'm sure I have enough. Perhaps another novel or two from the library?"

"Help yourself," he said, and moved on, without again pressing her to marry him before they traveled.

Only when the servants had cleared away dessert and set the brandy in front of him before departing did he change tack.

Rising when she did, he limped across to the sideboard and returned with another glass while she was still collecting her shawl and reticule.

"Join me?" he asked casually.

"That would hardly be proper."

"I don't see why it should make any difference which room we are in. Why is my joining you in the drawing room more proper than your remaining here, where we are comfortable?"

"I was not going to the drawing room, but to my own chamber."

"Well," he said, "it *would* be improper to join you there, so perhaps we could settle for here after all?"

She felt her face flush but refused to give in to embarrassment. They were friends, and if it came to arguments, she was quite capable of holding her own. She sat, and he inclined his head as though in appreciation before he sat, too, and poured brandy into each of the glasses. He clinked his glass against hers and sipped.

So, we are to be friends, she thought in relief.

"You said earlier that you do not wish to be married."

Or perhaps not. "I do not."

"Because the state is repugnant to you, or because you have lost your heart elsewhere?"

She dropped her gaze to her glass, away from his penetrating eyes. "The latter."

There was a pause. "May I know the name of this fortunate fellow?"

You, you ridiculous, foolish, wonderful... "No."

"You don't think it's possible you will get over him in time and love another?"

She raised her glass to her lips, letting the barest touch of brandy into her mouth. It was a curious flavor, an even more curious sensation of burning. "All things are possible."

"But you have not tried?"

She blinked. "How would you suggest I do that? Try to will myself into love with some passing stranger?"

"I was thinking of something more practical. A kiss, for example. Did your beloved ever kiss you?"

"No," she said shortly. "And I do not wish to discuss it."

"Don't you? I expect you wish he had. Has no one kissed you, then?"

She glared at him, wanting to wither him with a curt *"No!"* before stalking from the room. Incurable honesty, however, made her answer, "Yes. Zack Porter, the blacksmith's son."

"Did you like it?" The duke, damn him, seemed more curious than jealous.

"No," she replied. "It was wet, awkward, and uncomfortable. He was drunk, of course, but I made sure to avoid him in the future."

"Quite right," the duke approved, and she knew without looking that his eyes were laughing. "You can kiss me if you like. If it will help with your decision."

From sheer nervousness, she took another sip of burning brandy and pushed the glass away from her. "I don't know what decision you are talking about."

"Whether or not to marry me."

"Don't, sir," she pleaded. "I have made up my mind."

"Without even a kiss?" he said softly.

"Yes." She jumped to her feet, retrieving her reticule once more then looking around for the shawl. He stood in front of her, holding it in both hands, ready to put it around her shoulders. He was tall and broad-chested. Standing unaided like this, leaning only slightly against the table, he looked fit and strong and heart-wrenchingly handsome.

Without a word, she turned and shivered as he placed the shawl lightly around her. Then his hands closed gently on her shoulders and she wanted to close her eyes. *Don't. Please don't.*

And yet when he turned her, she let him. He gave her time to step away, to bolt or verbally slay him. But she did not move or speak. She ached to know, just once, what it would be like to feel this man's kiss. She had always recognized there was passion in him, almost frighteningly intense. And yet she was not frightened. She never had been.

His gaze dropped to her lips, and butterflies soared in her

stomach. He bent his head slowly, his lips parting just before they touched her mouth, soft and tender, barely a kiss at all. And yet it melted her. Light as a moth's wing, his lips caressed, and then fastened on hers.

Those butterflies dived, dragging heat and wonder in their wake. She tasted him, inhaled him through his silken, sensual mouth. No rushed, crushing assault like Zack's but a slow, sweet promise.

She wanted it to last forever. But when it ended and her eyelids fluttered open, he said huskily, "Goodnight, Olivia."

A goodnight kiss… What did that mean? She reached for what dignity she could muster.

"Goodnight," she managed, and walked quickly away to the door. She hoped he could not see her legs shaking beneath her skirts. She was in her own chamber, alone, before she dared to touch her lips. They seemed strange to her, irrevocably different just because he had kissed them.

RISING THE FOLLOWING morning, Olivia had no idea what to expect from the day. Excitement that wasn't quite dread had settled in her stomach, and she found herself thinking strange, unhelpful thoughts, such as, *What if he really does care for me?* And, *Married to him, I would have a chance to win his love…*

Washed and dressed, she threw open the window and sat in the seat below to let the breeze cool her cheeks.

Life had given her few advantages, although she was grateful for not starving. Aggie's care and friendship was one. Knowing Victor was another.

Knowing *the duke*, she corrected herself with severity. She must not get into the habit of thinking of him so familiarly.

It would be so easy just to marry him and see where it takes us…

She leaned her head back against the window frame and closed her eyes. Unforgivable temptation. She could be a good wife to him, an understanding helpmeet and friend. It was more than many marriages accomplished. She need not bind him with her love…and yet for her, anything else was unbearable. For him… He too deserved the chance to discover a great love, to find a happiness beyond mere contentment. As he spread his wings, he needed to be free to open his heart.

She touched her lips. *And if he still chooses me…in a few months, a few years…I could marry him then. Not now.*

With this decisive thought, she rose and began to brush out her hair. Aggie came in to help. Olivia had already told her about the proposed trip to Brussels, though not about the duke's proposal. Somehow, that was too personal to share with anyone.

Despite the decision she had made, her heart thudded as she walked toward the breakfast parlor. *Don't be there, don't be there…*

He wasn't there. The disappointment was like a blow. She laughed at herself and sat down to eat a solitary breakfast.

"Is His Grace well?" she asked the maid who brought fresh toast.

"I believe so, miss. He rode out early with Mr. Jenkins."

"Good. Thank you." Why did it feel like an anticlimax? She was behaving like a schoolgirl with her first crush on the dancing master.

Annoyed with herself, she set off for a brisk walk down to the village, where she spent the last of her money on delightful-smelling soap for herself and Aggie. She wondered if Anthony would stop her allowance now that she had disobeyed him. He might have discontinued the lease of the cottage. Why had she not thought of this before? She needed to make some provision for herself and Aggie that did not depend on the duke. She needed a paying position.

After they had found the truth about Anthony, whoever or whatever had killed the old duke, and whoever was attacking the younger.

On her return, she resisted going to the library. She had more or less finished what the duke had asked her to do, until he created more notes. She finished the novel she had been reading over a light luncheon in her room, and then, almost in desperation, went to the library in search of others to take with her to Brussels.

The duke sat on the sofa, casual in his old breeches and shirt sleeves, with the bright waistcoat unfastened. He held a letter in his hand with apparent distaste. As she entered, he dropped it.

"Olivia."

"Your Grace."

"Don't you think we could dispense with My Grace? My name is Victor, and you have used it before."

"How improper of me. I beg your pardon. I hope your letter is not bad news."

He wrinkled his nose. "I'm sure it is for someone. My aunt, Lady Hadleigh, writes that she is going to Brussels to sort out Her Grace's scandal."

"Will she not be some support to Her Grace?"

"God, no. They cordially dislike each other. But it seems we shall have quite the family reunion."

"When do we leave?"

"Whenever we can get passage, but I am hoping within the week." He held out his hand to her. "Will you come and sit with me?"

"I came to find a few novels to take with me," she said nervously.

"On the lower shelves at the back. My father had them placed too far up for easy reach in case the females of the house were tempted by such detrimental reading. We reshelved them."

"You and Lady Hera?" she asked over her shoulder as she crossed the room.

"And I suspect Her Grace added a few more."

Olivia found the shelves of novels and selected a few at random. "Have you written to Her Grace to tell her we are coming?"

"Not yet, but I will when I am more certain of dates. What have you there?"

"Oh, a couple by Mrs. Radcliffe," she said nervously, "and some Scottish tales. I'll just take them upstairs to go in my bag."

"Olivia." He caught her hand as she passed and tugged, firmly enough to pull her off her feet.

She landed across his lap, the books still tucked in one arm. "Your Grace," she gasped in shock. "I—"

"Victor," he said sternly. "Are you so skittish because I kissed you?"

She glared up at him. "Yes!"

"That is silly. You didn't mind at the time. Put down the books, Olivia."

In panic, she clutched them more closely, but he eased one out from under her arm and threw it to the far side of the sofa, after which it was much simpler to extract the others and set them aside.

"That's better," he murmured.

"Better for what?" she demanded.

He smiled, a gentle yet wicked smile. "Kissing you again."

He took her mouth with suddenness, this time, just as if he knew that his kiss was all she wanted in the world. Such a different kiss from the first, this was fierce and overwhelming, still unbearably tender yet with such open sensuality that her whole body, with which she had meant to resist him, liquified into utter desire.

His fingertips caressed her cheek, glided across her neck, and she found her palm against his rough, stubbly jaw. His hair was unexpectedly soft, his hand gentle now at her nape, holding her head steady for the onslaught of his bold, devastating mouth. So sweet to surrender, even sweeter to return the kiss, to move her lips with his and touch his tongue, taste the inside of his mouth.

"I like kissing you, Olivia Rainey," he muttered against her lips, and drew back enough to look down into her no doubt glazed eyes. His were thrillingly warm, almost smokey. A smile flickered. "I think you like kissing me."

"Why are you doing this?" she whispered.

"To persuade you to marry me. To show you we can find physical pleasure together as well as friendship."

She wanted to weep. "Don't you see, Victor? You cannot cut yourself off from more suitable women—"

"I don't want other women. I want you."

Pain and joy clawed at her heart. "You don't *know* other women!"

"I know you." He raised her in his arms and kissed her again.

She clutched him by the shoulders, the neck, but it seemed she could not even try to push him away. All she could do was cling to the remains of her good sense and, when she could speak at all, say, "And when you meet a suitable duchess? A woman you truly love? How much will you resent me for being in the way? I could not live with that."

He sat up, and she slid off his lap, though he kept his arm about her, holding her to his side. After a few moments of thought, he said, "I cannot promise things won't work out like that. I cannot promise no dashing and handsome man will sweep you off your feet. We are about to go to sea, enter an area where war is likelier than not. We could die. You want me to live, to spread my wings—well, this is how I wish to do it. With you. And if I have learned anything from my father's death, it is that one should not waste one's life on distant possibilities. *Carpe diem*, my sweet. Let us live for the day and see where it takes us."

She searched his face. "That is a good speech."

"I thought so. Quite spontaneous, too."

A breath of laughter shook her. "I like you too much."

"Too much for what?"

"Binding you, constricting you."

"No one shall constrict either of us," he said with a shade of grimness. "Not anymore." He threaded his fingers through hers. "Are we not in alliance?"

She nodded mutely.

"I may be a little…unworldly," he said, "but I am really not some fool who does not know his own mind. I want to marry you, and I believe we would have fun together in our alliance. If you believe otherwise, for whatever reason, I shall not constrain you. Only…" He drew in his breath. "For your sake as well as mine, you must not discuss this with anyone else."

"I know."

"Then you will think about it?"

"And you will take care until we leave?"

"Infinite care." He swept his hand boldly from her throat to her thigh, where it halted, sweetly warm and heavy. "I have too much to look forward to. I will make sure you do, also."

With a huge effort, she sat up, dislodging his hand, and moved to the other end of the sofa. "Then we had better continue with some decorum, Your Grace."

"We had indeed, Miss Rainey," he said austerely, while his eyes gleamed with the kind of mischief that left her breathless.

CHAPTER TWELVE

THEIR PLAN—AND VERY probably their safety—depended on providing the duke's enemy with no further suspicion of marriage between them. Therefore, over the next couple of days, they spent little time together except in the library and at mealtimes.

They did ride out that afternoon, with care, and Olivia found it a blessed relief to be away from the house. She also found a secret joy in his company. They made each other laugh, had much to discuss and argue over. But it was he who shortened the ride and kept his distance.

They understood each other from a mere meeting of eyes, and she left him behind while she hurried ahead into the house. She knew he would not join her for tea, and found herself thinking that if they were married, such things would not matter.

If he was safe, such things would not matter, she corrected herself.

She planned to spend the rest of the afternoon in her bedchamber, but no sooner had she changed out of her riding habit than a maid appeared with a message from the duke. They had morning callers, and he would appreciate her company.

The callers turned out to be Mrs. Naseby with her two offspring and their visitor, the elder Mr. Yates. Olivia suspected that the purpose was largely to make the duke more aware of Miss

Naseby without the Mountjoy girls outshining her. But if Victor was aware of the design, he gave no indication. He was his usual slightly abrupt self, but at least he retained his courtesy, while Olivia poured and distributed tea, with sandwiches and rather delicious cakes.

She found herself beside Mr. Yates. "Your son is not with you today, sir," she observed. "I trust he is well?"

"Only too well! He has run up to London to see a school friend. We expect him back tomorrow. Not quite polite to the Nasebys, but there, they are old friends and take us as we come. And of course they know I welcome all distractions for Tom."

"Distractions?"

"From his ludicrous engagement. Don't misunderstand me, ma'am, Izzy Merton is as dear to me as my own daughter—if I had a daughter—but she is flighty and mischievous and will lead him into all sorts of extravagances. Besides which, he is only just seventeen years old! Madness to marry so young without a feather to fly with. Merton and I have merely allowed the engagement in the belief they will each tire of it before they are eighteen."

Olivia smiled. "So unlike most parents, you hope he *will* get into mischief in Town, and realize he could not behave so if he had the responsibility of a wife?"

"That's the ticket," said Mr. Yates. "Or, alternatively, that it gives Izzy a disgust of him. But since I understand she is flirting her way through the British officer corps in Brussels, perhaps their understanding is already broken." He sighed. "Children are a trial, as well as a blessing, Miss Rainey."

"So I perceive, sir," she said gravely. She just hoped Tom would return in time to accompany them to Brussels. Though his father would clearly not be pleased. "You don't feel your scheme would work better if they were together and allowed to tire of each other?"

"That was the plan when we allowed the engagement. Made sense at the time, but Merton got nervous and packed his girl off to her aunt, who was going to Europe."

"Perhaps he should go to Europe, too."

"Perhaps. To be frank, I don't know what is best. But I feel it a good thing he has gone to London!"

The Naseby party stayed a mere half-hour before moving on to call on the vicar's wife. Olivia and the duke had a mere few moments' privacy while the guests were being shown out, before the servants would come to clear away the tea things.

"Did you know Tom Yates is in London?" she asked anxiously.

"Yes."

"What if he does not come back before we leave?"

"He will," the duke said, rising with the aid of his stick as the maids came in. He smiled beatifically and limped out of the room.

THERE WAS NO further attempt to dine without the presence of servants. Nor to linger and share a glass of brandy like friends after the meal. Olivia was conscious of a sense of loss as she rose to say goodnight. She wanted more time with him. If she was honest, she wanted another goodnight kiss.

"Take the brandy into the library, will you?" the duke told Jeremy the footman.

"Yes, Your Grace."

Olivia was already in the passage when Jeremy passed her with the decanter, speeding in the opposite direction toward the library. She took a step toward the stairs. Behind her, in the dining room, came the gentle clatter of crockery and cutlery, and the duke's uneven footsteps. Abruptly, she was pushed against the wall, the duke's hard body pinning her there while his open mouth slanted across hers.

Her nerves leapt in joy and anticipation, but there was no time even to do more than gasp, for the next instant, he was limping toward the library as if he had never touched her. The servants were emerging from the dining room with their burdens, and there was nothing for her to do but carry on toward the stairs.

Her lips, her body—everything—burned.

SHE WOKE IN the morning to the realization that the duke's behavior was not that of a man bent on polite courtship and a marriage of convenience. He really did want her. Whether because there was no one else—and she should allow that he possessed more discernment than that—his feelings were far more than chivalrous.

Lust. Men had lusts.

So do I, God help me.

She could not quite pinpoint the moment, but during that day, she realized she had actually begun to consider marriage to the duke. Becoming a duchess, just as her father had wanted, only with the aim of *thwarting* her father.

The day passed much as the one before, except without the shared ride. Nor did the duke join her for tea, though as she left the drawing room to take yet another walk, she all but ran into Tom Yates carrying a leather bag under one arm.

"Miss Rainey!" He paused to bow. "A pleasure!"

"Join us, Miss Rainey," came the duke's voice from the open door of the library.

Albert, who had been showing Tom the way, bowed and departed, leaving Olivia to walk beside Tom.

"How was London?" she asked.

"Busy," he replied. "And I'm glad to be back."

She realized that he bore with him the scent of horse, that he had not yet been back to the Nasebys' house, even to change. And with that came an inkling of his purpose in going to London in the first place.

"This is my library," the duke said, as though showing it off. He was standing just inside the door, and pushed it closed with his stick before waving Tom and Olivia toward the sofa. "We shan't be disturbed here. Glad to see you back. I hope you are not too exhausted?"

"Not at all. I felt like a whirlwind of useful activity!" Tom waited politely for Olivia to sit, then sat down beside her, and the duke dropped onto a straight-backed chair that had been previously placed to face the sofa.

Tom immediately emptied his leather bag of its contents, which were several documents. "From your man of business," he said, presenting two letters. "And from the bishop."

"Well done," the duke said, and Tom blushed with obvious pleasure as Victor unsealed and read the solicitor's rather long epistle. "Good. Passage awaits us from Harwich to Ostend, departing on Saturday morning. Rooms will be reserved for us in Harwich the previous night, accommodation for the journey from Ostend, and in the Hotel de Belle Vue in Brussels for our arrival. He has also asked his colleague in Brussels to try to hire us a house, but he believes it may be difficult with so many foreign visitors, to say nothing of the Allied armies. Excellent. A glass of brandy, Tom?"

"I would not say no."

"Allow me," Olivia said, going to the decanter. She felt slightly dazed. They truly were going to Brussels, and in only a couple more days. Inevitably, she would confront her father. But was there really a way to extract the truth from him?

"Can you keep the next departure to yourself?" the duke was asking Tom. "I don't like to ask you to be deceitful, but Naseby's servants may well talk to ours, and then everyone will know. Miss Rainey's safety here depends on our discretion."

"Of course," Tom said. "To be honest, I'd rather just leave a note, or my father will try to stop me going to Izzy. I'll have to grovel to the Nasebys, though."

"I'll be sure to emphasize your crucial role in my important plans," the duke said with only slight self-mockery. "To be frank, if things go as we hope, there will be an almighty scandal, but you should come out of it a hero."

Tom grinned and knocked back his brandy with the casual familiarity of a rather older man.

"Don't mention Harwich in any of the notes you leave behind. But be prepared to depart on Friday morning. I'll send you word what time, but it will be early."

"As you wish," Tom said agreeably. He set down his glass, stood up, and stretched. "I'd better get back to the Nasebys. Good luck!"

"You too."

When Tom had gone, Olivia said quietly, "Why is the bishop writing to you? What bishop?"

"The Bishop of London. He was known to my father. His office has supplied a marriage license. Now we need only pin down the vicar in secret." He raised his eyes from the documents still spread on the table between them and held her gaze. "Providing you agree."

The silence stretched. "It is madness, Victor."

His lips quirked. "Then you'll do it?"

Laughter caught at her breath. "God help us both, I will."

He reached across, and she laid her hand in his, like a promise. It didn't even frighten her, although perhaps it should have. Instead, gladness spread through her veins—as well as a new, ever-growing excitement.

THE FOLLOWING DAY, Mrs. Irwin appeared, grim-faced in the breakfast parlor, and closed the door on the servants before she marched over to the table and addressed the duke and Olivia, who were sitting there at a decorous distance from each other.

"I sent the footmen up to clean the chandelier in the hall. The chain that holds it to the ceiling was cut through."

Olivia stared at the duke in fright.

"Perhaps it had merely worn," he said mildly.

"No, the cut was clean. One good tug would have brought it down. And after what happened with Your Grace's illness..." Mrs. Irwin shuddered. "What is the household coming to?"

"Insanity," the duke murmured. "It could have fallen on anyone. Though, of course...I've seen that chandelier cleaned before. The footman can reach it by standing at the center of the first-floor balustrade."

"Then someone meant to watch you until you stood in the right place, and then tug the chandelier free?" Olivia said with horror.

"It's where I pace when I'm waiting for the carriage or for someone to join me. But the danger is enormous, both to the rest of the household by accident, and to whoever meant to climb up and pull the thing down on me."

Probably for the first time ever in front of her employer, Mrs. Irwin sank into the nearest chair. "This is intolerable! We must inform the magistrate—"

"Our man is desperate," the duke interrupted, sounding thoughtful rather than frightened. "But I think you might find one of the servants vanishes very soon without a word of explanation or farewell. When he does, you have my authority to go straight to the magistrate and raise a hue and cry."

"Do you know who he is, Your Grace?"

He blinked at her. "Who was cleaning the chandelier?"

"Jeremy and James."

"Probably not them, then. Is it safe for now?"

"We've taken it right down until the chain can be repaired."

He nodded. "Good. All will be well, Mrs. Irwin, believe me. I rely on you more than you can know."

She blushed with pleasure as she jumped up and curtseyed before hurrying from the room.

"Thank God there is only tonight to survive," the duke said, so lightly that Olivia glared at him incensed. "When I go, so will he," Victor said.

"And if he follows us?"

"We'll already be at sea."

OLIVIA'S LAST DAY and night at Cuttyngs was inevitably fraught with fear and uncertainty. She was afraid to leave Victor in case someone openly murdered him. She peered at every stair, surreptitiously tested the steadiness of every large piece of furniture that the duke was likely to pass. Even the bookcases in the library became threatening. Food tasted like ashes in her mouth, even though the duke was convinced poisoning would not be attempted again after they had shouted their suspicions so loudly.

"He might risk anything if he is going to bolt," Olivia argued.

"But he doesn't know he *is* going to bolt yet," Victor said. "No one, except Black and Aggie, know we are about to leave. That is our advantage."

Olivia prayed he was right. Her nerves were worn raw, and she slept little that night. Even so, it was Aggie who woke her early the following morning. Their bags were already packed. Admittedly, she was leaving with rather more than she came with. But Black appeared to carry them, and they hurried downstairs and across the hall, which looked curiously empty without its massive chandelier.

The coach awaited them at the front door. Not so unusual, since the duke occasionally traveled around the estate by this method. Victor was already inside. The coachman did look somewhat surprised as Black strapped a trunk and several bags to the vehicle, handed Olivia and Aggie into the coach, and climbed up onto the box.

Ten minutes later, the coach halted outside the village

church. The vicar, an elderly man, awaited them on the porch. He came forward while Black jumped down to open the carriage door and let down the steps for the women. Victor followed in his awkward yet efficient way. Black stayed with the coachman—who had not yet been ruled out of their suspicions—and Olivia and Aggie walked into the church.

"Your Grace," the vicar greeted his august visitor. "What a great pleasure to welcome you to the church. I understand you must be terribly busy, but it is an honor to attend you at any time of the day. Is there a particular way I can help you?"

"Indeed there is," Victor said, using his stick to close the church door behind him.

Tom Yates emerged from the shadows, much to the vicar's clear astonishment, and nodded amiably at the duke and Olivia.

Victor took the license from his pocket and presented it to the vicar. "This lady and I wish to be married."

The man's jaw dropped, though he recovered quickly. "Of course! It will be my joy. When does Your Grace wish to be married?"

"Now," Victor said.

The vicar blinked, as though awaiting further information.

"As in, right now," the duke said impatiently. "Don what vestments you need to. We have witnesses and a license and are in something of a hurry!"

Fifteen minutes later, Olivia, feeling almost as dazed as the vicar, emerged from the church into morning sunlight as the Duchess of Cuttyngham.

Black grinned as he opened the carriage door. "Congratulations, Your Grace," he murmured. "Wish you very happy, Your Grace," he added to Olivia, handing her in.

This time, Tom added his bulky presence inside the carriage, and Black, climbing back up to the box, gave the coachman his instructions.

"Two post-chaises awaiting us in Cuttyngham," Tom reported.

"You have been invaluable," the duke replied. "Are you sure you want to come with us now?"

"Lord, yes. I've left letters for my father and Mrs. Naseby, apologizing and pleading service to Your Grace as my excuse. I didn't mention Cuttyngham, Harwich, or even Brussels." Tom grinned. "Never thought I'd be assisting at someone else's elopement."

"We are not eloping," Victor said. "We are already married."

THEY STOPPED AT an inn in the town of Cuttyngham, where two post-chaises awaited. This time, the coachman climbed down to receive the duke's instructions.

Victor passed him a purse. "See to the horses and get yourself some breakfast before you go back to Cuttyngs." He extracted two letters from his coat and gave them to the coachman, too. "For Mrs. Irwin and Betts. Be sure to deliver them when you return."

John Coachman tugged his forelock. "Yes, Your Grace."

"Off you go, then," Victor said as the horses were led away and the man went off cheerfully enough for a slap-up breakfast.

The duke offered Olivia his arm, and they walked to the front chaise, where he handed her inside. Black and Tom were stowing the luggage in the second chaise, where Aggie intended to travel, along with Black. Tom looked undecided until the duke summoned him to travel in the first carriage.

Olivia was both disappointed and relieved not to be alone with her husband. Her marriage still felt unreal, like a dream or a story from someone else's life.

"What is the inn at Harwich like?" she asked.

"Comfortable, I believe," Tom replied.

"But the rooms we reserved are a ruse," Victor added. "As is the packet to Ostend. Just in case my would-be killer follows our trail to Harwich. In reality, we sail with the evening's tide."

"On what?" Olivia demanded, staring at him.

"On my father's yacht. It was an enthusiasm that quickly died, but I understand it was kept seaworthy and ready to sail at a moment's notice."

"Didn't you trust me?" Olivia blurted. "You did not tell me what you had asked Tom to do, and now this secrecy over the yacht—"

"I was trying to impress you," the duke said, just a little self-consciously.

She gazed at him in surprise. His unexpectedly shy smile dawned, boyish and self-deprecating, and she felt a rush a love so fierce that it hurt.

MRS. IRWIN STOOD in the kitchen, staring at John Coachman. By her side stood Betts, while Cook and most of the maids and footmen surrounded them with avid curiosity. John thrust two letters at her, and her fingers closed mechanically around them.

"What do you mean, they're not with you?" she demanded. "*Where is His Grace?*"

John sighed. "Last I saw of him was at Cuttyngham. He sent me for breakfast and told me when I'd finished, I was to take the coach back to Cuttyngs and give these letters to you and Mr. Betts."

Mrs. Irwin blinked at the letter in her hand, passed the other to Betts, and broke the seal of the one addressed to her. Her eyes widened as she read. Her jaw dropped, and she raised her eyes to Betts in disbelief.

"What?" Jenny demanded. "Where have they gone?"

"His Grace has married Miss Rainey," Mrs. Irwin said slowly.

"Well, that explains the church," John said, scratching his head.

"What?" exclaimed Albert the footman. He seemed to have gone white. "Then where have they gone?"

"On their wedding journey," Mrs. Irwin replied.

"There were two yellow bounders waiting at the inn," John said. "Must have been for His Grace. Mr. Black's with them, and Mrs. Arnott. And that young lad with the Nasebys—Mr. Yates."

"Well, good for them!" Jenny said warmly. "I call it romantic! And I don't care whose daughter she is, I think she's a lovely duchess."

"So she is," Frank agreed, grinning. "As for His Grace, no wonder he was looking so pleased with hisself!"

"Yes, but he'd no call to do it so secret, like," Jeremy said disgustedly. "Don't we get a holiday or nothing?"

"Certainly not if you question your betters," Betts said severely, then scowled at Albert's back as the footman strode determinedly to the back door.

"Here," Betts said sharply. "Where do you think you're going?"

"Out!" Albert snarled over his shoulder, and slammed the door behind him.

Mrs. Irwin, at once frightened and triumphant, exchanged glances with Betts. It was happening just as His Grace had said it would. Though she had never suspected Albert.

"Frank, Jeremy, bring him back," Betts growled.

"And then send to Sir Hugo," Mrs. Irwin added. "I think we've just found our poisoner, and the villain who almost killed us all with that wretched chandelier…"

CHAPTER THIRTEEN

THE DUKE'S YACHT was a fine vessel with, inevitably, luxurious accommodation below deck. Olivia was sent ahead with the captain to view the cabins while Tom and Black between them managed the duke's awkward descent of thc ladder.

"I hope this will do, Your Grace," the captain said, showing her a large sitting room with carpet on the floor and a highly polished dining table and chairs in the center. "Sleeping accommodation is through there, and there are other cabins for guests and servants at—er…the other end."

"Where do the crew sleep?" she asked.

"Oh, they have their own quarters. It doesn't take many of us to sail her, and I didn't have warning enough to take on servants."

"Of course not. Thank you, captain."

Aggie said, "Show me the kitchen, if you please, and I shall cook."

"Galley," the captain corrected her automatically. "Come with me, then."

As they left, Olivia crept forward through the doorway into a bedroom. A large, curtained bed dominated, causing a flush to spread through her whole body. She turned hastily away from the bed and went through yet another door into what appeared to be a dressing room, with a much smaller bed made up. Would Black sleep in there to help the duke when he needed it? Or would the duke sleep there himself? She had no idea how wedding nights were managed. Or any nights, really, for married people of the duke's rank.

Hearing the familiar sound of the stick, she turned to see the duke in the sitting room doorway, gazing around the larger bedroom.

"Liked his comforts, did His Grace," Victor remarked. "I wonder who he took on his voyages with him? It certainly wasn't my stepmother."

"I expect the captain could tell you."

Victor considered. "If I cared, I would ask him. Will you be comfortable enough here? It should only be for the one night, providing the weather holds fair."

She smiled. "I suspect the sea is likely to be a much greater source of discomfort than the furnishings! The movement is most odd, is it not? And we have not even set sail yet."

"According to Tom, Her Grace has a potion that helps. Though that won't be much use to us, sadly." He turned restlessly. "I'd like to go up on deck and watch the ship leave the port, but I don't really want us to be seen if our enemy is in pursuit."

"We can watch through the windows. We'll have different views from here, and the big window in the sitting room."

Black appeared with their bags, Aggie at his heels, and Victor and Olivia went back into the sitting room. Tom stuck his head in admiringly and was invited to come for a glass of brandy. He happily drank to the health of the bride and groom, and it suddenly seemed odd again.

I am a wife. I am a duchess…

Only a little later, the ship got underway. It started creaking in different ways, and as the sails were unfurled, its roll deepened. Olivia gave in to a much more childish excitement as they set sail, drawing out of the harbor in the dusk and pointing out to sea. The gentle roll made it difficult to walk at first, causing much amusement among themselves.

At Victor's request, the captain joined them for supper, which was served by Aggie and Black, and proved to be a welcome weight to steady Olivia's stomach. Afterward, she and Tom scrambled up on to the deck to admire the beauty of the sea at night. But while it caught at her breath, she did not stay long, for she missed Victor and knew he would not yet risk his dignity by being carried up to join them.

The food was all cleared away below. The duke sat alone in the sitting room, gazing out of the big window, though he gave her a quick smile when she entered.

"Aggie is waiting in there to help you undress, if you're ready to retire."

Again, the involuntary flush invaded her body. "I suspect Aggie is," she managed. "It has been a long day."

She went through to the large bedchamber, where Aggie had laid out her nightgown. Olivia avoided looking at it, and went up to Aggie instead, taking her by the hand.

"Thank you," she murmured. "I did not mean to turn you into a servant when we went to Cuttyngs."

"I was a servant when I first met you. I see nothing wrong with that. Though I must say, I never imagined you would be a duchess!"

"That *is* strange," Olivia said. "And I've no idea how it will work out. Think about what you would like, Aggie, while we try to sort out this business with my father. You know…you *must* know there is always a place for you with me, but if you would prefer a cottage in Cornwall near your sister, I'm sure the duke will oblige."

"Don't really know my sister anymore," Aggie said, staring hard as though defying tears.

Olivia squeezed her hand. "Think about it. And we'll talk again after the adventure!"

Aggie blinked and stepped nearer. "I think you've done right. I think he is a good man."

"I think so, too."

Aggie's fingers twisted, digging into Olivia's. "If he isn't, if it ever changes, if we are wrong—you will tell me?"

"Of course I will." Olivia hugged her and let her go. The things she wanted to ask Aggie, or even just blurt out to her, were nothing to do with the duke's goodness. And he sat only on the other side of the open door. "Go to bed, Aggie. But you'll come to me if you get sick?"

"On your wedding night?" Aggie said in disbelief. "Don't be daft."

Olivia's choke of laughter followed her out of the room. The duke was dousing the lamps in the sitting room. She sank onto the bed to wait for him, her heart drumming a fierce tattoo. Then she realized he had used the door into the dressing room.

Was that it? After all his courtship, he meant to leave her alone when they were finally married? Was that relief crowding into her brain? Or unbearable hurt? She rose, unsure what to do with herself, and the dressing room door opened.

Victor stood straight, in his shirt sleeves, without coat, waistcoat, or cravat. He held his stick lightly, casually, more like a somewhat rakish gentleman of fashion than the cripple he had been called. Her mouth went dry.

He said, "You must be tired, and you have had no time to adjust to our…status."

"I can say the same to you."

His lips quirked. "That is different. I have thought of nothing but this status for as long as I've known you. My question is, shall I leave you in peace until we have more privacy and you are better used to me?"

Olivia, who didn't think she could endure it if he left now, said, "Whatever Your Grace wishes."

"Are we back to My Grace again? Must I talk to you in the same style?"

"Of course not." She sounded cool and detached to her own ears—a considerable achievement when she was entirely churned up.

He came toward her, and she could not bear the doubt, the uncertainty, he was trying to hide. "Shall I kiss you goodnight and leave you?"

Victor's goodnight kisses, known and delicious... Mutely, she raised her face, heard his breath catch as his gaze dropped to her lips. He brought up his hand, cupping her cheek, and bent his head.

The kiss was soft, gentle. But her mouth opened at the first touch of his, as if it could do nothing else, and somehow everything deepened into a warm, tender sensuality. She clutched his shirt in one last effort to steady herself, and the blissful kiss went on and on.

When he raised his head, his breathing was uneven. "Remind me to go."

She twisted her fingers in the fabric of his shirt. "Don't you dare," she said.

A breath of laughter caressed her lips, and then his mouth was there again, and his arms wrapped around her, holding her close against his obvious hardness. Excitement galloped. His fingers were massaging her nape, making her gasp and press closer yet. Barely understood desires coursed through her as her hands found the hot, smooth skin of his back. She eased his shirt upward, and he let her go long enough to drag it off over his head before he seized her again. And now she had the wonder of his shoulders, the thick muscles of his arms, to stroke.

A little push sent her backward onto the bed, but he came with her, and his weight against her drove her wild. She hadn't even noticed him unfastening her gown and stays, but he rolled off her to pull them downward and away. While he kissed his way down her throat and across her shoulders, he untied her chemise, and she moaned as he cupped her breast and returned to kissing her mouth.

"You are so soft, so lovely," he whispered, his caresses growing more intimate across her naked stomach and hips. "Will you trust me to show you pleasure?"

She would trust him with anything, everything, as long as he didn't stop. She tasted his shoulder against her lips, her teeth and tongue, as his caress swept inward across her thigh to the sweet, heavy ache between her legs. She gasped at the intimacy, utterly beguiled by the bliss that grew and grew, and finally consumed her in joy.

Her mouth buried in his, she clung to him in wonder and gratitude.

"So that is what all the fuss is about," she whispered, even as she wondered how it involved men's pleasure and babies and—

"Not entirely," he said. "Only a very, very little." He reared up, unfastening his falls, and she was too stunned by her first sight of human male parts that she barely noticed him tuck her between the sheets, and himself with her, still wearing his pantaloons.

She reached out to caress him, and his hand closed around hers, showing her how. He was right. There was so much more to experience, and it all excited her, thrilled her, especially as he slid inside her. There was so much more pleasure, so much give and take, a hint of pain and friction, of sensuous rocking and intense, heady ecstasy that almost made her weep, because he found it in her, as she did in him.

WAKING CURLED AROUND a warm female body was a rarity for Victor. In fact, it had happened a mere handful of times in his past. Now, as then, he woke with rampant, heavy lust, but his feelings for the girl in his arms now were so much more profound and complicated. For sheer care of her, he could not give in to his desire again yet. He didn't even mind. He was smiling into her hair because he had brought her physical joy. And because he had found it in her.

Sweet and shy and unexpectedly passionate, she was everything he could ever want, in bed or out of it. How had life delivered him such luck? If he was honest, he had not expected his wedding night to go quite as well as it had. He had prepared himself for shock, a few tears, and a lot of coaxing. But the coaxing had been so natural, and her response shattering. And then she had fallen asleep in his arms, her cheek against his chest in perfect trust.

My God, I love you, Olivia Severne…

His arm must have tightened involuntarily across her body, for she pushed back in instant response. He smiled. "Good morning, Duchess."

"Good morning, Duke."

He could hear the slow smile in her voice, even before he leaned up on his elbow to press his lips to her temple, her cheek. She turned into his arms and gave him her mouth. The sweetest of tortures.

"Again?" she whispered against his lips. It might have been wonder, or suggestion.

"Not yet. Even I am not so selfish. We should rise and find coffee and breakfast and find out where we are."

"Now?" She sounded disappointed, and he smiled.

"Perhaps not *right* now." After all, there was no harm in kissing…

RUMORS WERE FLYING around Brussels that the French had crossed the border and invaded the Netherlands. Rosamund, once Duchess of Cuttyngham, now the wife of a mere Major Butler, was not overly concerned. There had been such rumors before, all eventually proved false. Giles and all the British she knew in Brussels had far too much faith in the Duke of Wellington to be afraid, let alone bolt.

"If you are truly anxious," Rosamund said to Mrs. Edwards when they gathered in the drawing room around midday, "you should probably go north and leave from Antwerp. That's what Giles told me."

"Major Butler has told you to leave?" Mrs. Edwards said in fresh alarm.

Rosamund laughed. "Not yet! In any case, I should not go without him. And until the duke is concerned, I don't think anyone needs to be." There were several dukes in Brussels these days, but only the Duke of Wellington never needed his full title among the British.

"Besides, we can't leave until after the Duchess of Richmond's ball," Izzy Merton said. "We can go after that, Fanny, if you like."

"No, I only wanted the duchess's opinion," Mrs. Edwards said. "After all, your parents would never forgive me if I exposed you to war."

"War is the only reason we're here," Hera observed. "Because Wellington and the army are all around the city, ready to invade France or to face Bonaparte if he invades the Low Countries."

"Well, lots of people were here on the Continent before Bonaparte escaped," Rosamund said. "But yes, I'm sure the Army of Occupation was a draw, and I suspect most British visitors would have gone home if they weren't fascinated by all the dashing soldiery and the excitement. And, of course, nearly every family has someone in the army."

Hera rose and paced to the window and back. "Why is Victor coming here *now*? Victor never goes anywhere."

"But there is no real reason why he shouldn't," Rosamund said. "His father told him he was an invalid, but he never was."

"I know that. But he's hardly coming for the balls and parties, is he? He doesn't do anything without a reason. I think he's found something about…about His Grace's death."

"Well, we'll be able to ask him soon enough. According to his letter, he should be in Brussels by this evening."

The door opened, and Mr. Edwards wandered in with Sir

Arthur Astley.

"Is it time for luncheon?" Mr. Edwards inquired.

"Almost," his wife replied, "though I feel we do nothing but eat these days, what with dining early to go to parties and then eating enormous suppers!"

"Dash it, is that a knock on the door?" Mr. Edwards demanded. "Who calls at this time of the day? I hope the servants have the sense to deny us."

"You are grumpy, aren't you, Uncle?" Izzy said, taking his arm. "You do need your luncheon!"

A flustered footman flew into the room. He was a local man and usually addressed everyone in French. Today, however, he said in stilted English, "They say they are the Duke and Duchess of Cuttyng-ham."

Mrs. Edwards peered at him. "You don't believe them?"

"Well, there's an infallible way to find out," Hera said wryly, striding to the door. "I believe I can still recognize my own brother."

The door, left ajar, was pushed wide open by a stick. "Your brother is relieved to hear it," Victor's unmistakable voice said, just as he entered with an unknown young lady on his arm.

Hera, brought to an abrupt halt, stared at him and grinned. They had never been demonstrably affectionate, although Rosamund knew the feeling ran very deep.

"Why, Victor, don't you look dashing," Hera observed.

"He does indeed," Rosamund said, going forward to give the young duke her hand. He took it and, rather to her surprise, kissed it.

"Your Grace."

"Mrs. Butler," she corrected him, with a tilt to her chin. "But I wish you would call me Rosamund. Hera does." Her gaze flickered to the unknown young lady on his arm. The footman had said *Duchess*—had he been mistaken?

At that point, with a cry, a whirlwind launched itself across the room and landed hard in the arms of the young man who had followed Victor into the room.

Rosamund blinked. "*Tom?*"

With both arms around Izzy, Tom could only grin at her over the top of his beloved's head.

"Izzy!" Mrs. Edwards wailed. "Where is your decorum?"

"She doesn't have any, ma'am," Tom said, extracting one arm from Izzy's hold. "How do you do? I think we met once, years ago. I apologize for the unannounced interruption."

"You came with Victor?" Rosamund said, bewildered, then her manners returned and she smiled hesitantly at the silent young lady on Victor's arm. "I'm sorry! Courtesy seems to have flown out of the window."

"Allow me to present my wife," Victor said, the faintest hint of color—and pride—seeping into his face. "Olivia, the Duchess of Cuttyngham. Olivia, my stepmother, the erstwhile duchess, Mrs. Butler. My sister, Lady Hera Severne—"

"Rivers," Hera interrupted.

Victor blinked. "I beg your pardon?"

"My name is Rivers now. I married Justin. The doctor. I wrote and told you, but I suppose you will have crossed with the letter."

"I suppose I will," Victor said, gazing at her in fascination. He let out a crack of laughter. "Well, good for you. I can see we have a lot to catch up with."

The new duchess, who had curtseyed gravely to Rosamund, turned now to Hera. Hera stared at her, frowning more in curiosity than dislike, though the expression was hardly welcoming. Before Rosamund could nudge her, the frown smoothed, and Hera threw out her hand.

"How do you do? What on earth possessed you to take on my brother? He won't notice your existence half the time."

"Well, I won't notice his when I'm reading, either," the duchess said, taking the proffered hand.

"Very proper," Hera said, amused.

"Back to the courtesies," Rosamund said hastily. "Allow me

to present our kind host and hostess, Mr. and Mrs. Edwards."

Victor troubled to bow, and he could do it with some grace while still keeping elegant hold of his stick. "I am delighted to make your acquaintance. My thanks for taking such care of my family."

Mrs. Edwards, her eyes wide, stammered, "No, no, I believe they have been looking after us!"

"And Sir Arthur Astley," Rosamund finished.

"Astley?" Victor said, frowning. "Were you not Hera's employer?"

The man smiled, a singularly sweet, slightly apologetic smile. "Actually, no. I was her charge."

Victor's eyebrows flew up. Even the new duchess looked worried. Which Rosamund understood only too well. Victor's tongue could be devastating.

"We escaped together," Sir Arthur informed him, blissfully unaware of his danger. "And with Justin's help, we came here."

"Luncheon is served, madame," the footman said.

"Then set extra places for our guests," Mrs. Edwards instructed him. "And we shall be through directly."

"Sherry's the thing," Mr. Edwards said, reaching for the decanter with relief, and another breath of laughter shook Victor. The boy had both grown and mellowed in some indefinable way.

"I know I should have the courtesy to leave you to your meal," he said, "but I find I am far too fascinated."

"Do you have somewhere to stay?" Mrs. Edwards asked. "I'm sure we could fit everyone in with a little ingenuity…"

"We're putting up at the Hotel de Belle Vue," the duchess reassured her.

"Oh, Frostbrook and Sophia are there," Hera said.

Victor, who had just accepted a glass of sherry from Mr. Edwards, paused to frown again. "Frostbrook and Sophia?" he said dangerously.

"Oh, they're married, too," the duchess said. "Those awful relations of Sophia's abducted her to force her to marry her unspeakable cousin, so Frostbrook was obliged to rescue her and bring her here."

"And marry her?" Victor demanded.

"They are perfectly happy, Victor," Hera said. "As I daresay you are."

Victor opened his mouth, closed it again, then said, "I feel responsible for her. I let her gallivant about the country with Frostbrook."

"I doubt you could have stopped her," Rosamund replied. "In any case, it was I who was responsible for her, and I abandoned her at Cuttyngs." Her gaze fell on Tom and Izzy, who now sat on the sofa, their heads very close together. "Izzy, you can't behave like this in public, you know. You are appalling your poor aunt and uncle."

"We are engaged," Izzy pointed out.

"In polite society," Mrs. Edwards said, glaring, "even engaged couples do not sit on each other's knees."

"At least, not where anyone can see them," Sir Arthur Astley said vaguely.

Victor gave another bark of laughter. "Put her down, Tom, before you put us all off our luncheon."

Mrs. Edwards set down her barely touched glass. "Shall we go through to the dining room?"

The meal was light—lighter than intended, since it had to stretch further—but the conversation was constant.

"So, how are you and Victor acquainted?" Rosamund asked the new duchess, having sat beside her for the purpose. Bizarrely, she still felt some responsibility toward her late husband's adult offspring. "The name Olivia seems oddly familiar to me, but I cannot think where I heard it recently."

"Miss Olivia Rainey," Sir Arthur said from the other side of the table. "Lord Frostbrook and Miss Wallace called on her before they left England."

"Of course!" Rosamund exclaimed. She frowned from Olivia to Victor. "But that would make you…"

"Anthony Severne's natural daughter," Olivia said calmly. Only a faintly heightened color betrayed her embarrassment. "I am aware you will regard it as a poor match for His Grace—"

"It is not a poor match," Victor interrupted with one of his spectacular scowls. "It is the only match. And if you imagine my family will criticize you… Well, my sister married a mere surgeon, and my stepmother the man who widowed her. There is no call for pot-and-kettle insults."

"Says the man who has just insulted all of us," Hera drawled.

A smile flickered on Olivia's lips. "Actually, you did, Victor."

"Well, I'm sorry for it," Victor said, not noticeably abashed. "But I won't have my wife impugned on Anthony's account."

"He's here, you know," Rosamund said.

"I do know," Victor replied. "That's why we came. He might still be a danger to you, if he suspects you might produce an heir to supplant him. He is most definitely a danger to me, and to Olivia."

Rosamund set down her fork, staring at him. "And you brought her here?"

"She was no safer at home," Victor said impatiently. "Anthony left at least one henchman behind. Besides, Olivia has as much of a stake in this fight as anyone."

Rosamund drew in her breath. "You had better tell us everything."

CHAPTER FOURTEEN

BY THE TIME they left the unassuming little house and climbed into the hired carriage, Victor had talked himself hoarse. He supposed he was unaccustomed to saying so much in such a short space of time. Or listening so much, come to that.

"It is a bit of a madhouse, isn't it?" he said to Olivia with some amusement.

"It gives the impression," Olivia said thoughtfully, "but it seems to me, everyone knows exactly what is going on."

"They are very open," Victor admitted, "not just about Tom and Izzy Merton, but about Rosamund and Butler and Astley. And no doubt you and me. And Rivers is sure His Grace was poisoned. I look forward to meeting him again. And Butler," he said with a shade more grimness.

Olivia said, "Only fair when they looked me over."

Victor glanced at her and took her hand. "Were they rude?" he asked ruefully. "If anyone was, I missed it, but I want to know."

"Of course not. As you pointed out, none of us is precisely scandal free. They were more…curious. Making sure I was not taking advantage. Which is reasonable. I *am* Anthony's daughter."

Victor grinned. "It's Anthony's reaction I'm looking forward to."

"Not alone," she said, "and not until we have made plans

with the rest of the family. Seriously, Victor."

"I know, I know. Tell you what, I think living in a town is just the thing. I shall walk more where the distances are smaller. After this carriage ride, of course. There is a park just opposite the hotel. In fact, there it is."

"We could be put down here and walk," she suggested.

"No," Victor said. He had much more urgent and pleasurable pastimes planned before dinner.

Arrived back at their rooms, he scribbled a note for Lord Frostbrook and sent Black off to deliver it. "Have the next few hours off," he said. "I shan't need you until six."

Olivia's eyes widened when he locked the door behind the valet. Her skin flushed. "What had you in mind, my lord duke?"

"A nap, perhaps," he said, approaching and taking her hand. He kissed her palm, lingeringly, and a smile of understanding trembled on her lips.

"Perhaps," she said breathlessly, and let him guide her into his bedchamber.

RUMPLED AFTER SEVERAL hours of love—and no sleep at all—Olivia could not actually be bothered getting up for a formal dinner with people she knew distrusted her. She wanted to stay in the cocoon of sweet, heady sensuality and not even think about unpleasant things like Anthony, her father.

But since she was not so irresponsible, she rose when Victor did. The gleam of his contented eyes and the secret smile he shared were delicious compensation.

As a result, she felt a new closeness to him as they walked slowly down the hotel stairs to the private room Victor had hired for dinner.

The hotel foyer was busy, with guests setting out for the evening, waiting for each other or making demands of the harassed hotel staff. A few people blatantly watched Victor's awkward descent, but he ignored them, and even managed the business with a certain grace.

In one of her surreptitious surveys, Olivia noticed a beautiful woman in Pomona silk gazing in his direction. The woman must have been well into her thirties, but she had presence as well as beauty. Olivia was not surprised that Victor's face had commanded her attention—he was eye-catchingly handsome—but the faint, almost soft smile lurking on her lips seemed inappropriate. When the woman shifted her insolent stare to Olivia instead, Olivia let her gaze pass casually on.

Before she could make any remark to Victor, a man's voice said, "Cuttyngham! It really is you!"

Lord Frostbrook, resplendent in perfect evening dress, strode toward them just as they reached the foot of the stairs, and Victor was able to hold out one surprisingly elegant hand. "Frostbrook. A surprise to see you here, too."

Frostbrook shook the duke's hand with what looked like pleasure, though his eyes widened when they swept over her. A frown tugged down his brow. "Miss Rainey! Somewhat more of a surprise."

"No longer. I have pleasure in presenting my duchess. I believe you know his lordship, Olivia."

"We have met." She had found him a little haughty if humorous, as he had filled her little cottage with his aristocratic presence. Now, since he seemed to be some sort of a friend to Victor, she extended her hand. "My lord."

"Your Grace," he said, bowing over her hand, though the eyes that bored into hers when he straightened were more piercing than friendly.

"We hear congratulations are in order to you, too," Victor said.

"Thank you. I'll just run up and fetch Sophia and we'll join you directly in the supper room, which is through the door at the far end of the foyer. I presume we are to have the Butlers and the

Rivers also?"

"The Edwards and Sir Arthur were already engaged, though Tom Yates might join us."

Frostbrook, his foot already on the second step, turned back in surprise. "Izzy's Tom?"

"The very same."

"Good God," he said in apparent amusement, and carried on up the stairs.

As Olivia took her husband's arm, she again caught sight of the beautiful lady in green, now passing through the door Frostbrook had declared the way to the supper room. A hotel servant opened it again for Victor and Olivia with an obsequious bow.

The lady in green still stood by one of the several doors off this passage, her hand wrapped around the arm of an expensively dressed military gentleman of distinguished years and impressive whiskers.

She looked up, directly at Victor, and smiled. Victor drew in a sharp breath, but he did not pause.

"This way, *monseigneur*," the hotel servant said, and threw open the door at the end of the passage. Olivia and the duke had to walk past the lady in green and her companion, who courteously moved aside for them. Olivia didn't see how Victor could possibly know the lady, and indeed he swept by, although at the last moment, he accorded her a curt nod.

There was no time to ask questions, for the Butlers and the Rivers already awaited them in the supper room.

"You know Dr. Rivers already," Rosamund said quickly, taking the arm of a tall, good-looking young man in unform. "This is my husband, Major Giles Butler. Giles, the Duke of Cuttyngham, and Her Grace the Duchess."

Major Butler was clearly conscious of the awkwardness of the moment, for a flare of color followed the line of his cheekbone. He bowed stiffly. "Your Grace. I can only say how sorry I am for the duel."

Victor met the serious gaze with his sardonic one, and the room seemed to hold its collective breath.

"It is like His Grace to leave a storm behind for everyone else to clear up." He held out his hand. "No more duels? You have Rosamund to consider."

"Absolutely no more duels," Butler said. He grasped Victor's hand and smiled, an amiable, boyish grin that gave Olivia some inkling of his attraction to the erstwhile duchess. There was mischief and humor in his eyes, but also a great deal of thought and intelligence. And just a hint of vulnerability. "I am very glad to meet you at last."

He bowed to Olivia, who also gave him her hand. "Major."

"Your Grace."

The Frostbrooks arrived at that point, and Olivia found herself briefly beside her ladyship, who had been Miss Wallace at their last meeting.

"So how did this happen?" Lady Frostbrook asked with a glance at the duke.

"Much like *that*, I imagine," Olivia said, nodding toward Lord Frostbrook.

Sophia laughed. "*Touché*."

"Shall we sit?" Olivia said to the company as a whole, since she was supposed to be the hostess. They took their places in a casual way. A waiter came in and poured wine, another served soup, while a troop of other servants brought an array of dishes, which they placed either on the table or on the sideboard behind it. They then departed, closing the door behind them.

"We thought it easier this way," Victor said. "Then we can talk undisturbed. Because we do need to talk." He reached for his spoon. "I don't think any of us doubts, at this stage, that Major Butler was not primarily responsible for His Grace's death."

Dr. Rivers waved his spoon. "He should not have died at all from so minor a wound, let alone so quickly. It could have been a shock to his heart, of course. He might have had some illness none of his family or doctors knew anything about. Because the odd thing is, I saw him fall the instant *before* the shots were fired."

"So did I," Olivia agreed.

"I aimed well to the left of him," Major Butler said quietly. "It seemed to me he fell into my line of fire. But that could be my conscience trying to acquit me of killing him."

"Not if the duchess and I saw the same thing," Rivers argued. "And Mac—Butler's second, who is admittedly not unbiased—agrees. For me, the question became, what could have made the duke fall *before* he was shot? Only when I encountered a patient near my home, who was suffering from the effects of laudanum poisoning, did it enter my head that the duke could have been poisoned before the duel. So that the duel itself became nothing more than a cover for murder."

Rosamund shivered. "A murder Giles might still have to pay for with his life."

"He neither ate nor drank that morning," Frostbrook pointed out.

Olivia laid down her spoon. "He did."

Everyone turned to her. She drew in a breath.

"I suppose you all know I am Anthony Severne's natural daughter. I used to go to the George Inn to receive his letters and, latterly, to meet him. That was why I was there the morning of the duel. I went to Anthony's room and saw the duke there. Someone gave him a drink from a silver flask. Although they were in Anthony's room, I did not hear my father's voice, or see him. I went back to my own room rather than interrupt them."

Sophia—Lady Frostbrook—said, "You did not tell us that when we spoke at your cottage."

"No, I didn't."

Victor reached over and took her hand.

She clung to his fingers, staring at the half-eaten soup. "I don't know if you can understand this. I was educated as a lady, but one without a family or anyone to talk to who was educated to the same degree. While I tried to be grateful, I was unspeakably lonely, neither lady nor fit to work at anything ungenteel. My father's sudden appearance in my life was everything I had ever wanted. Suddenly I had family. And family loyalty. He even…wished to arrange a marriage for me with Lord Dean, as Victor was at the time."

She smiled ruefully and raised her gaze to take in everyone at the table. "Don't worry. I was as aware then as I am now how unsuitable such a match was. But it was proposed to me in such a way as made it seem I would be helping Victor as well as Anthony—in fact, all my new family. Only, then there was the duel and what I had seen at the inn. And Anthony commanded me to go to Cuttyngs to meet my grieving family. I didn't go."

"Why not?" Lady Hera asked.

Olivia shook her head. "Too many things seemed wrong. The duel, Anthony's vengeance against Major Butler, the idea that I should go in mourning to the young man I had never even met and marry him… It was all wrong. I refused."

"What Olivia is trying to avoid saying," Victor added, "is that His Grace paid her money to marry me. Well, he paid it to Anthony."

"Why?" Rosamund asked.

"Because," Hera said slowly, "my brother is a poor, gibbering cripple whom no respectable woman would ever marry. He said that often enough. You heard him."

Rosamund stared at her. "You mean His Grace believed it?"

Hera wrinkled her nose. "Of course. Once he had said it, he had to."

Olivia grasped Victor's hand more tightly. "I understand he said it so often, and in so many ways, that *Victor* believed it. When I finally came to Cuttyngs—after putting Lord and Lady Frostbrook's concerns together with my own—it was to warn Victor of possible danger. To my shame, I still could not bring myself to voice suspicion of my father. I still hoped I was wrong. Victor, of course, thought I had come to fulfill the bargain of our fathers."

"It seems you did," Frostbrook observed.

Victor met his gaze. "If you ever repeat that, I may not shoot you, but believe me, I will find a way to ram your teeth down your throat."

"I might let you," Frostbrook said. It could have been apology, or acknowledgement that he was biding his time until Olivia should prove herself worthy or otherwise.

"I wanted to see what she would do," Victor said. He picked up his wine glass, twisting his long fingers about the stem. "I felt like a cat playing with a mouse, particularly when the accidents began."

"Accidents?" Hera pounced.

"A poisoning at dinner, and an obstacle stretched across the staircase to trip me. And the chain holding the big chandelier in the hall was cut." He drank and set the glass back down on the table without removing his fingers. "It was Olivia who saved me from the poisoning."

Hera leaned forward, staring at her. "Because you already suspected our father had been poisoned, too?"

Olivia nodded. "We could not narrow the culprit down much beyond that it was not Black, the valet, who was clearly upset and doing all he could to help. And Victor found out that both he and Albert the footman had stopped reporting to his father some time before he died. They were the late duke's spies in the household."

"And Gregson," Rosamund said with dislike. "In fact, Gregson is here with Anthony…" She frowned. "Anthony is open about wanting to inherit the title after you, Victor. He tried to make me sign some document to say that any child of mine born after my second wedding was Giles's and not His Grace's."

"Did you sign?" Victor asked.

Rosamund curled her lip. "Of course not. But I told him no child of mine would ever be brought up a Severne." She flicked an apologetic smile at Victor. "I exclude you from my contempt, but my children will be Giles's."

"So if Olivia did not set off this round of attacks on Victor," Hera said, scowling and looking rather alarmingly like her brother, "what did?"

"I think it *was* me," Olivia admitted. "Inadvertently. Whoever Anthony left behind knew of our fathers' infamous marriage plan, and also Anthony's change of heart. Anthony can no longer trust me. I disobeyed him. He does not want me to be duchess, since he doubts he would be able to control or milk the duchy through me. I suspect he has found Victor a much stronger character than he imagined, too. But Victor and I had become friends."

"Olivia helped me with my studies," Victor said, color tingeing his cheeks. "And in her actions when I was poisoned, she proved where her loyalties lay. I could not be allowed to marry her and produce heirs that might exclude Anthony."

"So," Major Butler said after a pause, "we believe it was Anthony Severne who poisoned the duke and killed him? And now wants His young Grace dead, too? Do we have proof? Or just feeling?"

"Feeling," Olivia said ruefully.

Frostbrook, who seemed to have been gazing at nothing in particular, suddenly said, "No. We have proof."

Major Butler said, "We do?"

Dr. Rivers said, "What? What do you know, Frostbrook?"

"On the morning of the duel," Frostbrook said, "I was waiting just inside the front door of the inn for Cuttyngham and Severne. I was impatient to get it over with. From the front door, you can see the beginning of the upstairs passage, and the first bedchamber door. Which happened to be Anthony's. From the corner of my eye, I saw a movement, like a swishing skirt vanishing along the passage. I ignored it at the time, assuming it was a maid keeping out of the way of the dueling gentlemen." His eyes focused on Olivia. "I suspect now it might have been you, after you had seen the duke drink from the flask. But I saw who came out of the room with His Grace almost immediately afterwards."

Olivia closed her eyes. Even now, she didn't want it to be true. "My father?" she whispered.

CHAPTER FIFTEEN

"ANTHONY SEVERNE," FROSTBROOK agreed. "Who else would be in his room? I even saw him patting his pocket, as though he had just put something there. Perhaps it would not convict a gentleman of murder, but with the rest of our testimony, it should be enough to prevent a murder charge against Butler."

"Oh, thank God," Rosamund uttered, covering her face with one hand.

Butler put his arm around her. "I'm sorry," he said to Olivia. "This must be hard to hear."

Olivia nodded, wordlessly, and rose to put the covered dishes on the table. Without a word, Sophia helped by clearing away the soup plates.

Hera spoke in a small, hard voice. "So Anthony killed His Grace. Can we link him to the attacks on Victor?"

"We—er… did a bunk," Victor said apologetically. "Olivia and me. We married in secret before Tom Yates and Olivia's companion and bolted for Harwich. It was the only way to ensure that we got safely away and kept the rest of the household safe from our attacker's increasingly reckless attempts. They were endangering far more people than just me." His lips quirked. "We also hoped it would inspire whoever he was to pursue us and so betray himself to the staff. With luck, Mrs. Irwin has already passed his name to the magistrate, but I have received no word as yet."

"Hopefully, he won't come here," Butler said. "We'll have enough to contend with, what with Severne and Gregson. And Bonaparte, who probably isn't actually in Paris anymore."

"Where is he?" Victor asked.

Major Butler shrugged. "We don't know yet, but I suspect it won't be long before we do. Rivers and I may be gone for days if and when we face attack. So we need to do something about Severne and his henchmen *now*."

"Has Your Grace any objections to having him arrested, tried, and imprisoned like any other criminal?" Dr. Rivers inquired.

"None." Victor shrugged. "It will make an almighty stink, scandal-wise, but I doubt any of us care much about that."

Rosamund frowned. "True, but we can't be too rigid about law breaking, or we have to give up Giles, too. He was dueling."

"But not killing anyone," Hera pointed out. "I suppose the alternative is, we take matters into our own hands and forbid him the country."

"Then he would have to pollute someone else's," Dr. Rivers pointed out. "The man is a menace. Even if we forgive him for murdering His late Grace, he cheerfully went after Butler to pay for the crime, knowing he wasn't guilty. And then the attempts on the present duke's life appear to me unforgivable."

"They are," Hera said harshly. "In fact, I would quite like to murder him myself."

"Form an orderly queue," Victor murmured.

Major Butler said, "Military plans normally last only until the action begins. Then modifications or entirely new plans are necessary. Despite a certain sympathy with the proposal, we *cannot* kill him. Unless in self-defense, of course. We should probably begin with the aim of bringing him to legal justice, for which we need solid proof."

"Witness statements," Dr. Rivers said thoughtfully. "A few incriminating documents linking him either to past crimes or future ones."

Victor regarded him skeptically. "And how would we go about acquiring these?"

Olivia raised her head. "Actually, I might have a few ideas there…"

ANTHONY SEVERNE WAS poor and bored. He wanted quite badly to go home, where there were several people—including his beloved cousin, the young duke—who could still be tapped for money. While in Brussels, among the foreign visitors and the local gentry—some of whom probably preferred Bonaparte to their uninspiring new king—he had become quickly known as a cadger. He wasn't sure he could bear to kick his heels here much longer. In fact, it had been a bad idea to come at all, because he had failed to prevent Rosamund's marriage, and to blacken Butler's name. Wellington himself supported the major, so Anthony was reduced to graceful silence.

His best hope lay in England, where he had left considerable instructions for all eventualities. But he knew that if anything happened to Victor—and God knew it was past time something did!—then Anthony's safest place was here, far from the crime. Just in case that fool Albert failed to make the killing look enough like an accident and the authorities began to look around at who would benefit.

The sun was no longer high when Anthony entered his lodging house, wondering where he could scrape a dinner invitation. Climbing the stairs, he acknowledged that he disliked his dingy lodgings, he hated the growing summer heat, and he hated…

He opened the door to his rooms, and found Gregson waiting for him, glass in hand. The villain had helped himself to Anthony's admittedly inferior brandy, though he jumped to his feet as soon as his master entered.

"The other thing I hate," Anthony said witheringly, "is servants who lounge about doing nothing but toping."

"Sorry, sir," Gregson said, with an incomprehensible air of excitement. "But..."

He was a groom by training, not a house servant, but even so...

Gregson started again. "Thing is, sir, I've been waiting here for hours, desperate to tell you at once."

"Tell me what?" Anthony asked wearily, throwing his hat onto the bed while Gregson helped him out of his tight-fitting coat.

"I saw His Grace!" Gregson said, removing the coat to the back of a chair.

Anthony threw back his head and groaned. "Do I not suffer enough without having to listen to your damned ghost stories?"

"Ghost stories?" Gregson peered at him in clear consternation, then his eyes lightened and he grinned. "Not the old duke," he said. "I saw his body myself, didn't I? No, I saw the young one, here in Brussels."

Anthony paused in mid-stride. "Victor?" he said. "Victor is in *Brussels*? Are you sure?"

"Course I'm sure."

"How the devil did he get here?" Anthony mused.

"Boy gets on and off his own horse, rides damned well, and jumps it over fences you and I would hesitate to risk. Besides which, he has a house full of servants and bags full of money."

Anthony scowled at him. "The question was rhetorical. Someone has been feeding his confidence more quickly than I had bargained for."

"That would be his duchess, I expect."

Anthony was not blind to Gregson's malicious jibes. In this case, he chose to ignore them. He sighed and sank onto the nearest lumpy chair. "Who in God's name married him?" Damn Olivia anyway. It was as well he had found out her unreliability before she married Victor. Now Anthony had a completely different set of plans.

"Don't know, sir," Gregson replied. "Never saw her. Just heard Black say, *Don't forget the duchess's smaller bag.*"

"It could be Rosamund's bag," Anthony said, "full of things Victor has brought over for her. Were they ever so friendly? Besides, he can hardly be delirious that she married Butler! Wonder if he knows yet about Hera's *mésalliance*?" He leapt to his feet, smiling. "I shall enlighten him. Where did you see him, Gregson?"

"Belle Vue Hotel, sir. Midmorning."

"See any of the other servants?"

"Only Black. The carriage was hired and driven by foreigners. Like the hotel staff. Which doesn't mean there aren't loads of Cuttyngs people here. I just didn't take the time to find out."

"Take the time now, Gregson. Spy out the lie of the land, as it were, while I prepare to call on His Grace…"

BEFORE THEY LEFT the hotel supper room, they had agreed on a few principles. Eventually, Victor had withdrawn his objections to using Olivia as bait for Anthony, providing she was well guarded.

"I will have to be," she said reasonably, "since the whole point is to provide witnesses for whatever indiscretions he is induced to drop."

"And you don't mind this?" Victor asked, softly, for her alone, as they rose to leave.

She met his gaze without fear, a hint of a smile in her eyes. "I have chosen my side and will fight for it to the last."

He tucked her hand into the crook of his arm and squeezed it. Arm in arm, they followed the others from the supper room and along the passage toward the main foyer. Most of the other parties appeared to have dissolved, although the door nearest the foyer was still open, releasing the convivial sounds of chatter and laughter. A flash of green caught the corner of Victor's eye, and he could not help glancing through the open door.

Yes, it really was her. Jezebel Jakes, in tasteful green silk, pearls at her throat and her ears, white gloves adorning her hands as she gave one to a departing guest with a gracious smile. She stood beside the same starched old military gent, but her gaze flicked up to Victor. Impossible to tell if her smile was for her guests or for him. Hell, did she even remember him as more than a vaguely familiar face?

Either way, she could really not be allowed to accost Olivia… He kept moving forward as if he had not seen her and walked through the door into the foyer, which was at least quieter at this hour. The farewells were being said among his own guests, who had warmed noticeably to Olivia, making Victor proud of all of them. Not that they discussed anything private, only vague plans to meet and walk, go shopping, or ride beyond the town walls in the Allée Verte.

"One moment," Victor murmured. "Wait with my wife a second, will you?" As though he had left something behind, he limped back through the door to the supper rooms. The others had looked slightly surprised, but Olivia's glance had been worryingly…opaque.

Fortunately, Jezebel saw him at once, and he only had to lounge at his own supper room door for a moment before she emerged from hers, closing the door behind her.

She smiled hugely at Victor. "Bless my soul, it *is* you! Ain't you grown up handsome? Though to be sure, you were gorgeous as a young 'un, too!" Without warning, she threw her arms around his neck and bestowed a smacking kiss on his cheek.

Victor owed her at least a hug in return, and he gave it, briefly, before catching her hands and dragging them down. "What are you up to, Jez?"

"Up to being a married lady," she said, in completely different accents to those she had greeted him in. "I'm a vicomtesse, now.

And my name's Jessica, not Jezebel."

"Is he good to you?"

Jez laughed. "Is *she* good to *you*?"

"She's more than I could ever have dreamed of," he said quietly.

Her gaze grew at once shrewd and rueful. "And you want to be sure I won't rock the boat? Can't, love, can I? Got me own marriage to consider!" She gave him a playful little shove toward the door. "Back to the missus," she said cheerfully, and winked before pinning a haughtier expression to her face and sailing back into her supper room.

Victor couldn't help grinning as he returned to the foyer, though he straightened his face before joining the others. The last goodnights were said, and he and Olivia made their way upstairs.

"Did you spy some old friends?" Olivia asked.

"What makes you think so?"

"The lady in green was looking at you earlier."

"Well, I'm a handsome fellow."

Her face softened, and she laid her cheek briefly against his arm. "You are, Victor, and you have no idea."

"I'm beginning to," he said. "In fact, right now, I have several ideas..."

ANTHONY COULD NOT quite believe his luck. Peering from behind the double protection of a pillar in the hotel foyer and a news sheet in French that he could not even read, he had at first been uneasy to see Rosamund and Hera and their husbands emerge from the private supper rooms, closely followed by the once-haughty Lord Frostbrook and his bizarre choice of bride—Rosamund's one-time companion, for goodness' sake! What was the world coming to?

And then, at last, came Victor, leaning only lightly on his

stick, and on his arm…Olivia.

Anthony almost did not recognize her. It was not the fashionable gown, nor even the new, more elaborate hairstyle. It was something about her expression that threw him, that almost fooled him into ignoring her.

But no, that was definitely his daughter, the treacherous little minx—and she cut him out before marrying the duke on her own. Well, that would not wash!

Unexpectedly, Victor abandoned her with the others and limped in his quick yet awkward way back the way he had come. Anthony folded his newspaper and strolled about the edge of the foyer, keeping his person well away from his cousins' or Frostbrook's line of vision.

When he reached the door through which Victor had just vanished, he opened it a crack as though meaning to go through and then changed his mind, walking rapidly away again toward the front door. But he was smiling, because he had only needed that crack and that moment to see all he needed—Victor holding the hands of a luscious woman Anthony recognized more easily than his own daughter. Done up like a sow's ear in jewels, silks, and lace, she was undeniably Jezebel Jakes of Covent Garden.

Most definitely, there was ammunition here, and he, Anthony Severne, the future Duke of Cuttyngham, was just the man to fire it.

ALTHOUGH OLIVIA HAD noticed the woman in green and suspected Victor of going back to talk to her, she was not truly concerned. Every man had a past. Victor's, thanks to his father and his voluntary isolation, was presumably less populated than most, but he was not obliged to tell her everything. After all, she had not told him about the curate two Christmases ago.

Perhaps he would even introduce the green lady at some

point when he was more comfortable. For now, she reveled in the new closeness of marriage, rejoiced in its intimate pleasures, and fell increasingly in love with her husband. Even simple things, like enjoying breakfast together, were new and cherished experiences.

Black brought Victor a note with breakfast. He broke the seal only after the first few mouthfuls. "From Dulac," he said, after a moment. "Our man of business in Brussels. He says there is a house available in the Rue Royale, very close to the hotel, overlooking the park. Apparently, the previous tenants were English and have just scampered for home."

"Do you suppose they know something we don't?" Olivia asked.

"No. We just have more reason for staying. But perhaps we should consider leaving as soon as Anthony is dealt with. Shall we bother going to see the house?"

"Does it come with its own servants?"

"Apparently so."

"Then we should go and look. A house would be more comfortable." And safer from Anthony.

"Very well, I'll tell him we'll go at midday, shall I? I want to take a walk in the park first, to be seen as we agreed last night."

"Shall I come?"

"Come this afternoon instead, after we've viewed the house."

She was not offended. She liked to see him spreading his wings, going for a walk without her clinging to his arm as though she were holding him up. "You have to take Black, though," she warned.

"I will. And Frostbrook will be lurking around too, along with whoever has been dragooned from the Edwards household. What will you do?"

"I believe I shall compose a note to Anthony, inviting him to tea this afternoon. Then we can have people lurking in your bedchamber, listening."

"Do you really think he will incriminate himself?"

"He might, if he is sure enough that we are alone."

He stood up and went to her, turning up her face to kiss her. "Take care, my sweet. No chances."

"Likewise."

When Victor and Black had gone, and Aggie had taken away her laundry, Olivia sat down by the rolltop desk and pulled a piece of paper toward her. After some thought, she lifted the pen and began to write.

She had only completed the first sentence beyond her greeting when a knock sounded on the sitting room door. Assuming it was the maids come to clean, she rose and unlocked the door, opening it to discover instead a man.

Her stomach dived. For she was not ready to meet him… Dear God, would she ever be ready?

"Olivia," Anthony said fondly. "May I come in?"

Chapter Sixteen

Somehow, she managed to smile. "Of course! I heard you were here and, in fact, was in the midst of writing to invite you to tea."

"Is that why you are keeping me in the passage?"

There was nothing for it but to stand back and invite him in with an embarrassed laugh. "Sorry, Aggie has not yet tidied, and I wanted to impress you!"

"Oh, I am impressed," Anthony assured her. "In fact, you had me completely fooled. I truly thought you an innocent maiden, too frightened to marry the cripple for money."

She had to bite back her fury and hope he saw her heightened color as embarrassment instead. "I was never frightened."

"And so you thought to get one over on me, and marry him without allowing me my share?"

"Do sit down, Father, and stop talking nonsense," she said briskly. "Whatever happened between you and the late duke was clearly nothing to do with me, because I don't recall receiving any money whatsoever. But here I am, Duchess of Cuttyngham."

She sat, as elegantly as she could, in one of the armchairs so that he could not sit beside her.

He sank onto the sofa, resting one arm along its back, and regarded her. "Why did you not obey me and come to Cuttyngs when I summoned you?"

"I doubt anyone is receptive to romance in the first bleakness of mourning."

"My dear Olivia, if you still imagine Victor ever mourned his father, you do not understand him in the slightest."

She raised her eyebrows. "And you do? You imagined you could make him marry me, and then keep me from his bed, while you took over the running of all his estates and other wealth!"

A faint flush rose into Anthony's carefully expressionless face, but he waved the accusation aside. "So there are hidden depths to my little cousin. Is he eating out of *your* hand, daughter?"

This was not happening as they had planned last night. Someone should have been listening, noting the conversation. Anthony had found her too early, and she had lost the advantage before they had begun. He had known they were at this hotel, had probably seen Victor leave with Black at his heels and known he was safe. He would discount Aggie, as he always had, though Olivia wished quite hard that she would return now.

"Well, is he?" Anthony pushed. "Eating out of your hand?"

Olivia forced herself to meet his gaze. "I brought him here to Brussels, did I not? To you."

It was the right note, at last. Anthony relaxed, revealing how tense he had been up to that point. "Well, I wish you had not. He was better in England."

Where your man could murder him? She might have won an admission by asking why, but there was no one to hear. She could not waste the words she needed him to say, for in all probability he would never repeat them.

She gazed back at Anthony, feeling helpless panic rise. This man, so easily overlooked by his noble relations, had murdered at least one man without a qualm. Being his daughter would not save her if he even suspected that she might be carrying Victor's child. Desperately, she cast around for something to say while keeping her face bland and just a little submissive.

When a knock sounded at the door, her relief was intense. "Enter," she called, hoping it was Aggie.

But it was Sophia, Lady Frostbrook, who swept through the door. "Good morning, Your Grace! I wondered if you might care to—" She broke off, smiling politely as her gaze found Anthony.

"Lady Frostbrook, how kind," Olivia said, rising. "I suppose you must be acquainted with Mr. Severne?"

"Indeed," Sophia said, inclining her head.

Anthony rose somewhat more lethargically. "Ah yes, the mysterious companion who reappeared as Lady Frostbrook. The dowager countess must love you."

"She will learn to," Sophia replied, not remotely put out. She turned back to Olivia. "I came to see if you would like to take a walk? Perhaps look in some shops? But if you are engaged—"

"Oh, you may discount me," Anthony assured her, already strolling for the door. He smiled at Olivia, making her flesh crawl with sudden fear. "We can talk later, my dear. Good morning!"

Olivia waited until the door shut behind him before she sat back down with a bump, urgently putting her finger to her lips to warn Sophia. She did not put it past Anthony to be listening at the door.

"A walk sounds just the thing," Olivia said. "I barely know the town at all yet. And I brought very few gowns that will be remotely suitable for all the fashionable parties you mentioned. Would you like tea before we set out, or—"

Sophia caught on. "Oh, we could have coffee at one of those places with tables on the street!"

"What an excellent idea. Let me just fetch my bonnet."

Five minutes later, they were outside and crossing into the park. "I'm so glad you came," Olivia admitted. "I had no idea he even knew we were here. But I'm sure he waited until Victor went out."

"I think he did. Frostbrook saw him in the foyer while His Grace was leaving, and expected him to follow the duke. When he didn't, Frostbrook ran up to warn me before he went after His Grace. I came as quickly as I could."

"He appears to be at least one step ahead of us. So maddening after all our careful planning! There was no one but me to hear his admissions."

Sophia was silent as they walked along the leafy path. "Do you think he knows of our alliance?"

Olivia shivered. "If he was skulking in the foyer this morning, then he could have been there last night, too. He was not surprised to see me as the duchess, so he must have known. We thought we had the advantage in that he would underestimate us. I think instead we have underestimated him."

ANTHONY WAS REALLY quite pleased with himself. He had no intention of letting Olivia act except in subservience to him.

Perhaps he should have kept a closer eye on her growing up, but frankly, children were not his favorite creatures, and although he paid for her upkeep and education, partly through her mother's extortion and partly with a view to the future when he might need a grateful female on his side, he had had no real interest in her.

Her mother had been a grasping whore, too, who had washed her hands of the girl as soon as she extracted the means from Anthony to look after her. Anthony had been very young and green at the time, but even so, he had regarded it as something of an investment. Recalling her existence as he regarded his finances one day, he had begun to form his plan to control the dukedom—which, sadly, necessitated being rid of the cousin he had served so faithfully for years. Old Cuttyngham had been stubborn beyond belief, and tight-fisted to boot. He could be manipulated but never defrauded.

His heir, Victor, on the other hand, was an unworldly cripple—scarcely the idiot his father thought him, though much more vulnerable and therefore malleable. Or at least so Anthony had imagined, until Victor had thrown him out of the house along with the Hadleighs and all the other hangers-on.

In the circumstances, Olivia's betrayal hardly mattered when he needed to get rid of Victor anyway. But now that he had discovered her true nature, he was rather proud. He hadn't quite decided whether or not to let her live. It would probably depend on the marriage settlements, which he would discuss with her later.

After sending Gregson off to find out what he could about the marriage from Black, Anthony himself went in search of Jezebel Jakes—now, apparently, the Vicomtesse de Beaujardin. It seemed the vicomtesse associated largely with the native population in Brussels and had little to do with the officers of the occupying army or the other British visitors who had swarmed into the town since the peace last year. The vicomte, appointed a colonel in the Netherlands National Militia, was devoted to his wife.

Anthony was amused enough to knock on her door, well before the usual hours of polite calling. He almost expected to be turned away, but she consented to receive him in a tastefully furnished sitting room.

"Monsieur Severne?" she said in perfectly French-accented English. "I am the Vicomtesse de Beaujardin. Is there some way I can help you?"

He grinned as the door closed behind him. "Jezebel, you are magnificent."

She sighed, and her accent reverted to type. "I thought you must have found out. But if you make trouble for me, Severne, I warn you—"

"Don't trouble yourself. I am not interested in your little foreign escapades. I am more interested in your relationship with my young cousin."

She curled her lip. "Weren't you always? How is he? I hear he is duke now."

"You know perfectly well that he is. You saw him last night."

Her eyes fell. "That was a surprise. Though I am glad to see him looking so well. Who is the little wife?"

Anthony smiled. "My daughter."

Jezebel's eyes flew back up to his. "Really? How very well managed of you."

"I thought so."

"Are you warning me not to come between them?"

If anything, he was rather hoping for the opposite, but he had no wish to play all his cards at once. "I suspect that ship has sailed," he said wryly, and she did not disabuse him, merely smiled her secret smile. "He could not keep his hands off you last night." For which Anthony was profoundly grateful. If Victor was pursuing Jez, then it seemed likely Olivia was withholding marital favors. She was, it seemed, still a useful daughter to him.

"I am fond of the boy. What do you want, Severne?"

"Oh, just renewing an old acquaintance."

"My respectability is important to me," she said carefully.

"And to me," he said with a smile. He bowed and left without another word, knowing he had made his point. When he sent instructions, she would obey, or Anthony would burn her pathetic respectability to the ground with a mere few words in a very few carefully chosen ears.

OLIVIA LOVED THE house. It was spacious without being overwhelmingly grand or ornate, it was spotlessly clean, and the servants, who seemed all to have learned at least a smattering of English, were clearly efficient. Moreover, since it overlooked the park and was so central, Victor could practice his walking and be relatively close to everywhere else. And to top it all, he had discovered that the Duke of Wellington himself had his residence and headquarters only a little farther along the road.

"I think we should take it," Olivia said. "If you like it?"

"I do. Black and Dulac are talking to the servants about security and what important people we are. We cannot have any strangers admitted to the house." Victor took her hand. "Don't look like that. We won't have to live like this forever, only until Anthony is dealt with. In the meantime, we might as well be comfortable in a pleasant house, surrounded by good friends and obedient servants."

Dulac bustled importantly into the drawing room. "I believe this will admirably suit Monsieur le Duc. The servants have all been here for more than a year, and are eager to serve a new master now that their old one has departed so suddenly. To be frank, they were afraid for their livelihoods and are relieved enough to serve you well, whether they like you or not."

"Is that your impression also, Black?" Victor asked, glancing at the door where the valet lurked.

Black nodded. "Seem to be decent people."

"Then we should probably get them started moving our few things from the hotel."

"Maybe I should invite Anthony to tea tomorrow instead," Olivia said worriedly when they were alone. "They seem to dine so early here, and my nerves would not stretch for a whole hour."

"Write to him this afternoon, once we are settled."

"Sophia was suggesting we go to the theater this evening."

"Why not?" Victor said, as casually as if he was used to going to such places. And yet Olivia knew he had never been in his life. Sadness, anger, and happiness mingled so intensely in her heart that she was afraid she would weep.

WITH THE AID of their new servants, Victor merely took over payment for the theatre box rented by the previous house tenants, and so he and Olivia were able to invite Rosamund and Hera, the Frostbrooks, Tom, Izzy, and Sir Arthur—thus allowing the Edwards, Rosamund said, an evening of well-earned peace.

Victor was ridiculously excited about going. He knew this was rather childish and would have been embarrassed by his sad lack of experience had Olivia not confessed that she had only been twice herself, once as a schoolgirl and once with Aggie on quarter day. And they had been decidedly provincial theatres where they had sat in the cheap seats, not in the rarified atmosphere of the private boxes above that housed the wealthy.

"I just hope the stairs are not steep enough to embarrass me," he said ruefully.

"We shall manage," Olivia said, as though it were her problem as much as his. She smiled shyly. "Actually, I got you a present while I was out with Sophia—it might help." She moved to the window and took something from behind the curtain.

She came back to him holding out a smart walnut walking stick with a carved gold head. Victor's throat closed up. No one had ever given him such a gift, something that not just acknowledged but *glorified* what he had always seen as his disability.

"You don't like it," she said, her voice light yet curiously flat.

He pulled himself together, reaching for the stick. "It is the handsomest cane I have ever seen." He ran his hand over the elegant, curved handle and the polished wood shaft, then used it to lever himself upright beside her. He put his arm around her and kissed her. "Thank you," he whispered.

Both her arms came around him, holding him close in gladness and relief, and yet again he thanked God for this amazing, caring woman.

Despite his anxieties concerning Anthony and Olivia's safety, Victor found he was enjoying this spreading of his wings, the gathering of simple experiences most people took for granted—walking in a public park, going to the theatre with his wife, accepting invitations to parties.

"The Duchess of Richmond left her card at the new house," Olivia told Rosamund, "though neither Victor nor I have ever met her!"

"She can be kind," Rosamund said. "She was to me. And of course she will want as many dukes as she can get at her ball! She did invite you, did she not?"

"Not yet."

"Will you go, Victor?" Hera asked. "For I'm sure she will invite you."

"Probably," Victor said, his attention moving to the stage with growing excitement as the curtain went up.

It was only at the first interval that he noticed Jez, the Vicomtesse de Beaujardin, sitting in a box on the opposite side of the stage, with the military gentleman who seemed to be her husband, and a few other local worthies. He let his gaze move on at once, though it struck him she was taking a huge chance. If Victor, who never went anywhere, recognized her, would not many of the British visitors? She had been an actress on the London stage, with a certain amount of fame, latterly. And he had hardly been the only man to whom she had granted intimacies for a price.

It was all rather sordid to him now, and he didn't want it touching Olivia at all. But years ago, Jez had been his nearest thing to a friend, and he truly wished her well. At least most of the theatregoers here were Belgian.

Those few that were English made a point of claiming acquaintance with at least one of Victor's party—usually Izzy—and dropping into the ducal box to be introduced to the new duke and duchess. Their expressions amused Victor, from avid curiosity to astonishment and even disappointment. Of course, he was always at his best sitting down. In the second interval, he took himself for a walk along the corridor to ease the stiffness in his leg.

He had not gone very far, giving a polite nod to the few people he encountered, when, without warning, someone grasped his elbow and tugged.

Since it was his stick arm, he lost his balance utterly and painfully, falling against a surprisingly soft body before he landed with a bump on a hard chair. In the dim light, he blinked up at Jez.

They were at the back of an unused box, the door to the corridor closed, and the curtain drawn to hide them from the stage side.

In sheer fury, he gave her the glare that withered his servants and reduced them to gibbering. But Jez was made of sterner stuff.

"Don't try to freeze me to death with that look," she said. "I'm not here because I want to be, and my risk is greater than yours. Now shut your cakehole and listen."

"I haven't said anything at all, and you—"

"Victor, love, that cousin of yours came to see me," she interrupted. "He means me no good, but I suspect it's you he's after. Sooner or later, he's going to hold my past over me to make me do something against you."

Victor curled his lip. "He is a worm. But don't worry. He's about to have such a spectacular fall that no one will give credence to anything he says."

Jez smiled dazzlingly. "Why, Victor, love, you've found your teeth."

He grinned evilly and heaved himself to his feet. "Don't haul me around like that, Jez."

"You didn't used to mind."

"Begone, woman. Thanks for the warning—and the risk. I'm more grateful than you'll ever know."

She nodded. "You look after your little duchess," she said, and swept past him out of the door.

WHILE OLIVIA WAS glad to see Victor enjoying himself in activities most people considered ordinary,. she was not happy that he wandered off alone. Catching Tom's eye, she rose and slipped from the box, with Tom obediently at her heels.

A few people were milling, chatting, between boxes. Olivia glanced one way and then the other.

"There he goes," Tom said as a walnut walking stick vanished around the corner. They quickened their pace and reached the corner just in time to see the duke all but fall into an empty box. The door shut quickly behind him. Olivia gasped in distress, and as one, they hurried up to the box.

Olivia would have barged straight in, but Tom caught her hand, and she realized it would at least be sensible to know how many people were in there with him. Her heart thundering, she put her ear to the door.

A teasing female voice, not in the least threatening, was saying, "...Victor, love, you've found your teeth."

There was movement within. "Don't haul me around like that," Victor said, sounding not in the least put-out.

In fact, he sounded amused, almost...playful.

Understanding, jealousy, a thousand possibilities, all struck her at once. It was as well Tom had heard the approach of other people and tugged her away from the door.

"There is no danger to him," she managed, nodding civilly to those walking past. "It seems to be a friend."

Before she could hustle Tom away, the friend emerged from the box. Although she wore a dusky pink today, Olivia knew her at once for the lady in green.

Something seemed to be squeezing painfully at her heart. She rubbed it absently. "You go back to the box, Tom. I'll make sure His Grace hasn't hurt his leg."

Tom frowned but nodded and turned reluctantly away. Olivia took three paces to the box and went in.

Victor was already on his feet, holding his stick. He had been gazing into space, lost in thought. At the apparently unexpected sight of Olivia, his whole face lit up and he smiled, surely without guile or inhibition. Her pain eased, shifting into a more bearable form.

"Olivia," he murmured like a caress.

She waited a few moments in silence, for him to tell her who the woman was. He said nothing, though a slightly puzzled expression crossed his face. He offered her his arm, and she took it because there was nothing else to do.

When they returned to the box, the curtain had already risen on the next act.

CHAPTER SEVENTEEN

"WELL?" ANTHONY SNAPPED at Gregson when the man finally entered his room, weaving slightly. Gregson, clearly, had been in the tavern. "What did you learn? Are they really married, and if so, when?"

Gregson peered at him owlishly. "Black don't like me much. Didn't want to talk. But he did say the duke and duchess married in the Cuttyngs village church, and it was the day that they left England."

"So they've been traveling ever since," Anthony said with some satisfaction. Olivia would have been more easily able to keep her bridegroom at arm's length. Which still left last night at a decent hotel, and tonight in their newly hired house.

Anthony had an invitation to tea with Olivia tomorrow. Which was how he knew their address. They had a fine house overlooking the park, close to the Duke of Wellington himself, while Anthony… He cast a disgusted look around his cheap room with its slightly musty smell and discolored wallpaper. Perhaps Olivia would invite him to move into their house. *They must have a great deal more space then they need, even if Hera goes to them too.*

Although living there would make the crime easier, it would also bring him too close to it. He would need people to swear he was not in the house when it happened…

"Whose idea was it come to Brussels?" he asked Gregson.

"Olivia's or the duke's?"

Gregson shrugged, showing a tendency to sink onto the nearest chair until Anthony glared at him and he straightened again. "Black didn't say. Mentioned some accidents at Cuttyngs, though."

Anthony's eyebrows flew up. "Accidents? What sort of accidents?"

"Bad food, with only His Grace affected. The chandelier in the hall cut so it was ready to fall."

Anthony closed his eyes. Really, one was hampered on all sides by idiot henchmen. Who would have believed either of those events accidents if the duke had died? "So the duke is suspicious? Of whom? Is that why he left England?"

"Black didn't say."

Anthony sighed. "What else have you found out at my expense?"

"The Belgian viscountess has been in Brussels since the end of last year, or at her old man's estates to the east. Don't see how she could have been having an affair with the young duke."

"But they could have arranged to meet here," Anthony pointed out.

Gregson shrugged without interest.

"Oh, go to bed," Anthony snarled. "I hope you're more use tomorrow!"

IF IT HADN'T been for the nagging fear, the hurt, that seemed to stiffen her whole body, Olivia would have liked coming home to their first shared home as its mistress. There would have been satisfaction in sending the servants to bed, climbing the stairs to their private apartments, and closing the door on the world.

Now, she closed the bedchamber door in silence and watched as Victor turned up the lamp and lit a few more candles. Her heart was heavy and frightened, and she seemed unable to move.

The hours of marital intimacy spent with Victor had quickly become necessary to Olivia, not just for the addictive physical pleasures but the ever-increasing closeness between them. He had even let her see his twisted leg, touch it, as though he finally understood that she loved all of him. It was trust. Or so she had believed.

Now… Now, she no longer knew what she believed of him or herself. She was glad Black and Aggie had both been told not to wait up for them, for her first instinct was to hide.

She had a bedchamber of her own, though they had agreed she would, for all intents and purposes, share his. Her things were here. She could, of course, take a few away with her to the other room, enough for tonight. It would give her time to cry and think, away from his persuasive, beguiling person.

But it felt like crossing an imaginary line. Setting a precedent. A boundary to the love that had grown so quickly and become so precious, at least to her.

At Cuttyngs—it seemed a lifetime ago!—she had vowed to win his love. She thought she had. But the incident at the theatre with the woman in green—the Vicomtesse de Beaujardin, according to Izzy—had proved their affection and trust were not so advanced as she had naively imagined.

I am not a child to sulk because my new toy does not work as I want it to.

Undecided, she waited, unmoving, as Victor sat down on the side of the bed, watching her.

"Is something wrong, Olivia?" he asked.

No, nothing is wrong. I believe I shall sleep in my own room tonight. Goodnight, Victor. Even unsaid, the words terrified her, hovering on the edge of her lips and tongue, the beginning of coldness, distrust, and dishonesty.

"I don't know," she replied, walking slowly across the room at last. She sank down on the bed beside him, touching at shoulder and thigh, and some burden seemed to ease. She took his hand in both of hers and looked up at him. "Who is the lady in green to you? Madame de Beaujardin?"

He blinked, and she knew she had taken him by surprise, but almost at the same time, a gleam of amusement began to form in his eyes. "I should have known better than to try to keep her from you."

"Why did you?"

His gaze fell to their joined hands. "At first because she is not respectable, and I didn't want her contaminating you. And then because I realized the shame was mine, and I did not want to own it."

"What shame?" she asked, bewildered. Surely, he'd had no opportunity to accumulate any.

He brought his other hand over hers, playing distractedly with her fingers. "I told you about my father's phase of buying women for me."

"To humiliate you. But it didn't work as well as he'd hoped because the women liked you."

"They were paid to like me," he said cynically. "But one became…a friend. She wrote to me. She even came back without my father's knowledge, and I smuggled her up the back stairs." His gaze lifted to hers once more. "It was not an innocent friendship."

She swallowed. "I do not grudge you it, Victor. But what does this have to do with the Vicomtesse de Beaujardin?"

His smile was lopsided. "Because she was not always the vicomtesse. She was an actress called Jezebel Jakes. I almost didn't recognize her when I saw her in the hotel yesterday. It may be hypocritical, but even *I* knew that one doesn't introduce women like Jez to one's wife."

"And now?"

"I've been trying to work out how to pass on what she told me without mentioning her." His frown vanished. "So actually, I'm relieved to have it in the open. Apparently, Anthony recognized her too and is preparing to use her against me. She has her secrets to keep from her own husband, the vicomte, and Anthony imagines she will be easily manipulated."

"I don't see how she could hurt you anyway! Are there any gentlemen so pure that they have no disreputable women in their past or present?"

"I don't know enough gentlemen to say. Do you mind? That Jez is here?"

She drew in her breath. "I mind that you tried to keep her from me. I don't want secrets between us, Victor."

He tugged her against his side, his arm around her shoulders. "Neither do I," he said.

She swallowed, unable to relax yet until it was all said. "Will you maintain your…friendship with her?"

He jerked back as though she had struck him. "You mean make her my mistress again?" he said harshly, his eyes raking hers. "Why in God's name would I do that? Are you so tired of my attentions already that you would push me into her arms for peace?"

Olivia felt her mouth fall open. Without warning, tears sprang into her eyes. "Victor, I would *die* inside if you went to her!"

"So would I," he said savagely, and fell on her mouth in the fiercest kiss she had ever imagined. He pushed her backward, dragging her beneath him, his hands urgent, demanding. She surrendered utterly with equal parts relief and joy, and then, as his mouth and his fingers gentled into sheer sensuality, she returned his caresses eagerly and let passion consume them both.

THE MORNING BROUGHT cards of invitation to the Duchess of Richmond's ball.

"It's to be the event of the season," Lady Hera told them, dropping in during the morning to see the house. "Both because she beat the Duke of Wellington by holding her ball days before his own and forced him to cancel, and because it will probably be the last party before the soldiers march away."

"Do you know something?" Victor asked.

"No. Only rumor," Hera said, pacing over to the window and back. "But Justin is on edge, and Giles's duties have certainly intensified."

"Will they be allowed to attend the duchess's ball?" Olivia asked her.

Hera cast her a crooked smile over her shoulder. "Oh yes, most of the British officers will be there, including Wellington himself. Part of it is showing a calm face to the people who might otherwise panic, but he genuinely doesn't seem to be troubled just yet. Whatever the rumors of French movements, he obviously knows otherwise. So, has Anthony accepted your invitation to tea?"

"Not yet. But I suspect he will come." Olivia jumped up and went to the internal door that opened into another, smaller salon. "I thought Victor and our witnesses could wait in here, with the door slightly ajar, while I try to make him say or write something incriminating."

"Someone not related to us would be best," Hera said. "Frostbrook and maybe Mr. Edwards."

Victor scowled. "We'll need a constant cycle of people, because I don't trust him not to come early again. And the servants have been advised to look out for anyone loitering or watching the house."

Hera nodded. "Good." She opened her mouth as if she would say more but closed it again. "I'll go back and organize a schedule. Be careful."

She left without any further farewell, somewhat to Olivia's surprise. Victor was frowning after her.

"She's afraid," he said.

Her husband was an army surgeon, attached to Giles Butler's regiment. Olivia had heard something of the story of their marriage, which, in many ways, was as sudden as her own. Like Victor, Hera did not wear her heart on her sleeve, and like him she must have been damaged by the old duke.

"Everyone is afraid," Olivia said soberly. "We are so absorbed in our own little stage, in finding the truth of one death and preventing another, that it is too easy to forget the huge tragedy waiting in the wings."

"Wellington is not afraid," said Victor, who had met the great man during his walk in the park that morning. "Perhaps because he knows what will happen. He only fights if he knows he will win. But then, he has never faced Napoleon Bonaparte in person before."

Unconsciously, Olivia moved nearer Victor. "And whoever wins, men will still die. No wonder Rosamund married her major while she could."

"There is nothing we can do about Bonaparte," Victor said, taking her hand. "But we can deal with Cousin Anthony."

IN FACT, IT was not Cousin Anthony who came early that afternoon, but everyone else. Olivia received a positive deluge of people, mostly British, most of whom had overlooked the social norm of leaving cards before visiting. Lady Sarah and Lady Georgianna Lennox, two of the Duchess of Richmond's lively daughters, entered with Rosamund and a very young Guards officer, which seemed to open the floodgates for the curious, the friendly, and, no doubt, the biggest gossips in Brussels.

The influx of so many fashionable and aristocratic strangers almost overwhelmed Olivia. In the circumstances she was almost desperate for the continued support of Rosamund and Hera, for the etiquette of tea was buried in schooldays, and Victor had even less experience than she. Besides, it would have looked odd if he had clung to her side all afternoon. Rosamund kept her calm, and

Hera kept the fresh teapots ordered, while Izzy Merton transferred innumerable cups of tea wherever Rosamund told her.

Olivia, a smile stretched on her lips for so long that her jaw ached, could barely recall who was who, let alone make sense of the snippets of gossip, whether imparted to her or overheard.

"It's going well," Rosamund murmured. "They might have come from curiosity, but they like you. Victor, of course, fascinates them."

Victor was almost permanently surrounded by groups of curious men and avid women of all ages. Frostbrook seemed to keep one eye on the situation, but even so, Olivia fully expected the duke to explode in temper. He had been far too isolated in his life to deal easily with this number of people, who must have included the malicious as well as the toadying.

Yet the explosion never came. Whenever Olivia could spare an anxious glance in his direction, he seemed perfectly at ease, sitting or standing among a tea-swilling group looking unexpectedly elegant with his walking stick and his frown and his wild, dark beauty. So far as she could tell, he remained courteous throughout. He seemed to say little, though when he did speak, in short, no doubt sardonic bursts, it seemed to produce either sage nods or bursts of surprised laughter.

He was most certainly holding his own, and, oddly, it was this more than anything that calmed the worst of Olivia's anxiety.

With a squeak of dismay, Lady Georgianna bounced to her feet, seizing her sister by the hand. "Duchess, forgive us for taking up so much of your time! We have been here almost an hour—which must, of course, be the fault of your wonderful hospitality rather than my own scatterbrains and bad manners. I hope we will see you at my mother's ball tomorrow evening?"

"Indeed, we look forward to it," Olivia said, rising to offer her hand. Which was when Anthony Severne walked in and looked momentarily taken aback to see the crowded drawing room.

The Lennox ladies curtseyed and dragged their Guards officer with them to the door. Victor, who had risen to make a civil farewell, had clearly seen Anthony, too.

Anthony lingered by the door, bowing and exchanging pleasantries with Lady Sarah as she departed. His advance across the room was something of a stately progress. It struck Olivia that he probably wanted Victor to limp across the room to welcome his heir.

"Does the world know I am his natural daughter?" Olivia murmured to Rosamund.

"Of course. You had to come from somewhere. Brazen truth is sometimes better. And any blue blood is generally better than none, even when none comes with marriage lines."

Olivia went forward to meet her father, her plans once more in helpless tatters. The quiet afternoon she had meant to use to persuade him to incriminate himself had vanished into this bright, social circus. No one could have overheard him saying anything from the next room, and so everyone of the "alliance" was in here, overstaying their welcome, as only Lady Georgianna seemed to have noticed.

Anthony saw her coming and extricated himself from his current companion to meet her. "Well, my dear," he said fondly, taking her hand and bending to kiss her cheek, which he had never done before. She had to fight her instinctive rigidity in response and disguise the shiver of revulsion. He was her father. She should not feel like this. For a moment, the tragedy appalled her.

Then she could smile and take his arm, leading him through the throng toward where she had last seen Victor. "I'm so glad you could come."

"I did not expect you to be entertaining so early in your visit."

"Nor did I."

"Never underestimate the curiosity of so-called polite society," he drawled, thereby removing any satisfaction she might have felt in the afternoon's social success. "How is poor Victor coping? I expect he has gone to lie down. I'm sure a foreign library will do just as well for the purpose."

"That would be somewhat rude to our guests."

"Victor is rude," Anthony said.

"Not so often," Olivia said, trying not to be annoyed on Victor's behalf. In fact, she began to wonder if Anthony had not done more than go along with the late duke's cruelties to Victor. Perhaps he had also encouraged them. An uncontrollable shudder passed through her, but fortunately the circle before them parted, and Victor's back was visible, encased in a well-tailored blue morning coat and loose pantaloons that didn't hide his twisted leg, but disguised it to some degree.

One of the occasional, Victor-inspired shouts of laughter sounded. Olivia could recognize them now from the note of surprise that tended to mingle with the amusement. Then Victor turned quite casually, with the aid of his new walking stick, and looked directly at Anthony.

Whatever the sight did to her father, it sent Olivia's stomach diving. With his too-wild, too-long raven hair, and the smile just dying on his sensual lips and in his amazing, mischievous dark eyes, he was every inch the romantic, Byronic hero.

There was no way to tell if Anthony recognized that. Certainly, she heard his sudden catch of breath, but then he laughed and held out his hand.

"Good, God, Victor," he said in amusement. "Haven't you scrubbed up decently? Marriage must be good for you." Anthony had stopped, clearly intending to make Victor limp the last few paces between them.

But Victor was no longer a child, and he vastly outranked the cousin who had never troubled to win his affection.

He didn't move, except to smile with equal amusement. "Of course it is, Cousin. Did you doubt it?"

Which left Anthony with the choice of staying where he was with his hand held out to the air like a fool or moving forward again. Especially when Olivia dropped his arm.

Anthony smiled and stepped forward, but Victor did not raise his hand until his cousin stood right in front of him. Their hands clasped.

"Of course, I never doubted it for a moment. I trust my daughter takes good care of Your Grace?"

"As you see," Victor said pleasantly, dropping his cousin's hand. There was no point in arguing with Anthony's attempt to imply a nurse's care rather than a wife's.

"Come and sit down, sir," Olivia said, returning to her place. "Here is Rosamund keeping me company."

"Another delightful surprise," Anthony said, smiling thinly as he bowed to Rosamund, who lifted one eyebrow.

"Really? Did you not know I was still in Brussels?"

"Of course. I merely find it unexpected that you cling so close to the ducal family."

"Don't be silly," Rosamund said, smiling. "Hera and Victor are my stepchildren."

"Not anymore," Anthony pointed out.

"In my heart," Rosamund said gravely, and behind her, Hera laughed, attracting Anthony's attention.

"How do you do, Cousin?" Hera said carelessly.

"Tea," Olivia said, handing her father a cup. "A little pastry, perhaps?"

It was as well, she thought, that he had not arrived an hour ago and found her flustered and anxious on her own behalf and Victor's. Or was it? Perhaps discovering her overwhelmed and in need of instruction would have suited their purpose better. As it was, Anthony had a view of his grumpy, crippled nephew quite at his ease among the elite of Society, including young and mature ladies, army officers, and noblemen. And he must have seen that Olivia was at least holding her own, although Rosamund's and Hera's presence so close must have betrayed her lack of confidence at least.

She could use that. Somehow. Her guests appeared to be departing now, in twos and threes. To her surprise, most bade her more than a courteous farewell. There were genuine smiles and expressions of desire to know her better. Olivia must, she supposed, have been wittier than she knew while trying to make civil conversation at the same time as remembering names and faces and making sure everyone had tea.

"Thank you for allowing us to call without any notice!" a smiling young matron said to her on departure. "It has been a delightful afternoon. I do hope we'll be able to renew our conversation at the Duchess of Richmond's tomorrow?"

What conversation? Olivia wondered. "I look forward to it," she assured the lady.

"I should hope so," said the lady's husband. Olivia wished she could remember their names. "You have promised me the first waltz, Duchess!"

Olivia could not recall that either, but she kept smiling as they walked away.

"Do you go the duchess's ball, then?" Anthony sounded surprised. "I'll escort you, if you like."

"Thank you, sir, but there is no need," Olivia replied. "Victor will escort me."

"*Victor* is going?" Anthony looked both astonished and amused. "Why?"

"Why not?" she countered.

"It's a ball," he said dryly. "The purpose is to dance."

"Oh, the duchess has promised novel entertainment on top of dancing."

"And will Victor enjoy sitting among the non-dancing dowagers and elderly gentlemen?"

"Probably, if that is what he chooses," Olivia said a shade tartly before she recalled that she was meant to give the impression of still being Anthony's to command. "Excuse me, I believe I must just bid farewell to..." To whoever the middle-aged couple with the daughter was.

CHAPTER EIGHTEEN

VICTOR WAS IMMENSELY proud of his wife. He knew from the slight stiffness of her posture that she was terrified of the influx of highborn strangers come to gawp and pry. His every instinct was to go to her, to support her, but he had to trust her to manage her part while he attended to his own. He was relieved to see Rosamund and Hera close enough to her to help iron out any social difficulties and take her part. And at least worrying about her meant he had little chance to feel his own awkwardness.

He did what he had always done on the few occasions he had been tolerated in public. He listened and said little unless he was asked, and then he said exactly what he thought in whatever manner he chose. This seemed to win him a few friends, who, amusingly enough, regarded him as a wit or as someone wise in social and international affairs—Victor, the man who had never before been beyond the boundaries of Cuttyngs. Well, he had certainly read more books and papers than most, and they appeared to be standing him in good stead.

He was pleasantly surprised to encounter several amusing and clever men among his guests. He was even more astonished to realize that several handsome young matrons were trying to flirt with him, while the girl he caught staring at him looked at his face, not his game leg, and blushed, smiling, when their eyes met.

He shoved all the experiences to the back of his head for

future consideration, for as soon as Anthony arrived, every nerve seemed to spring into alertness, like a soldier on watch for the enemy.

Anthony was testing the water. He adopted some of His Grace's tricks, like forcing him to walk across a room while family, servants and the odd favored guest all gawped at the spectacle. Victor still cringed inside at the memory of those occasions—lurching across the room like some ungainly animal, while the old bastard pretended to encourage him with words like *Hurry up, boy, we don't have all day even if you do*, or *Walk straight, for God's sake. You did better when you were six years old!*

His mother had allowed it and watched, unmoving. Hera had stared straight ahead, lips thinned as a child's should never be. Servants, tutors, and guests, including Anthony on many occasions, had looked on according to their nature, with pity or amusement or satisfaction at Cuttyngham's misfortune in heirs.

It was how Victor had first met his father's second duchess, Rosamund. He still remembered Rosamund starting toward him and His Grace holding her back with one sharp word. For a few unguarded moments, her expression had been appalled, angry, and then she had smiled at him, treating him as though he were normal. He had taken it for pity, which was almost as offensive as revulsion. But she had not joined in the ritual humiliation of the formal dinner, either.

That was the last shameful walk, the last public humiliation. Somehow, Rosamund had convinced His Grace not to do it in public. Which didn't spare Victor privately but was still a considerable relief. Life had been slightly easier after that. Rosamund had been able to change a few things that neither he nor Hera could, insisted on the servants' respect, and occasionally fought and lost his battles, like that to obtain His Grace's permission to go to Oxford.

That she had tried meant a huge amount to him and to Hera. He recalled the wonder of realizing they had a friend in the house. It was too late, of course. Neither he nor Hera had any idea how to reach out to a friend. They expected *her* to know, as they did with each other. She made a few overtures, especially in the first year or so, but he had been too ignorant to respond as he should have. And besides, by then she was a victim too.

All this flashed through Victor's mind when Anthony paused as though delighted and fondly held out his hand to Victor from a distance of several yards. Victor's leg was stronger now, thanks to his regimen of exercise and practice. Obeying the older man's summons could have been accomplished if not with grace then at least with a certain amount of aplomb.

But the act was sheer insolence on Anthony's part, well beyond discourtesy. A deliberate reminder of his father to sap his burgeoning confidence? Or had Anthony always been the devil whispering in His Grace's ear to encourage every cruelty under the guise of trying to make the cripple stronger?

If it was a declaration of war, Victor won the opening skirmish and deliberately ignored his heir thereafter, when what he wanted to do was rip Olivia from his side and knock him down. Which would hardly convict the man, either of murdering the old duke or making the attempts on Victor's own life.

As the room gradually emptied, Victor noticed Frostbrook taking his leave of Olivia, and walked to intercept him. "I'll come with you to the door," he said amiably. And if he wished, Anthony could watch that. He was fairly sure no one else did.

Beyond the drawing room doors, they turned as one, not right to the front door, but left toward the smaller salon connected to the drawing room.

"Nicely managed," Frostbrook murmured.

"That was Olivia. I couldn't have brought myself to be civil." Quietly, Victor opened the door to the smaller salon, and found his sister and stepmother already there, along with Sir Arthur Astley, who had been in Hera's care during her brief period as a paid companion. Victor had to agree the man was very far from helpless, let alone insane. In fact, he rather liked him—he was well read, devastatingly logical, and even witty in an understated way that appealed to Victor. But as a witness...

"I thought we had agreed on Edwards," Victor muttered, not best pleased. "I like the man, but there is a vagueness about him that—"

"Astley is better," Frostbrook interrupted, still low-voiced. "He recalls, verbatim, everything he reads. Or hears."

Victor closed his mouth and withdrew his objections.

As they had planned, Rosamund and Hera sat near the passage door, ready to rush into the drawing room should discreet rescue be necessary. Sir Arthur sat on a chair directly in front of the connecting door to the drawing room. Frostbrook walked up to join him.

Rosamund and Hera nodded to Victor. He nodded back and left the room, moving as quietly as he could toward the footman at the front door.

"Do we still have guests, Jean?" he asked, loud enough for Olivia and Anthony to hear the sound of his voice at least.

"Only Monsieur Severne, Monsieur le Duc."

"Then you may go about your other duties, and I shall enjoy a well-earned rest," Victor said, and moved back down the hall, tapping his stick more noisily. His nerves screamed in fear and outrage because he had allowed himself to be persuaded, and left Olivia alone with Anthony.

"SO, WHAT ARE your plans, daughter?" Anthony asked her when they were finally alone.

Olivia swept past him and sat on the sofa nearest the connecting door. Her heart beat foolishly fast. What if he did not choose to sit beside her? His voice would probably carry far enough to be heard in the next room, but her allies there could not risk opening the connecting door a crack if there was any risk he would see it happening.

"In what sense?" she asked, just to say something, though it was hardly clever.

"Every sense," he replied dryly, coming toward her. "You have married him. Now, what do you mean to do?" He sat beside her, flooding her with relief.

"I am the duchess," she said clearly. It was their agreed watchword. Hearing it, someone would ease the connecting door open a tiny crack, enough to overhear even quietly spoken speech. Olivia met Anthony's gaze and hurried on. "I mean to be a good wife. And a good daughter."

Anthony's thin lips stretched into a smile that did not touch his eyes. "I hoped you would say that."

"Did you doubt me?"

"You did not come to Cuttyngs when I told you."

"We have discussed that, have we not? It would not have answered. Victor is not an imbecile, sir. He would hardly have been susceptible to a strange woman making advances while he buried his father."

"Don't be foolish! He was delighted to bury his father."

She held his gaze, almost afraid to breathe. She had not intended to get to this point so soon, but the opportunity could not be ignored. "So, in effect, you did Victor a favor?"

Anthony did not look away. "What is that supposed to mean?"

"It means, sir, that I am *not* foolish. I know Dr. Rivers and later Lord Frostbrook talked to you about the possibility of the late duke being ill at the duel and dying *before* the shot was fired, in effect falling *into* Major Butler's line of fire, which would otherwise have missed him."

"Rivers is Butler's friend and trying to exonerate him from a murder charge. Frostbrook, I am beginning to think, has always been under the duchess's thumb."

"Rosamund's? If Frostbrook is under anyone's thumb it is Lady Frostbrook's, and he seems to rather like that. I have no doubt he has his own reasons for pursuing the mystery, but the point is, I know both he and Dr. Rivers spoke to you about their suspicions. And you told them the late duke ate nothing and drank nothing before the duel."

"So I did," Anthony agreed softly. There was a warning in his eyes, but she could not afford to be cowed.

She lifted her chin. "You lied."

"Foolish child," he said indulgently, although his eyes remained hard as agates. "You cannot know that."

"I can. I saw you through the half-open door of your bedchamber. You gave him the silver flask from your pocket, and he drank from it."

"Trust me, it hardly made him falling-down drunk."

"No, it poisoned him, didn't it?"

Anthony's nostrils flared, for she sounded far too accusing.

Forcing herself, she laid her hand over his on his lap. "I tell you this because it is what they now believe," she said urgently. "Not only Butler and Rivers, but Frostbrook, too."

"And Victor?"

"Victor requires proof."

"Which, of course, he will never find," Anthony said, his fingers curling like claws around hers. "Will he, daughter?"

"Of course not," she said, as though affronted. "Without me, they have only suspicion and guesses. But you need to be aware of the danger." *Speak. Tell me now that you did it.*

But the silence stretched between them. Behind her father's opaque eyes, she had no idea what he was thinking.

"Thank you," he said at last.

She waited, but there were no more words. *Damnation!* "What would you like me to do?" she asked.

His eyes dropped to their joined hands, and he released her. It took all her will not to rub her fingers, for he had all but crushed them in his grip. "I don't know yet," he said slowly. "But when I send you an instruction, you must be ready to act immediately. This time, you cannot afford to imagine you know better than me."

"No, sir," she said humbly.

Frowning, he raised his eyes to hers. "One thing you might do now. Get me a list of all the medicines Rosamund Butler keeps."

Olivia blinked. "Why?"

"Because it might help. But if it is beyond you—"

"Of course not. I know she will be happy to tell me all about her herbs."

Anthony nodded and rose to his feet. "Good. Then we'll talk again tomorrow, at the Duchess of Richmond's ball. I will probably have instructions for you then."

"Very well." She rose with him, allowing a trace of genuine anxiety into her voice. "You will not make me into a bad wife, sir, will you?"

Anthony's lips curled into a sneer. "That rather depends on your definition. Just keep him from your bed for another night and we are there."

While heat scorched her face—not least because of those listening in the other room—as Anthony strolled across the floor and let himself out, not bothering to close the doors behind him. Her straining ears caught his footsteps in the hall and the opening and shutting of the front door.

Only then did she rush across to the window, to be sure he had gone. She saw him striding across the road toward the park, looking jaunty and almost happy.

She heard the faint sound of the connecting door being pushed open. Victor came through first, hurrying, and she ran to him, seizing him in a tight hold as though she could thus remove the stain, the uncleanliness of her father, and keep Victor safe.

"Well done," he whispered in her ear.

"He didn't say it," she muttered into his neck, and drew back an inch or two to peer at the others over his shoulder. "I couldn't make him say he had done it."

"You couldn't have pushed him further," Victor said.

"Not now," Frostbrook agreed. "His Grace is right. You won

Severne's confidence, I believe, and next time he will say more. In the meantime, what he did say is interesting enough."

"He is interested in Rosamund's potions," Olivia said, drawing herself out of Victor's embrace and threading her fingers through his to keep the physical connection.

"I heard that," Rosamund said with a hint of grimness.

"Do you suppose he stole something of yours to poison His Grace with?" Hera asked her.

"I had very little at Cuttyngs," Rosamund said, "and none of it would have given His Grace as much as a sore stomach unless he'd swilled it by the bottle." She drew in her breath and regarded the others. "What I did have were a lot of botanical books and herbals. Most were from the Cuttyngs library, but I had taken them to my own sitting room so that I didn't disturb Victor while I studied."

Victor looked uncomfortable but seemed to force the feeling aside. "You think he used your books to study how to make the poison he needed? Was he in the habit of invading your sitting room?"

"No, he more or less ignored me when he was at Cuttyngs. But he wandered the house at will. He could have been in there while I was out walking or in the stillroom… In fact, I frequently left books in the stillroom, too. It annoyed Mrs. Irwin."

"It wouldn't annoy her now," Olivia said. "It was one of your preparations that saved Victor, and she will be forever grateful."

"Really?" Rosamund said.

"Really. She loves Victor. I think they all do, now the shadow of the late duke no longer hovers over them like some malign god."

Victor flushed. "You exaggerate, my dear. Except the malign god part. Anyone for a walk? I feel the need of fresh air."

"Oh, me too," Olivia said fervently.

CHAPTER NINETEEN

BY THE FOLLOWING day, a certain air of suppressed excitement in Brussels could no longer be put down solely to the Duchess of Richmond's highly anticipated ball. Rumors that the French had crossed the border and defeated the Prussian army thrilled the Bonapartists among the townspeople yet caused a mere ripple on the surface of their everyday lives.

Olivia, influenced by the British visitors who had called, felt no cause for alarm. Inevitably, there would be another battle, but, according to Giles Butler, who arrived in Brussels with Dr. Rivers in time for the ball, Wellington's intelligence networks were second to none, and if there had indeed been an attack on the Prussians, it was a mere diversion.

In fact, when Olivia and Victor called at the Edwards's house, Major Butler's main concern seemed to be Anthony. "What does he want with a list of Rosamund's herbs?" he wondered, his good-natured face split by a frown.

"Perhaps to steal something to do away with me," Victor said dispassionately. "Or even to deflect blame from himself by casting it on Rosamund."

Major Butler's frown became a scowl.

"Name some medicines that contain nothing harmful," Olivia suggested, seating herself at Rosamund's desk. "I'll give him the list tonight and tell him I couldn't ask for more in one day without rousing your suspicions. If I make it thorough, with all the ingredients and purposes of each potion, he'll think I'm trying and yet will learn nothing."

"I'm glad you're on our side," Major Butler said with apparent respect. "But we need to plan the evening carefully, so that His Grace is never left unprotected, and someone is always close enough to overhear whatever instructions Anthony gives the duchess."

"Don't waltz with him," Sir Arthur said to Olivia. "No one will be able to overhear enough."

"Alcoves are useful," Hera said casually. "One can skulk outside and overhear much. Or antechambers. If we know in advance, we can hide behind curtains or something."

Dr. Rivers blinked at his wife in some surprise. "Isn't this all a little farcical?"

"Much of life is," Hera replied.

"What we cannot do is have another meeting of the whole alliance," Victor said, "because I'm fairly sure Gregson will be watching my movements at least. So if we plan now what to do, we can pass it on to the others as opportunity arises…"

ANTHONY HAD BEEN secretly appalled at how close he had come to disaster. He had never imagined Cuttyngham's friends, let alone his enemies, coming to the conclusion that the duke had been poisoned before the duel. At least only Olivia knew for certain.

But Anthony did not trust anyone, least of all his daughter, who had let him down once before. He allowed that she might have been right, and she had certainly achieved marriage to Victor without his help. The question was, *why?* Because she still desired to do her father's bidding, as an obedient daughter should? Or did she just want to keep him sweet while she kept all the lovely Cuttyngham wealth to herself? Victor certainly hadn't greeted him like a loving cousin welcoming his heir after weeks apart. Olivia could change that…or not.

By the morning of the Duchess of Richmond's ball, he realized Olivia had one major disadvantage. Even were she foolish enough to tell the world about old Cuttyngham's death, her story was so bizarre that no one would believe her. And if they did, well, the widow who had married his killer was an expert in herbal poisons.

And if Victor had to die in a similar way, then this time Anthony would be nowhere near him, and all it would prove was that the Severnes were addicted to foolish duels. With the French already over the border, no one in Brussels would be persuaded to examine the stomach contents of a silly English duke. And once Anthony was duke, no one at home could touch him, save the House of Lords, and they would not sully their hands with such nonsense.

Victor's death would bring all Anthony needed. The dukedom, providing the life of comfort he craved and banishing in one stroke all his debts and financial difficulties. His succession to Cuttyngham would clip Olivia's wings and make her entirely unnecessary, a mere illegitimate fortune hunter who had run out of luck. Though he might allow whatever marriage settlements had been made to stand. If she behaved well.

The rest—Butler, Rivers, even Frostbrook, the traitor—were either scandalous nobodies or eccentrics who would be ignored in England without proof. And here in Brussels, everyone was far too busy with approaching war.

Oh yes, it was time to set another little duel in motion. While there was still time.

Accordingly, Anthony lurked outside the house of the Vicomte de Beaujardin until he saw that gentleman leave, walking smartly toward the town center with his stiff, military bearing. Anthony hurried after him. It took longer than he expected to fall into step beside him. Anthony had to allow that the man was fit for his age.

"Monsieur de Beaujardin, is it not?" he said, touching the brim of his hat.

The old colonel cast him a glance and twitched his whiskers before replying in heavily accented English. "It is, but I don't know you, do I? Among the English, I know only army officers."

"Then we have many acquaintances in common," Anthony said smoothly. "I have the somewhat dubious honor to be the cousin of the English Duke of Cuttyngham."

The vicomte waved a dismissive hand. "I do not know him."

Anthony raised his eyebrows. "The vicomtesse does."

A wave of furious color swept through the older man's whiskers. "Do not dare to mention the name of my wife in such a manner!"

Anthony held one hand in a gesture of submission. "Monsieur, I would not dream of impugning the name of your lady wife." *Pah!* "Allow me to explain. The duke my cousin is, in many ways, an unfortunate young man. He was born a cripple, sickly and simple, and so his family kept him isolated from the world. It was a tragedy in more ways than one, when his father died suddenly, and he inherited the dukedom and all the wealth and power that goes with that."

"I fail to see what that has to do with me or my wife!" snapped the vicomte.

They had reached one end of the park, and Anthony indicated a nearby bench in the shade. "Shall we sit a moment, monsieur, and I shall enlighten you?"

For an instant, the vicomte clearly meant to refuse and keep walking, and Anthony resigned himself to a further forced march along the length of the park. Then the man spun around and plonked himself on the bench.

"I can spare you two minutes, no more. Please do not waste my time. I have important affairs to see to that affect my country and yours!"

"Of course, monsieur." Anthony bowed. "I would not trouble

you at such a time for anything less than a matter that must be even closer to your heart."

"Get on with it," the vicomte barked.

"Very well. It shames me to admit that my cousin the duke has become, in a remarkably short space of time, entirely dissolute. In short, the power has gone to his head, and too much wine has addled what few wits he has left. And so he believes every woman of whatever rank is available to him. And for that reason, even with his physical disadvantages, no woman is safe anywhere near him. He is, sir, a menace, because he plays first upon pity and then he strikes."

The vicomte's lips curled in contempt. "You should have him locked up, monsieur!"

"Believe me, I am taking steps, with the help of his poor wife and sister. But that does not help anyone now. I merely want you to be aware of an incident I witnessed at the Hotel de Belle Vue, only the other day."

The vicomte's gaze snapped up, as Anthony had known it would, at mention of a place he had actually been with his wife.

"What incident?" he asked with suspicion.

"My cousin's family dined there on the same night as you and your lady. He made some excuse to leave us, and when I went to find him a few minutes later, I found him assaulting your wife."

"Assaulting my wife?" The angry color drained from the vicomte's face, leaving it almost white. "But she said nothing of this!"

"I expect she was afraid to. Who would believe a cripple had such strength? Do not be *too* afraid, monsieur. I got to him before he had done much more than seriously alarm the lady. No lasting harm was done, if you catch my meaning."

The vicomte was not so mealy-mouthed. "You mean he did not rape her only feet from where I and her friends were dining? My God, this is intolerable!"

"It is," Anthony agreed. "And I could not live with myself if I did not make you aware of what happened and apologize with all my heart. I daresay you will have to leave the town soon, to fight, but I would suggest you make arrangements to keep your wife as safe as possible. I am sorry for it, but obviously there is no way to demand satisfaction of him for the insult—"

"Oh, is there not?" de Beaujardin said wrathfully. "There, you are wrong. I will be discreet, but I shall shoot this puppy for his insolence."

"It is your right," Anthony replied.

"From what you say, it is the only way my wife or any decent woman can be safe from this monster! Where do I find him?"

"I doubt his servants will admit you," Anthony said, "and, in truth, you should probably leave the matter to me."

The vicomte glared at him. "Because you have done so well so far? Oh no, monsieur. This one, I arrange myself!"

"Perhaps if you see him, you will feel differently. I understand he attends the Duchess of Richmond's ball this evening. Are you not invited?"

"We are, but my wife does not wish to go. Too many English, she said..."

"I expect she was afraid of meeting my nephew the duke," Anthony said, which was, he rather thought, a masterstroke. And he was right.

"Confound the snake! I will deal with him. Good day, sir." The vicomte jumped up and strode off down the path, leaving Anthony gazing after him with a smile of pure delight on his lips.

Really, people were just too easy to manipulate.

ON HER WAY home from the Edwards's house, Olivia had her final ball gown fitting. Her life, which had been taking surprising directions for some weeks now, took on a dreamlike quality. How could half her mind be consumed with the fairytale beauty of her gown, and her husband's reaction to it, while the other half worried so fearfully over Victor's safety and the possibility of the distant war coming closer?

She felt like an observer in a dream where nothing you did made any difference. When she tried to tell Victor, he actually laughed. "My dear, you have already made all the difference in the world. You always will."

Which at least had the effect of enchanting her. He did love her a little… And yet such was her perverse nature that that was no longer enough. A little affection and gratitude were so much less than she wanted. She wanted his whole heart. But at least she had a beginning, and she had the undoubted, smoldering admiration in his eyes when he wandered into her room just as she stood up from her dressing table.

There had been little time for the dressmaker to adorn the garment with extravagant trimmings, so Olivia had chosen this one for its flowing, simple shape and its flattering neckline. The gold silk gown was worn over an ivory lace slip, and the effect was gorgeous, even worn with no jewelry at all, since she had none.

But Victor surprised her with more than the intensity of his admiration. He held her gaze as he moved toward her, his eyes glittering and exciting, and she wondered with some anticipation if he was not about to undo all Aggie's work. They could always be late to the ball…

He took her hand and raised it to his lips before turning it and kissing the inside of her wrist. Then, rather to her surprise, he released her hand and leaned over her to open a drawer in the dressing table.

"I brought you these. I hoped you'd find them for yourself and be delighted. Though it strikes me you might have found them and hated them."

Uncomprehendingly, she dragged her gaze from his face to the open drawer. A leather jewel case lay on top of her chemises.

"Oh, Victor," she murmured with a catch in her voice as she reached for the box. Opening it, she discovered a gorgeous and unusual design of necklace of gold, with two strings of pearls between interlinked gold chains. There were delicate matching earrings and a bracelet.

With surprising dexterity for a man who had so little experience of the world, he placed the necklace across her breast and fastened it at her nape. She donned the earrings, which clung and dangled, and he clasped the bracelet about her arm.

She stared at her reflection. The surprisingly beautiful figure she had seen before seemed to have become astonishingly regal. "Oh, my… Is it me?"

"You are the duchess," he said. "My duchess."

"I am still Olivia," she said anxiously.

He bent and brushed his lips across her nape, making her shiver with desire. "That will never change," he murmured against her skin, before he straightened and offered her his arm. "I believe the carriage awaits."

The hired carriage of the previous tenants was at their disposal, along with the horses and stables. Since "the alliance" had insisted Olivia and Victor did not walk alone into the duchess's residence, they collected the Frostbrooks from the nearby hotel and drove to the Richmonds'.

Olivia had known it would be a huge and crowded event, but even so, she was not prepared for the colorful, glittering throng that met her gaze beneath a massive array of candles. Bright military unforms, of red, blue, and gold braid, mingled with the soft white and delicate pastel shades of the young girls' gowns and the deeper colors of the matrons. Among them, by contrast, were dotted the sober black of civilian gentlemen's evening coats and satin breeches. Everywhere, shining jewels caught the candlelight and sparkled.

Involuntarily, standing in the doorway, Olivia tightened her hand on Victor's arm. For a moment, she met his gaze, and saw mirrored there her own amazement, anxiety, and impulse to retreat. Then a smile flickered in his eyes.

"We are the true debutants here," he murmured, and she smiled back.

At least with the ballroom on the ground floor, Victor had no stairs to negotiate. They began their slow progress, under many pairs of jaded eyes desperate for entertainment, or at least novelty, which the reclusive new duke seemed likely to provide. Those who had met him yesterday must have spread the word, however, for Olivia read nothing unkind or malicious in the faces turned toward them.

The Duke and Duchess of Richmond welcomed them graciously.

"The Duke of Wellington has not arrived yet," the duchess informed them, "but we do expect him!"

"Which means," Victor murmured as they moved forward into the heaving ballroom, "that no French attack is imminent."

But everyone knew it was coming. As Olivia and Victor passed from group to group, much of the talk was of war. The young, untried officers were cock-a-hoop at the chance to have a go at Boney and cover themselves in glory. The veteran officers, like Major Butler, who had been in the Peninsular army, seemed more resigned than vocal, and Wellington's staff officers smiled and said nothing much was happening yet but there might be action tomorrow.

"Oh, God," Victor uttered as he presented Olivia with a fresh glass of champagne. His gaze had gone beyond her head. "It's my Aunt Hadleigh…and she has just seen us."

Olivia turned quickly to see a determined middle-aged woman with a pinched face bearing down upon them, a stout, somewhat apathetic gentleman on her heels. They both looked astonished.

"Victor!" the lady exclaimed. "How on earth did *you* get to Brussels?"

"His Grace's yacht, a carriage, and several teams of horses," Victor replied.

"I suppose you have come to take Hera away from That Woman. Unfortunately, there's nothing can be done about the wretched marriage, but for God's sake, take her back to England and keep her out of Society's way for a while. A long while!"

Olivia could feel Victor icing up. "How do you do, Aunt?" he said frigidly. "Uncle. My dear, allow me to present Lord and Lady Hadleigh."

Lady Hadleigh was looking outraged, which appeared to prompt her husband to say, amiably if condescendingly, "Victor, my boy, etiquette requires you introduce a lady of lesser rank to your aunt first. Can't be expected to know, but there it is."

Victor stared. "Can I expect either of you to be at least civil when I introduce you to my wife, the Duchess of Cuttyngham? Apparently not."

"Wife? Duchess?" spluttered her ladyship, staring at Olivia as though she had grown horns. "What nonsense is this?"

Victor sighed. "I should have known better."

Lord Hadleigh, looking very flushed, said, "Wish you both very happy, of course, but Brussels is not the place to be just at the moment. The war is almost upon us, and between ourselves, I don't expect Wellington to put up much of a show against Bonaparte. Overrated, don't you know. Thing is, we're leaving for Antwerp tomorrow. You should come with us."

"I trust you'll have a pleasant journey," Victor said coldly, and turned his back on them both. "My family always said *I* was rude," he confided quite audibly to Olivia, who let out a very strange noise between a cough, a snort, and a giggle.

Victor grinned at her, his eyes dancing with mischief. "And that should keep them away for the next few years at least."

THE RICHMONDS' GUESTS were there to dance, and dance they did. Her confidence already bolstered by the compliments of "the alliance," Olivia waltzed first with Major Butler.

"I have not seen Anthony," she murmured to him. "Is he here yet?"

"Haven't seen him either, but I'm sure he will come."

"Where is Victor?" she asked with sudden fear when she saw that he had vanished from his place by one of the long windows.

"Two windows along, with some ladies and a junior officer. Edwards is close by."

Tom and Izzy floated past, arguing spiritedly, but with eyes for no one else.

"I'm not sure how much reliance we should place on *them* tonight," Olivia said.

"Enough. At least when they're not dancing. Stop worrying, Duchess. We are all here."

"Sorry." She forced herself to relax. "And in the circumstances, I feel you should use my name. To me, Rosamund is the duchess!"

It was as this dance ended that Olivia again saw the lady in green. She wore a different gown but of the same shade, and she looked magnificent on the arm of her husband. A twinge of jealousy surprised Olivia, but mostly, she felt warmth toward the other woman who had helped Victor in the only ways she could, treating him with humanity and, so far as Olivia could gather, genuine affection.

However, it was in no one's interests to draw attention to any connection between them, so she forced her gaze on to find Victor.

"I'll take you to him," Giles Butler said. "Shall we fetch some champagne on the way?"

There was a strange, hectic gaiety to the evening that infected Olivia as much as anyone else, though perhaps for slightly different reasons. She began to enjoy herself. She sat out the complicated quadrille, which she had never learned at school, but her second dance was with the charming, devil-may-care son of a marquis, who made her laugh by claiming to be an ordained clergyman. By then, she had almost forgotten about Anthony.

Until, as she whisked through the crowd in search of Victor, a hand closed around her wrist and yanked her into the alcove at one end of the room.

CHAPTER TWENTY

THE CURTAIN FELL, shutting out the ballroom, giving Olivia the unpleasant illusion of being completely isolated from Victor and her other friends.

"Well," Anthony murmured, releasing her wrist and raking her from head to foot with his supercilious gaze. "Don't you look the part in your ball dress? The perfect duchess! The jewels help, of course—a gift from your devoted husband?"

"Indeed," she managed, while she tried to control the sudden, rapid beating of her heart.

Was anyone close by to listen? She could not recall who should have been "on duty" with her at the moment, but the plan had been to take Anthony to the little antechamber at the other end of the ballroom. Here, there was nowhere to sit, to lull him—or herself—into any sense of comfort. The Duchess of Richmond had unmarried daughters and clearly was not going to make flirting in alcoves easy. Which really was not important right now.

Anthony's lip curled. "Trying to buy your favors? You will make sure to hold out a little longer?"

She met his gaze. *You really are a stupid, nasty little man. Why did I ever want you to be my father? That you are sickens me.* "Leave my husband to me," she said shortly. She opened her reticule. "This is what I have so far. It is a very partial list, but I could not keep her any longer without arousing suspicion. I shall go to her again tomorrow."

He took the folded list from her and, without even glancing at it, placed it in an inside pocket of his coat. "Ask her about heart medicine. After all, isn't a weak heart one of Rivers's original theories as to how the late duke died?"

Olivia widened her eyes. "You want to blame *her*?"

"She did marry the man who seems so reluctant to accept the blame himself."

"I don't understand," she said, somewhat weakly. She just could not think of another way to encourage him to expound and incriminate himself, although she was not even sure anyone else was listening. What scared her even more was the fact that Anthony either did know he was safe from eavesdroppers or didn't care. Anyone passing the alcove might have overheard and understood his remark about the late duke's death.

He was regarding her with a sort of knowing condescension. He even reached out and pinched her cheek, just a little too hard. "Yes, you do, my dear. Yes, you do. Run along now."

Dismissed like a schoolgirl, there was nothing she could do but walk out. She could still feel the imprint of his fingers on her cheek. No doubt it would show red and make her appear unbecomingly, even scandalously, flushed. She felt pathetically relieved when Tom and Izzy materialized on either side of her.

Izzy chattered away about dances and dresses, though in the middle of it, her voice dropped. "Is Your Grace well?"

Olivia nodded and let her ramble a little while she absorbed with unspeakable relief that they were approaching Victor, seated with a few older men and one of Wellington's staff officers. Sir Arthur Astley lurked nearby.

"Did you hear?" she asked Tom and Izzy. "Did anyone?"

"Mostly," Tom said. "But he revealed only ill will. Hardly an admission."

"Well, we never thought it would be easy." She cast a quick smile at each of them. "Thank you!"

Izzy and Tom vanished, and Victor rose to his feet with the other gentlemen, who stayed to converse a little before wandering off. Olivia sat down, and so did Victor.

"He does want to blame Rosamund," Olivia said. "And he's interested in heart medicine."

"We'd better see what Rosamund and Rivers make of that," Victor said. "Did he hurt you?"

She shook her head. "He appalled me. Made me ashamed. But he did not hurt me."

Victor took her hand, careless of anyone who might see such unfashionable marital affection. "He can't. He is nothing, and you have all of us."

She clung for an instant, then released him. "We are fortunate in our friends."

"We are. Another waltz is about to begin. I wish I could dance with you."

His words and the gentleness of his eyes warmed her heart. "We can dance alone, if you wish."

"Under moonlight?" he asked, a smile tugging at his lips.

"Why not?"

"I shall hold you to that. In the meanwhile, if I am not mistaken, here is Dr. Rivers come to waltz with you."

Hera plonked herself into Olivia's chair. Sir Arthur had wandered away and appeared to be leading a lady onto the dance floor. Frostbrook stood now with a group of people on Victor's other side. That much of their plan appeared to be working, at least.

Dr. Rivers, a tall, somewhat sardonic man of formidable intelligence, took Olivia in his arms, and they began to dance.

"Heart medicine," Olivia said with a bright smile for any observers. "He is interested in heart medicine."

The doctor was an excellent dancer, but at this, his foot faltered, though he recovered quickly. "Digitalis," he breathed. "Deadly nightshade. Foxglove. A little can solve heart problems. Too much is fatal. It tastes bitter, but in sharp spirits, if he was already upset, perhaps he would not have paid attention."

"You mean… Could that have been how the duke died?"

"It could, but we'll never prove it without digging the old…devil up." The doctor turned her in the dance, and she glimpsed Victor limping into the card room, which had been set up off the ballroom.

At Victor's side was a much older military gentleman with bushy whiskers. With a jolt, Olivia recognized him as the Vicomte de Beaujardin. Unreasonably alarmed, she raked the ballroom for a sight of his wife, and found her gazing in the direction of the card room too. Her face was white, and just for an instant, her expression was terrified.

VICTOR RECOGNIZED THE vicomte immediately, though he hid his surprise to be approached.

"You have the custom not to speak until you are introduced," the older man said with mild contempt. "But I am sure you will excuse me, since we have so many mutual friends."

Something about the vicomte's stiff posture and fierce eyes prevented Victor from offering his hand, though he did incline his head by way of a bow. "Cuttyngham."

"Colonel Vicomte de Beaujardin. But I imagine you know that."

"I believe you were pointed out to me."

"Perhaps when we dined at the same hotel," the vicomte said. "Will you join me in a hand of piquet?"

Victor did not really care for card games, but a tutor had once taught him the rudiments of piquet, and he had played a few times with Hera since. "Why not? I should be glad to."

The vicomte muttered something indistinguishable beneath his breath. It might have been "You won't be."

Intrigued now, and carefully not looking toward Jez, who

seemed to be very much not looking toward him and her husband, he accompanied de Beaujardin to the card room.

De Beaujardin sat at one end of the table for two at the side and picked up the waiting pack of cards with a hint of impatience, while Victor lowered himself awkwardly into the small space left and propped his stick against the table.

The vicomte dealt the cards. "It will not be a long game. In fact, we need not play, except for show. You may go as soon as you have answered me with the names of your seconds."

Victor blinked. "Seconds?" he repeated, assuming he had misunderstood, or that the vicomte had a problem with English. "We can speak in French if you prefer."

"I do not prefer." De Beaujardin set down the cards and lifted his gaze to Victor's. "You have insulted my wife, and I demand you give me satisfaction."

Victor, who had half expected to be grilled about the vicomtesse's past, stared at him. "I hope you will be satisfied when I tell you I have never insulted the lady in my life. Neither would I ever dream of doing so."

"You insulted her, sir, by forcing your attentions on her at the Hotel de Belle Vue three nights ago."

"I did no such thing," Victor said calmly. "And if you think about it, you will realize there was no possible time I could have done so."

"You were seen, Monsieur le Duc!"

"Ah. I wonder by whom?"

"It matters not! What matters is that I right the wrong."

"There was no wrong. But allow me to guess the identity of your informant. My cousin, Mr. Anthony Severne?"

The vicomte blinked rapidly, as though surprised, but he was not deterred. "Precisely. Your own cousin. He has told me all about you, Monsieur le Duc!"

"Oh, I'm sure he has. My only surprise is that you have chosen to believe any of it. Have you spoken to your wife, for example?"

"Most assuredly not! Nor shall I. We will manage this discreetly, and I will shoot you. If you die, I shall be glad."

Victor held his gaze. "I won't meet you, monsieur."

"You think I or the world will excuse you because you are crippled?"

The word stung. But only because his father had used it so often in malice. "A malformed leg does not prevent me from shooting straight. And for your information, there is nothing to excuse. I shall not meet you."

De Beaujardin's face twitched with fury. He began to peel off his glove, and Victor knew without doubt that the vicomte meant to strike him with it in front of everyone in the card room. The story would spread with delight throughout the ballroom, hurting Jez and this old martinet as well as Victor. And, most of all, hurting Olivia.

This was no place to discuss anything.

"Stop," Victor said softly.

De Beaujardin paused, flexed his fingers, and smoothed the glove about his hand once more. "Well?"

Victor seized his stick and eased himself to his feet. "Lord Frostbrook will call upon you tomorrow. At least we agree upon dis—What the devil is that infernal noise?"

He was not the only one roused from the card room. Everyone was leaving and pressing toward the door to the ballroom, where the Duchess of Richmond had laid on a novel entertainment for her guests.

To the deafening skirl of bagpipes, a band of Scots soldiers marched across the ballroom with a magnificent swagger, kilts swinging, drums beating.

Olivia's hand slid into Victor's, and together they watched the display. The troop divided and reformed in groups, dancing energetic reels to their own music. After that, they showed off their famous sword dance, agilely leaping and stepping over the deadly blades without ever touching them, or even looking at them.

They were applauded with loud appreciation and awarded refreshment while many of the bolder guests even flirted with them. They were young, only private soldiers and sergeants. Some swaggered at the attention. Some blushed. And then, on a curt command, they formed up and marched off again, pipes wailing once more in competition with the huge cheers of the duchess's guests.

Victor grinned at Olivia. She brushed at her eyes, and he saw to his consternation that she was all but weeping. "What is it?"

"I don't know," she whispered. "They are just so young, so full of life, and it's as if they are marching straight off to war."

⋙⋘

IT WAS NOT long after the Gordon Highlanders marched away that the Duke of Wellington arrived, looking casual, elegant, and amiable, as though he hadn't a care in the world. The more nervous among the guests seemed to relax at the very sight of him, and Olivia found herself hoping that his presence meant the rumors of imminent war were somewhat previous. The duke himself seemed mainly intent on amusement and flirting.

Only then she observed the staff officer approaching his commander with definite purpose in his step. The duke's affable expression never changed as he listened. He merely nodded, uttered a few words in reply, and returned to his conversation.

But whatever was said on either side, everything changed. Word spread among the uniformed guests like a game of Chinese whispers, and officers began to make their way to their hostess to give their thanks and excuses. Clearly, they had been ordered to rejoin their regiments immediately.

As dancers left the floor, the music stopped. Watching the understated exodus, Olivia felt a coldness wrap around her heart and spread through her veins.

"It begins," Victor said, materializing beside her.

For once, she had forgotten to keep watch on him, but as she took his arm, she was conscious of deep, guilty gratitude that he was not one of those leaving.

All the officers departed quietly and without fuss. A few made more tender farewells to wives or sweethearts, although in such publicity, this was necessarily limited. For once, no eagle-eyed parents objected to an officer kissing the hand of an unmarried girl, or the special smile she bestowed upon him. They might never have allowed her to marry him, but the fact that it might well be the last time she saw him crushed all petty matters of etiquette and excessive propriety.

As the young officers strode away to the Duchess of Richmond, Olivia saw Anthony making his own farewell. And then her eyes were caught by the unbearable sight of Rosamund and Giles Butler.

He held her, still waltzing, just for a few steps, speaking soft, gentle words to her while she gazed into his face as though memorizing every line. She did not weep or plead, and when he released her and kissed her hands, she smiled at him, her lips moving in private farewell.

Giles turned and strode away from her. Not far from him, Dr. Rivers stood beside Hera, his face bearing a curiously similar expression to Giles's, as though only part of him remained here. The rest was already on his duty, on the battle to come. Hera held his hand tightly, but she did not weep either. She was gazing at him as though she was somehow imparting some extra strength to him. His hand lifted, and he brushed her cheek with the back of his knuckles.

And then, abruptly, her attention was seized again by Giles, who seemed to have just caught sight of Olivia. He veered toward them, the frown on his handsome brow vanishing as he paused beside her and Victor.

"I'm afraid I have to go now. We've been ordered back. I know you will look after Rosamund for me."

Olivia nodded mutely.

"Count on it," Victor said, offering his hand.

Giles smiled and took it. "The French fooled us. It was no feint. They really did beat the Prussians back, and now they're coming at us. But don't worry. The duke has everything in place."

There was only one duke now.

"Be safe," Olivia said, giving him her hand.

He grinned as he bowed over it. "Count on it," he said, and strode out of the room.

Dr. Rivers nodded to them but did not stop.

There was a moment when the remains of the alliance stood together in silence—Rosamund, Hera, the Frostbrooks, the Edwards, Tom and Izzy, and Sir Arthur Astley. There seemed to be nothing to say, and when the orchestra started up again, they drifted apart once more.

The dancing continued, everyone going through the motions of a suddenly depleted ball. But the heart had gone out of it. Wellington had left quietly. Victor sent for their carriage, and they took their leave of their distracted hostess.

"We pray for them all," said the duchess, whose own family was deeply involved. "And we have the duke." She did not mean her own husband.

The Frostbrooks joined Olivia and Victor in their carriage for the return journey. But everything was different now. There were troops in the streets, British and German, Dutch and Belgian. And when they came to the park, both sides were almost blocked by marching soldiers and by supply carts and wagons. The park itself was full of horses.

"We would be better walking," Frostbrook said, with a quick glance at Victor. "If your leg is up to it?"

"I'll cope," Victor said, perhaps acknowledging that whatever he suffered now was so much less than what was about to be visited upon so many of the men marching past, and those spilling out of their billets all over the town, waved off or even accompanied by their native hosts.

Victor gave instructions to the coachman, and then they all got out and made their way along the street, as far as the Place Royale and the regiments gathering there to march out of the town. Victor and Frostbrook took off their hats, and Olivia and Sophia smiled and waved at them because it was all they could do.

Olivia, feeling both proud and oppressed by galloping tragedy, was reluctant to go home. She knew she would never sleep. For one thing, the noise in the town was immense. Drums and trumpets summoning the military reserves sounded constantly, mingling with the rattle of cart wheels, the sounds of horses on the move, and the interminable shouting of orders and greetings and messages of good luck.

Much later, in bed with Victor, Olivia realized that her fear for his life and Anthony's malice had faded into the mass of terrible anxiety for *all* the young men facing death now. Making love with him brought tears as well as pleasure, but it seemed to be as necessary as breathing, an affirmation of life.

CHAPTER TWENTY-ONE

VICTOR WOKE THE following morning with the feeling he had forgotten something. Most important of all his joys and responsibilities was his wife, lying sound asleep in his arms, her bright chestnut hair spread across the pillow, her skin smooth and untroubled in slumber. She was exhausted by the sheer emotional turmoil of last night, and yet when they finally got to bed and he had resolved with some difficulty to let her sleep undisturbed, she had thrown her arms around him and clung, her embrace changing subtly to one of almost desperate sensuality.

He loved her passion. He loved her courage and her compassion and everything that made her Olivia, all with such intensity that it hurt to gaze at her.

But this time, he *would* let her sleep. Gently disengaging himself, he slid out of bed, grabbed his stick, and limped silently into his dressing room to wash and dress without disturbing her.

Black was already there, laying out morning clothes. "Good morning, Your Grace. You'll have seen the troops leaving town?"

"Yes, they've gone south toward Waterloo," Victor said distractedly. What had he forgotten in all the excitement of approaching battle? As he dragged his face out of the washing bowl and smothered it in a towel, the rest of the ball came back to him. *Damn it, I forgot about de Beaujardin!* "Can you find me some coffee, Black? I need to go out before breakfast."

"Very good, Your Grace."

In fact, Lord Frostbrook forestalled him by arriving as Victor limped downstairs. It was not so easy in this house to bump down on his rear, which was actually good for his leg. It would never be straighter, but it was definitely stronger.

"Frost, I was just coming to see you," Victor greeted him. "Come and have breakfast."

"Is all well?" Frostbrook asked, following him into the breakfast parlor, where flustered maids were hastily ferrying about cold meats and cheese and bread.

"Yes, I just remembered something I should have told you last night."

On her way out, a maid poured fresh coffee and fled.

Frostbrook closed the door behind her and sat down, helping himself to everything on offer. "What did you forget?"

Victor spread butter on the dense bread and laid a thin slice of cheese across it. "Do you remember Jezebel Jakes?"

"Actress?"

"That's her. Or was her. Now she's a viscountess—the Vicomtesse de Beaujardin, in fact."

Frostbrook laid down his fork. "Damn. I thought I saw a likeness there. Assumed I was mistaken. Not that I ever met the lady, but I've noticed her about the town. And she was at the ball last night."

"Thing is, I have cause to know her from her previous incarnation," Victor said. "I regard her as a friend, still. Anthony knows, and has been making mischief, getting her husband to believe I either seduced her or assaulted her. He wasn't terribly clear on the accusation, just on the challenge."

Frostbrook stared. "He challenged you to a *duel*?"

"I'm afraid I named you as my second."

Frostbrook swore. "Then you accepted it? After all you said about your father's idiocy? Even knowing Anthony—Anthony blasted Severne!—had put him up to it?"

Victor sighed. "I did *try* to wriggle out of it, assured him it was untrue and I have every respect for the lady, but he wouldn't have it. When he was clearly going to cause a scandal by slapping me with his glove, I gave in and accepted. I decided it was more discreet to speak to him later without half of Brussels watching. As it was, I think I got away with it, but I forgot to warn you last night that he's expecting you to call."

"I doubt he is now," Frostbrook said. "I suspect events have rather overtaken you both, and he is with the army. But I'll call and see. If he's there, I'll explain the situation."

"I told him to speak to his wife, but I don't suppose he did."

"Why, did you tell yours?"

Victor flushed slightly. "No. I was distracted."

"I think we all were. Sophia meant to mention to you that she saw Anthony leave the ball almost as soon as the first soldiers. Do you suppose he has taken fright and fled the town?"

"Part of me hopes so, because I can't be bothered dealing with his triviality right now." Victor sighed. "But we came here to discover his guilt and draw his claws, finish it one way or another. It might take longer than we hoped."

"It might." Frostbrook polished off what was left on his plate and reached for his coffee. "After I've seen de Beaujardin, I'll just call by Anthony's lodgings. There's certainly no sign of him or the groom skulking around here or the park. What will you do?"

Victor shifted restlessly. "Go to the Edwards's house, once Olivia wakes. Rosamund will be in bits, and I doubt Hera is much better—she loves her surgeon. I was going to ask them to remove her, but it strikes me there will be more distractions where they are."

"It is a bit of a madhouse," Frostbrook agreed, setting down his cup and rising. "My regards to the duchess, and I'll let you know the results of my labors. Oh, you will keep up the precautions we agreed, at least until we know for sure that Anthony has gone? Take Black and one of the footmen with you wherever you go."

Victor nodded curtly, irked by the necessity, though he remembered to thank Frostbrook on his way out.

THE REST OF that day and the one after were largely spent in anxious waiting. Frostbrook reported that de Beaujardin had left town to join his men, though he had been efficient enough to leave a note for Lord Frostbrook with his servants, a curt message that he would receive him upon his return.

"And Anthony appears to have bolted," Frostbrook told everyone when he found them at the Edwards's house. "His rooms have been cleared out, and Gregson is gone too. They owed a month's rent."

"I'll pay it," Victor said resignedly.

"And take it off his allowance," Hera advised.

"Before you stop it all together," Rosamund added. "Apparently the Hadleighs have gone, too."

Olivia was surprised to find the women so strong, so normal. She suspected she would be a useless, nervous wreck in their position, especially Rosamund's, but then, she had not knowingly married a career officer, or an army surgeon famous for going onto the battlefields to administer to his patients.

"They have probably all fled north to Antwerp," Sir Arthur said. "A lot of English people have."

"Perhaps we should, too," Mr. Edwards said anxiously, looking from his wife to his niece. "Perhaps I am being irresponsible to remain."

"No," Mrs. Edwards said after a moment. "We shouldn't flee until it becomes absolutely necessary."

"Well, watch out for your horses," Frostbrook advised. "I've posted guards on mine. But, like you, we shall stay until there is no choice."

Rosamund and Hera would stay, whatever happened, which meant Victor and Olivia would, too. It was never said, merely understood.

There was a battle fought that first day. Olivia knew, because she heard the guns in the afternoon, distant yet booming omens of disaster. Frostbrook, Sir Arthur, and Tom rode out in search of news and found only rumor and roads blocked with baggage carts. Olivia went with Rosamund, Hera, and Sophia to help collect bandages and medicines for the wounded who were inevitable now.

The following day, they did the same, although by then many horrifically wounded soldiers had limped back into Brussels or been carried there in carts. There had been battles. The Prussians had been beaten and fallen back. Others called the battles mere skirmishes, but no one could give the whole picture. Rumors of defeat and of victory abounded. But no one could be sure.

All Olivia knew for certain, as she accompanied Rosamund with her bandages, salves, and medicines, was the horror of injury, wounds she had never imagined and had no idea how to treat. Her heart was full of tears she could not shed. All she could do, like everyone else, was try her best.

In the afternoon, as if things were not bad enough, thunder rumbled and the heavens opened.

ANTHONY, WEARING A smelly, oiled cloak with a hood, walked through the park as though going about his everyday business. Which he was, in a way. Peering through the trees, he saw no movement outside his cousin's house. No one came or went, no carriage awaited. But the shutters were open, and occasionally he was sure he glimpsed a face at an upper window. Victor and Olivia were still here.

Good girl.

Anthony had taken his possessions, and Gregson, and cleared out of his lodgings to a quiet, unfashionable hotel, where he had taken rooms under the name of Mr. Anton. Largely because the damned war had got in the way of his plans.

At the ball, he had discovered he actually trusted Olivia to do her duty. But the sight of Victor, puny, crippled Victor, trying to pretend he was normal and mixing with the elite of Society, infuriated him. Mostly because Victor hadn't looked puny or crippled at all. He had not danced, but he had moved around with his elegant new cane, limping but certainly not lurching. Dressed in severe, formal black, with his black brows and untamed hair, he had looked like some ridiculous Byronic hero, almost *handsome*. The ladies had appeared to flock about him even more than the distinguished gentlemen seen all too frequently in his company. It was curiosity, of course, but it had not looked like pity to Anthony.

The boy had grown. Even Anthony had to admit that. There was no way he could ever have controlled the dukedom through Victor, even with Olivia's help. And so he had been delighted to see his new plan working so well. He had seen the Vicomte de Beaujardin accost Victor and even observed them surreptitiously in the card room—until the infernal racket of the Gordon Highlanders had interrupted the whole proceeding.

But just when he was sure the challenge had been made and accepted, the damned war got in the way. De Beaujardin was forced to abandon the duel for his duty, and God knew when or if the chance would arrive now.

In fact, Anthony had panicked. But at least he had not bolted for Antwerp and England, like the Hadleighs and so many others. And now he had a new plan in place.

He walked as far as Wellington's all-but-deserted headquarters, then crossed the park and walked down the other side. Rain was trickling down his neck as he drew level with Victor's house and walked across the park toward it.

This time, he was rewarded by the sight of a waiting carriage and horses, and an open front door. A footman ran out with an umbrella, but Olivia, emerging from the carriage, seemed to be soaked already. Dripping, she walked into the house with bent shoulders and dragging feet, as though exhausted.

Where was Victor? Had he been in the house alone all this time? Hardly alone. There were still too many damned servants. The time was not yet ripe. But it would be.

What Anthony really needed was chaos.

THE NEXT DAY was Sunday. Again, Olivia went with Rosamund, Hera, and Sophia to give what help she could to the wounded, who only grew in numbers. She was appalled to see so many Highlanders lying injured and dying, possibly some of the same young men who had entertained everyone so recently at the Duchess of Richmond's ball. Their regiment had clearly taken a terrible pounding, and that was before the main action that everyone said would be fought today.

Some news was clearer now, of course. The Prussians, defeated at Ligny, had been forced to fall back, and Wellington, who had held the crossroads at Quatre Bras, had retreated with them, as far as the village of Waterloo, in order to maintain communications between the allies. But Olivia heard no guns.

"Perhaps the French have surrendered," she said hopefully.

Rosamund, Hera, and Sophia regarded her with blatant disbelief.

"The wind is in the wrong direction," Rosamund said. "I doubt we would hear anything from Waterloo."

Instead, the proof of the battle arrived throughout the day in carts full of muddied and wounded, young men with horrendous injuries that Olivia could never imagine anyone surviving. Some dragged themselves, dazed and semiconscious. Many fell in the street. There was no time for nausea or even panic. She could not prevent the terrible pity, but she could do her best to clean and stanch bleeding and bandage. Sometimes, all she could do was give a sip of water, or hold some poor boy's hand so that he did not die alone.

Not far away, she saw a vaguely familiar young man doing much the same. She had danced with him at the Duchess of Richmond's ball. Young, handsome and well dressed, he walked among the wounded, frequently dropping to his knees to give a drink from the flasks he carried. Once, he put his arms around a clearly dying soldier, as Olivia did with the youth whose head now lay on her lap.

Moving away when the boy had died, helpless tears streaming down her cheeks, she wiped her face with the back of her hand and turned to the next man. Someone was already with him, a woman who spared her a curious and compassionate glance.

"Your Grace is not used to so much blood," she said.

Olivia blinked and recognized Jezebel Jakes, now the Vicomtesse de Beaujardin. Olivia moved past her to the next soldier, who had a gaping wound in his stomach. She all but swayed to her knees, reaching for the spirit bottle and the bandages.

"Is anyone?" Olivia said, and tried to smile at the poor soldier. "There, let me try to make you a little more comfortable. Take this water…"

The young man lost consciousness, but still breathed as she cleaned and bandaged him.

"I believe you are a friend of my husband's," Olivia said, more to distract herself than anything else.

"I wondered if he would tell you that. Did he tell you also how we met?"

"Yes." In this place, in this situation, it did not even hurt.

"But you do not hate me?"

Olivia paused for an instant, turning her head toward the other woman. "Hate you? For being the only humanity in his life?"

"*Then,*" the vicomtesse said, rising to her feet. "Not now. You'll pardon me when I say that the old duke deserved to be shot—along with that cousin constantly whispering in his ear like some malevolent demon."

"Anthony?" Olivia said.

"I'd have shot them both myself if I could have got away with it. I still would, even after all this blood… This poor lad is dead, God rest him…"

⁂

ANTHONY HAD WISHED for chaos, and by late afternoon he had it. The good people of Brussels who had begun by going about their normal Sunday amusements, sitting on pavement cafes beyond the walls, enjoying coffee and luncheon and wine, quickly threw open their doors to the wounded who limped into the town in increasing numbers during the afternoon, littering the streets with bodies and blood. Front doors and back doors were left open as servants and masters ran out into the streets for news of the battle no one doubted was being fought.

Anthony watched Olivia set off, thick as thieves with Rosamund and Hera and Sophia Wallace, the companion who had become Countess of Frostbrook. Like yesterday, they had volunteered to help the wounded. According to Gregson, the other denizens of the Edwards's house were driving around the town, picking up soldiers who could no longer walk, and collecting supplies of medicine and bandages to deliver where needed. Frostbrook had gone out, too, driving his own curricle, which he had brought all the way from England. He was, perhaps, on the same errand. Anthony didn't much care. Victor was as unprotected as he was ever likely to be.

It had never seemed worthwhile to watch him. There was nothing the cripple could do in this chaos except await news from his friends.

Anthony hurried from the Hotel de Belle Vue, which he also kept under observation, back along the road to Victor's house. A gaggle of servants were gathered on the edge of the park, anxiously gossiping. But Victor's front door was wide open.

Anthony strolled up and quite casually entered the house. The hall was empty, though from the kitchen he could hear muffled voices exclaiming in the mixture of French and Flemish you frequently heard in the town. The public rooms were all on the ground floor, he knew from his previous visit, so with his hand to his inside coat pocket, he glanced in at the empty reception room. The drawing room, dining room, and breakfast parlor were equally unoccupied.

Anthony crept up the stairs. Victor must be in his private apartments—which were easily spotted because they were the only ones entered by double doors. He listened for only a moment, then, hearing no voices or even movement, he went smartly inside, closing the doors behind him.

He was inside a small sitting room, which had another door leading onto the main bedchamber. Victor's chamber, presumably. A coat and cravat had been dropped on the bed. There was a masculine dressing room on one side, also deserted.

Damn Victor—has he gone out, too? Did I miss him? What good does he imagine he can do for anyone? Or had he gone to fetch Olivia? That would be annoying. Irritated, Anthony opened the cupboards and drawers of the main bedroom, looking for money if nothing else. Then he would simply wait for Victor, since he was already in the house. Wrapped in his voluminous cloak, no one would recognize him, even if they saw him bolting out of the house when the deed was done.

Anthony frowned. He found himself staring at ladies' chemises in a drawer. Yet on the dressing table, a gentleman's sleeve buttons, a carelessly thrown cravat pin. And the pearls Olivia had worn at the Duchess of Richmond's ball.

A horrible suspicion began to form in his mind.

He strode to the bed, yanking back the coverlet. A gentleman's nightshirt was folded neatly on one pillow, a lady's confection in lace and ribbons on the other.

The blood sang in his ears. He was back to the beginning.

Even with Victor dead, Olivia, the treacherous little bitch, could be bearing his child.

Red spots of fury flashed in front of his eyes. How could he have been so blind?

Well, there would be nothing for her now. He'd turf her out of every ducal residence, make sure she had the bare minimum of everything. And if it turned out she was carrying—well, surely there were ways of dealing with that, too.

Abruptly, a familiar sound caused his head to jerk up once more. The tap of a stick on the wooden floor, then muffled by the sitting room carpet.

Hastily, Anthony stepped behind the bedchamber door. Even here, the signs of Olivia's betrayal were obvious. A heavy, masculine dressing gown hung side by side with a smaller, feminine one. Ignoring the fresh upsurge of rage, Anthony peered through the doorway.

Victor had removed his coat and thrown himself onto the high-backed chair at an elegant desk, though he was not doing anything. Resting, perhaps. He loosened his cravat and tossed it aside, then, with obvious pain, stretched his bad leg, twisted and ugly, out in front of him.

Perfect, Anthony thought savagely.

He slipped his fingers into his inner pocket and closed them around the dagger he had taken from a wounded soldier in the street. Letting the cloak fall silently to the floor, he advanced through the door toward the unmoving Victor. Without collar and cravat, his nape was exposed, making the boy peculiarly vulnerable.

Which was just how Anthony wanted him.

ROSAMUND, ALMOST GRAY with exhaustion, refused to leave the makeshift hospital. Olivia knew why. She was afraid Giles would be brought in and she would not be there.

"There will be other such places, closer to the battle," Hera said. "If Giles is hurt, Justin will have him. Come home now."

"You will be no use to him if you are too exhausted to nurse him," Olivia added. "And we are all too tired to be useful here anymore."

Lord Frostbrook, his arm around Sophia, was already leading the way to his curricle, a bizarrely smart conveyance for a world full of blood and death. For some reason, it made Olivia smile as she and Hera pulled Rosamund with them.

Tom and Sir Arthur were on the box of a closed carriage, hailing them. "We're under instructions to bring you all home," Tom said, clambering down to open the door and lower the steps. "Up you go!"

Olivia had just set her foot on the step when she saw Jezebel de Beaujardin again, her shoulders stooped with tiredness, looking vaguely about her as though for a vehicle, and then, head down, she began to walk.

"Madame," Olivia called on impulse. "Let us take you home."

The woman hesitated, then trudged toward them, and Tom handed her inside. Olivia made the introductions, adding, as the carriage began to move, "You look exhausted, madame."

"Not exhausted, anxious. One of the injured saw my husband fall. I don't know if he is alive or dead."

On impulse, Olivia took her hand, but there was nothing she could say.

The vicomtesse looked at her. "Did you know my husband challenged yours to a duel?"

"*What?*" Fear snatched at Olivia's breath, and then, almost at once, belief in her husband reasserted itself. "Victor won't fight him. Anthony Severne must have riled your husband with lies."

The vicomtesse uttered a word that one did not hear in polite society. Olivia only knew of it because she had once overheard the blacksmith's son after mis-aiming a hammer.

"Ignore him for now," Olivia advised. "He has left Brussels."

Jezebel stared at her. "No, he hasn't. I saw him this morning, in the park, near Wellington's residence."

Something seemed to thud into Olivia's stomach. "Where is Victor?" She wrenched open the window and shouted the question to Tom and Sir Arthur.

"At home. He sent us to you," Tom called back.

"Oh, hurry, hurry!" Olivia pleaded in a sudden frenzy of anxiety she could not explain. "You must hurry!"

Obediently, Sir Arthur whipped up the horses.

VICTOR HAD BEEN driving around the town all afternoon, transporting the wounded and medicines. It was time, probably, to drive out toward the village of Waterloo and bring back whoever he could, and discover the truth of the battle. Any news from wounded soldiers had been indecisive and partial, since they had seen only the mixed fortunes of their own companies. His instinct was to stay, but if the French were coming, as one group of fleeing hussars had yelled at him, he had to think of Olivia and Hera and Rosamund.

As he sat at his desk to think, he grasped his stick to make rising simpler. His leg throbbed, but it was easy to ignore the pain. It would not stop him going out again. But he needed to see Olivia before he did, to hold her and be sure of her safety. His heart ached with pride in her for what she was doing.

As though the thought had conjured her, he heard a faint movement from the bedchamber behind him. He almost smiled before it came to him that he *always* knew when she was close. There was something in the air, more than her subtle perfume. And now, he smelled the very unsubtle stink of old, oiled cloth.

His nerves, attuned to Olivia, seemed to switch suddenly to a flare of warning. He tightened his fingers around the head of his cane and jerked around.

Cousin Anthony, only a couple of feet away, flew at him, a wicked-looking dagger raised to stab downward. Aiming for the neck, the kill. The knowledge flashed through Victor's mind at the same instant as he whipped up his cane, crashing it into Anthony's wrist. Anthony cried out in astonished pain as the dagger flew out of his hand, and Victor brought the stick back down, hard against his cousin's shoulder.

Anthony grunted, falling to one side, and Victor used the cane to haul himself to his feet.

"A new trick," he taunted Anthony. "I thought you wanted to finish me off in a duel, like you did His Grace."

"Couldn't wait," Anthony said with peculiar viciousness, and lashed out with his boot, kicking Victor's bad leg from under him.

Victor collapsed on the floor in excruciating pain, giving Anthony the time he needed to snatch the dagger back up and leap to his feet.

But Victor was used to pain, to moving and thinking through it. "Afraid de Beaujardin might die in battle before he can do your dirty work? Jez would never have let him, you know. Neither would I. How did you persuade my father to it?"

"I heard the officers talking at the George Inn." Anthony, dagger in hand, advanced on him. "I knew some of them had served under Colonel Landon, and His Grace despised all Landons. I neither knew nor cared why. All I did was make sure we shared the parlor with the officers and waited to see what would happen."

Anthony kicked him in the hip, but, ready for it, Victor had jerked away from the worst of the blow and now lashed out with his good leg, bringing Anthony crashing to the floor.

"Opportunistic," Victor said, flinging up his cane to defend himself. "But it worked perfectly. What of the poison, though? You must have studied hard to get the quantities just right."

Anthony laughed, grasping the stick held between Victor's hands with both of his. "Foxglove leaves. It's different for everyone. I admit I took a chance. I was afraid to use too much in case he dropped dead at my feet, so I erred on the side of caution. Then—Christ, your arms are strong."

"They've had to be to compensate for the leg. Then what?"

"Then I was afraid I hadn't given him enough to affect him at all. I hoped he would fall in company and everyone would think the stress of the duel had stopped his heart." Anthony gave up trying to wrest the stick from Victor and staggered to his feet. "And it's true he began to look pretty ill, particularly during the pacing. I saw his face, though Frostbrook seemed more concerned with Butler's aim." Anthony kicked the cane out of Victor's hands and fell on him. "I never dreamed it would work so well that he actually died in the moment of firing. I had a perfect culprit in Butler."

Victor threw himself away from the dagger's downward swipe and snatched at his cousin's wrist. "That's why you had him pursued so relentlessly. No one would look at your part in it all if Butler was paying for the crime. And I suppose if it wasn't for Dr. Rivers, none of us *would* have looked. We were all too delighted to see the old bastard gone."

Anthony's hand shook with the effort of keeping his hold on the dagger. He could not force the blade down, but Victor could not make him drop it either.

"And you fell straight into my trap by marrying my daughter," Anthony said, with a sudden push downward.

Victor laughed in his face, only just managing to prevent the plunge of the dagger. "It was *you* being trapped, Anthony. Olivia loves me. She was working with all of us to make you confess, to make you pay."

His taunts had the desired effect, weakening Anthony's efforts just enough for Victor to heave upward and roll over his cousin. Now he had both hands around his cousin's wrist while Anthony bucked beneath him.

"You have no proof," Anthony gasped. The dagger fell from his grasp, and Victor sent it spinning across the floor beneath the desk. "And you'll never be safe! I have a man at Cuttyngs who'll never rest while a cripple masquerades as the duke! And you'll never even know who he is."

This time, it was Anthony who rolled, then scrambled to his feet, looking desperately around for Victor's cane or some other weapon.

Victor laughed. "Inefficient Albert?" he said, though he had heard it only yesterday from Mrs. Irwin's letter. "He bolted the same day we did and is now sitting in a magistrate's prison, desperate to tell all he knows in the vain hope of saving his own miserable life."

Anthony's shock might have won Victor the second he needed to haul himself upright with the aid of the desk, but he hadn't bargained on the fury it would inspire in his cousin. Anthony flew at him before he was even stable, knocking him across the desk, and then closed both hands about his throat and squeezed.

Anthony's face was purple, his eyes almost insane with rage. As Victor tried to break his grip, the blood surged noisily in his ears, like voices. Was this really the end? He would die after all at the hands of his stupid, greedy, entitled cousin? It was no consolation that the authorities would now charge him with murder. Olivia would be in terrible danger until they caught him, and if the French had won the battle, God knew how long it would be before such matters could be dealt with. He could not bear never to see Olivia again.

He *would* not bear it.

With a huge roar of effort that was probably all in his head, not in his strangled throat, he tore Anthony's arms apart, jerked up his good knee, and kicked his cousin in the chest so hard that he flew across the room, cracking his head on the wall with a sickening thud. Anthony crumpled to the floor.

Gasping in huge, racking, agonizing breaths, Victor tried to haul himself upright. But he must have been hallucinating, for Olivia's soft hands helped him, held him. Her beautiful face swam in front of his, tears cascading down her cheeks. She was real. He could smell her, feel her lips on his hands, his face.

The room, suddenly, was full of people. His friends of the alliance, servants... Frostbrook and Sir Arthur lifted him and laid him lengthwise on the sofa. Hera was pressing a glass of water into his hands.

Gradually, his blurred vision and his blurred brain sharpened. Bizarrely, Jez Jakes stood at the back of the room, gazing at him. Anthony had vanished.

"Where did you take him?" Victor asked hoarsely.

"The servants removed him to a room at the back of the house," Frostbrook said. "He's dead, Victor."

Victor paused, a fresh nightmare opening before him. "I killed him."

Frostbrook gripped his shoulder. "He struck his head against the wall with appalling force. Even if you meant it to happen—and it was something of a freak occurrence—no one could dispute it was self-defense. All of us and several of your servants saw him strangling you."

"It's over, Victor," Olivia whispered, still clinging to his hand. "It's over."

AS IT HAPPENED, even the battle was over by then, though Olivia didn't know it until later. Victor was in no state to drive out toward the battlefield, as he had intended. But Frostbrook and Sir Arthur went, because the scale of the battle was only just becoming apparent, with the appalling numbers of wounded still pouring into the town in carts and wagons.

Like others, Olivia and Victor threw open the doors of their house, and the servants spread mattresses and makeshift beds in all the public rooms. Rosamund, Hera, and Sophia stayed to help where they could, while Lord Frostbrook went looking for a doctor, and Sir Arthur went in search of news in the gathering dusk.

The vicomtesse went home to await her husband or more definite news of him. Victor pressed her hand, and Olivia had no room for silly, petty jealousy, only understanding.

It was dark, though no one had yet retired when Frostbrook and Sir Arthur returned together.

"It's victory," Frostbrook said grimly. "Though at terrible cost, by all accounts. We need a spare room, Duchess. We've found Butler."

And then Giles stumbled into the house, heavily supported by Dr. Rivers.

With a cry, Rosamund flew to her husband, and his free arm closed around her. The other hung awkwardly at his side, and his thigh and hip were stained dark. His filthy, bloodied face was full of pain, and when he closed his eyes, holding Rosamund for an instant, tears coursed down his face, making terrible, anguished tracks down the dirty skin.

"Mac is dead. Elton is dead." It was as though the words had been repeating themselves in his brain and he could say nothing else.

"Them and thousands of others," Rivers uttered, his pain-racked gaze finding Hera on the staircase.

Rosamund found the strength to draw back from her husband. "Can you climb the stairs?" she asked briskly. "We should see to your wounds before we mourn."

GILES TURNED OUT to have a couple of nasty saber cuts on his arm and hip and many bruises, but nothing life-threatening, according to Dr. Rivers, providing care was taken.

The doctor, who had wanted to see to the wounded in the downstairs room, was persuaded to leave them until morning. He was too exhausted to do more than sleep.

Olivia didn't think she would ever sleep. So much death, so

much injury and tragedy. And yet it was a great victory, surely ending the war forever. The French were utterly routed, fleeing with the allies in pursuit. And Victor was safe. She hugged the last around her heart as she wrapped him in her arms and lay still.

Darkness enfolded them, but there was no silence. Not in the house and certainly not in the streets.

Victor said, "It was you."

"What was me?" she asked in surprise.

"Who gave me the strength. I thought I had lost, and he would kill me, but because of you, I couldn't give in. Not without seeing you one more time. And another and another." He turned suddenly, looming over her, taking her face between his hands in the darkness. It didn't seem to matter that they could not see each other. "I couldn't even remember if I had ever said, if I had ever told you how much I love you? That you are everything. *Everything*. Not just for giving me the strength and the courage to change my life, but by being you. You don't need to love me back, but I need you to know. Today taught me that much wisdom."

"Oh, Victor," she whispered. One arm was trapped by his body, but with the other, she stroked his hair, his bristly jaw, his lips. "I have *always* loved you. From the moment I saw you on that great horse, coming at me over the hedge. I was so afraid I would lose you today when the vicomtesse told me Anthony had never left, and then, when I saw him with his hands at your throat..." A sob escaped her, and tears coursed down her cheeks once more. She clung to him. "I could not bear to lose you, Victor, ever..."

She needed his kiss, and reached for it, but his hands still held her face.

"You love me?" he repeated with a caution that almost made her laugh. "Me?"

"Oh, Victor, who else would I love? I could give you a thousand qualities in you that I admire or like, but in truth, I don't know what makes it love. It just *is*."

Gradually, she felt his smile in the darkness. "Why, so it is for me. My beloved."

"My beloved," she whispered, and now he kissed her, long and achingly gentle.

Then he eased down beside her once more, and, holding each other, they somehow slipped into exhausted sleep.

IN THE MORNING, there were horrendous bruises on Victor's throat, though he made light of them, no doubt in comparison with the battle-injured all over the streets and in their own house.

Olivia found Dr. Rivers already attending to the wounded downstairs, issuing instructions to his helpers—servants and otherwise. Hera was there, as were Rosamund with her potions and Sophia bringing water and soup and whatever their patients could manage in the way of food.

Strangers were here too, and those she only vaguely recognized, like the rakish young man she had danced with at the Duchess of Richmond's ball, whom she had seen comforting the wounded yesterday. He crouched by the side of another wounded soldier, holding his hand and talking to him quietly.

"Lord Rupert Grande," Frostbrook murmured. "He's an ordained clergyman. In fact, he married Sophia and me. And Lady Hera and Rivers."

"Not such happy work today," Olivia whispered.

"Comforting work," Frostbrook corrected her, as Grande's head bowed. Olivia thought his shoulder might have shaken, as if in some silent sob, for she rather thought the soldier had slipped into death. Lord Rupert rose to his feet and moved on to the next bed.

"I would never have thought he had it in him," Frostbrook murmured. "Such a crisis brings out the best in people."

Around midday, they sustained a visit from the Vicomte de

Beaujardin.

The old soldier looked completely unhurt save for a bump on his head.

"I'm very glad to see you safe, monsieur," Victor said, offering him a seat in their makeshift sitting room upstairs.

The vicomte did not sit but stood stiffly, offering his hand. "I owe you an apology, Monsieur le Duc. I was completely taken in by your cousin, but my wife has now explained the matter to me more fully."

Victor searched his eyes as he took the outstretched hand. Olivia thought the older man was pleading, not for himself but for understanding over his wife's past and, perhaps, for Victor's discretion.

"Your wife is a good and kind woman," Victor said quietly. "And in the only sense that truly matters, she is a great lady."

A smile stretched the vicomte's lips. "Why, so I believe. Thank you, Monsicur lc Duc."

MUCH LATER, WHEN the Edwards arrived with Izzy and Tom and Sir Arthur, Rosamund declared that Giles wished to receive visitors, and everyone trooped into the wounded man's bedchamber. Giles looked pale, but incredibly handsome and romantic, propped up on pillows with his arm in a sling to prevent him moving it and opening the long, deep cut Dr. Rivers had stitched.

Everyone perched casually where they could—on the bed, on window seats, chairs, and stools. A footman left a tray of glasses and a decanter in front of Victor and departed.

"I know we are unlikely all to be much together again," Victor said. "Rivers and eventually Butler will have duties that keep them busy. Astley wants to go home, and so do the Edwards. Olivia and I will leave soon on a proper wedding journey, and I believe the Frostbrooks have similar plans."

While he spoke, he splashed brandy into each glass, and Olivia ferried one to everyone, two at a time.

"I wanted to say thank you for your alliance," Victor said quietly, as Olivia sat on the arm of his chair, as close as she could get without jostling his arm. "And for your defense of a man you barely know. For your support of my stepmother and my sister, and for theirs of Olivia. And yours."

"Don't be maudlin, Victor," Hera said lightly.

But Victor didn't laugh, or even smile. "It has to be said, even if only once." He raised his glass. "To absent friends, and lost friends. To all of us."

There might have been a shudder, a few shaky voices, and tight throats. But the hands that raised the glasses were strong, and the laughter, when it came, was genuine, reaffirming amongst all the tragedy, the beauty of life, love, and friendship.

EPILOGUE

August 1819

TOWARD THE END of her summer house party at Cuttyngs, Olivia opened a glittering ball by waltzing with the highest ranking nobleman present—apart from her husband—who happened to be the Earl of Frostbrook.

After the first steps, Frostbrook took a quick glance around the airy ballroom, all fresh flowers, glass, light, and open doors. "You have made a huge improvement to this event. But I suppose you are tired of hearing that."

"Oh, no," Olivia said. "Many of the old duke's cronies are appalled. I'm not sure they notice the decoration. They just still can't get over the idea of holding the autumn ball in the summer."

Frostbrook laughed. "A bold move. But this must be the third time you have done so."

"Yes, we have turned the autumn celebration back into what it used to be—a local event, with an open day for the tenants and workers and neighbors."

"It's good to see you and Victor so…*at home* with your guests and your life here."

Olivia glanced up at the gallery, where her three-year-old son was grinning and madly waving at her, as were Frostbrook's twin sons, and Rosamund and Hera's daughters. The younger babies were already asleep, with Olivia's nursemaid in charge, while the Frostbrooks' nurse had brought the older children to see the opening of the ball. Olivia smiled at them with a tightness in her throat that came from pride and gratitude and sheer love.

"Do you realize it is the first time we have all been together since Waterloo?" she said. "I know it's difficult for Rosamund to come back here, but it is wonderful to see her and Giles so well, positively shining with adventure! And Justin and Hera so contented and caring…"

"I think Hera is still flabbergasted by how you have turned this joyless mausoleum into a beautiful and comfortable home. I don't think I ever realized how much Cuttyngs lacked laughter and sheer life…" He broke off with a quick, self-deprecating smile. "But then, Brookwood was a little like that until Sophia took it in hand."

"Sophia thrives as your countess," Olivia said warmly.

A tinge of color spread along the fine bones of his handsome face. "I suspect it is rather the other way around. I see things differently with her."

Olivia smiled. "Victor was delighted to have your support in his bill to reform—"

"Yes, well, let us not talk politics here," Frostbrook interrupted hastily. "Let us just say I am no longer the blind old reactionary my wife once accused me of being. But I still like order."

"What, even a summer ball instead of an autumn one?"

He grinned. "It is radical, but it appears to work. Was it deliberate to make this a Waterloo reunion?"

"No, it just worked out that way. I wasn't sure Rosamund and Giles would be home in time. And Sir Arthur was away traveling until last month. But when I heard Tom and Izzy were married, I could not help but invite them, along with him, and the Edwards. And we ran into Lord Rupert Grande in London a few weeks ago." She did not mention that Victor's aunt and uncle, Lord and Lady Hadleigh, had declined the invitation, as they did every year, much to Victor's delight.

"It has been a pleasure, your party," Frostbrook said. "It still is."

This time it was Olivia who blushed.

As the dance ended, she waved openly to the children in the gallery, much to their excitement and the amusement of several guests. Then she flicked an eyebrow at the nursemaid, who began to herd them all back to the nursery.

After the pleasure of waltzing with an old and valued friend, Olivia went about her duties as hostess, introducing prospective dancing partners, spending time with the great and the good and the neglected, making sure the champagne kept flowing and that supper was on schedule. They had become familiar duties over the four years since her marriage, so that now she performed them with ease. Even the duty conversations were no longer merely duty.

As she moved around the room, she was aware of Victor performing his own hostly tasks, usually on the other side of the room. She liked that awareness, but she no longer felt the need to cling to him. There was contentedness even in mere, distant presence. And she had the third waltz to look forward to. It had become tradition.

She managed a few quick words with friends. Rosamund, looking almost carelessly beautiful in a simple gown that was far from new, said, "This is lovely, you know. I wish I had had your courage when I was duchess."

"You were married to the old duke," Olivia said. "I have Victor."

Rosamund smiled. "I'm so glad you do. And that he has you." And she went off to dance with Lord Rupert Grande.

Only then did Olivia realize that the third waltz was about to begin. She rustled off across the floor, and out the first open door to the brightly lit terrace, as though ascertaining that the servants had kept the area as it should be. Since it was a waltz, the few people taking the air on the terrace were making their way back inside. Tom and Izzy grinned at her and resumed their argument, so she was smiling as she walked to the end of the terrace, and then, glancing quickly around her, fled down the steps and positively ran around the unlit path to the rose garden.

This was a much more charming area now. Sweet scented and colorful, it was bordered by climbing roses. Rose trees were surrounded by smaller plants, and a rose-lined path led into a central grassy area where a round stone bench now stood to one side. With the distant music drifting over the ballroom, it seemed almost enchanted.

Victor stood there, too, both hands leaning on his cane as he gazed up at the moon and stars. They seemed to please him, for a smile lurked on his sensual lips. He was as handsome as ever in his severe evening dress. His hair, although recently cut, still managed to look untidy and tangled, and yet it suited him, gave him the wild, almost piratical look so at odds with the dull isolation of his early years.

"I thought you weren't coming," he murmured, looking at her at last.

Her heart turned over. "I was talking to Rosamund. I'm so glad they all came."

"So am I," he said. He propped his stick against the bench, and she walked into his arms.

They had perfected the movement in Italy, during the wedding journey they had begun in the weeks following Waterloo—a private waltz, a slow, gentle stepping and turning that required his balance, and her support, and a perfect understanding between them. He had his own grace, and he liked to dance. She loved the closeness, the feel of his arms and the movements of his body, too close for public dancing but wonderful alone.

It was their stolen moment, their indulgence in the midst of duty, even duties like the ball, which gave them both pleasure. This was special, a reminder of the foundation of all they had built here and all they would achieve together, even the promise of their children.

Slowly, lightly, she laid her cheek against his shoulder and turned with him, following his steps. She felt his lips in her hair and realized with disappointment that the waltz was ending. She raised her head and he kissed her, long and tenderly.

There was no need of words, but she said them anyway. "I love you."

A smile lit the softness of his eyes. "And I love you."

Another light, brushing kiss across her mouth, and then, reluctantly, he turned her once more so that he could reach his treasured walnut cane. Then he offered her his arm, and together, strengthened and renewed, they strolled happily back along the paths to the terrace, the ballroom, and their guests.

About Mary Lancaster

Mary Lancaster lives in Scotland with her husband, three mostly grown-up kids and a small, crazy dog.

Her first literary love was historical fiction, a genre which she relishes mixing up with romance and adventure in her own writing. Her most recent books are light, fun Regency romances written for Dragonblade Publishing: *The Imperial Season* series set at the Congress of Vienna; and the popular *Blackhaven Brides* series, which is set in a fashionable English spa town frequented by the great and the bad of Regency society.

Connect with Mary on-line – she loves to hear from readers:

Email Mary:
Mary@MaryLancaster.com

Website:
www.MaryLancaster.com

Newsletter sign-up:
http://eepurl.com/b4Xoif

Facebook:
facebook.com/mary.lancaster.1656

Facebook Author Page:
facebook.com/MaryLancasterNovelist

Twitter:
@MaryLancNovels

Amazon Author Page:
amazon.com/Mary-Lancaster/e/B00DJ5IACI

Bookbub:
bookbub.com/profile/mary-lancaster

www.ingramcontent.com/pod-product-compliance
Lightning Source LLC
Chambersburg PA
CBHW071437200726
48294CB00002B/677

* 9 7 8 1 9 6 1 2 7 5 4 3 0 *